A Book of Lost Songs

A Novel

Mark J. Mitchell

A Book of Lost Songs

A Novel

HISTRIA
FICTION

Histria Fiction

Las Vegas ◊ Chicago ◊ Palm Beach

Published in the United States of America by
Histria Books
7181 N. Hualapai Way, Ste. 130-86
Las Vegas, NV 89166 USA
HistriaBooks.com

Histria Fiction is an imprint of Histria Books. Titles published under the imprints of Histria Books are distributed worldwide.

All rights reserved. No part of this book may be reprinted or reproduced or utilized in any form or by any electronic, mechanical or other means, now known or hereafter invented, including photocopying and recording, or in any information storage or retrieval system, without the permission in writing from the Publisher.

Certain characters in this work are historical figures, and certain events portrayed did take place. However, this is a work of fiction. Names, characters, places, and incidents are either the product of the author's imagination or are used fictitiously. Any resemblance to actual persons, living or dead, is entirely coincidental.

Library of Congress Control Number: 2024944150

ISBN 978-1-59211-504-4 (softbound)
ISBN 978-1-59211-521-1 (eBook)

Copyright © 2025 by Mark J. Mitchell

Part One
The Cities of the Plains

1
The Gift

"What is light," I wonder as I top the dusty hill. "Is it the grace of God himself illuminating every beloved, all too human soul? Or is it a piercing beam from a dark lamp that stabs through summer darkness, sending vermin scattering, leaving only the old and slow to be crushed under my monk's sandal?"

The shadows become sharp, the sun pouring down from the east. The stony slope is steep but there is a path that I can follow. Each pebble is set in high relief. My shadow stretches long in front of me. I am glad to be leaving the North; I am looking forward to more familiar mountains than these. I am through with the North now; I hope I never return.

I keep the path with difficulty. The mountain rocks poke through my worn sandals. The animal behind me kicks small stones my way. I am not going back to the place I left. I am not returning to the discipline of the cloister. I am going home.

As I make my way down this steep morning slope, kicking scree before me, I realize that I no longer know what day it is. I have forgotten so much.

I remember the day it all began, Saint John's Day. The vigil had been long and the night short. Matins had come early and I was sleepy. I knelt in my cell and recited prayers for our blessed Saint Dominic to help me discharge my duties that day. I wanted to be worthy of the habit I wore. There was a cough outside the open doorways and I turned to see Fra Pedro.

"Fra Itzal," he said sheepishly. He was thin and sickly, his face marked by pox. His parents had given him to the Church, hoping to save his soul if not his body. He was younger than I and newer to the priory.

"Good morning, brother."

"The abbot has asked for you," he stated flatly.

I rose from my knees, nodded the boy forward, and followed him down the hall. Our sandals scraped softly on the stone flags. His slight limp broke the rhythm of our steps. I wondered what might be wanted of me. I didn't remember any offense, but it was possible to be unaware that you required correction. We crossed out into the bright morning light and made our way around the cloister to the abbot's door. Pedro bobbed his head, crossed himself, and left me there.

I hesitated for only a moment before realizing there was no point in putting things off. I knocked gently on the heavy door and it swung open on well-oiled hinges.

"Fra Abbot," I said, not seeing the big man for the bright light that streamed through the window like cream behind him. "You sent for me?"

"Come in, come in, Fra Itzal. You may sit." There was a stool on the side of his table closest to me. I sat.

He burst into a fit of dry, painful coughs. I sat nervously, praying for his health. The brother physician did not think this abbot was long for his office.

There was a large, leather-bound codex on the table. The abbot slid it toward me.

"Do you know what this is, brother?" he asked.

It was obviously a book. I didn't know how to answer him.

"Open it," he ordered. I did.

It was lovely. Beautiful vellum pages, folio sized. The top half of each page was lined with four-line staffs. The bottom half was blank.

"It is a book for music, Fra Abbot."

"Very good, Fra Itzal."

"It must be very precious."

"It is. It is a donation. A gift to us, but it comes with conditions."

"What conditions, Fra Abbot?" I asked since it seemed expected of me.

"The donor moved out of the North, from the other side of the mountains many years ago. He is now old and about to die. He had this book made."

I waited. The coughing started again. It was no good fetching him water when this happened, all of us knew that. The only thing to do was sit, uncomfortable, until the poor man could speak again. I looked down at my feet as the coughs gave way to gasps, then breaths.

"What do you know of the North, Fra Itzal?"

"Nothing, really, Fra Abbot. I am from the West, myself. Over in Navarre."

"I know. That is one of the things that makes you qualified for the task I have in mind. You speak the language of the Basque folk?"

"It is the tongue I was born to. I can also read it."

"I know that as well. Also that you can speak and read the tongue they call Occitan. The language used in the North."

"Yes, I can. I read and write Occitan. I also read and write what they call French, although I cannot speak it. And Catalan. I have a few words of what they call Castilian. And Latin, of course."

"Of course, my boy, of course."

I bridled at the "boy" but held both my temper and my tongue.

"I am told that you know something of music as well?"

"A bit, Fra Abbot. I have a guitarra latina, and I can play that."

"Can you write down music? In a book like this?" he asked me.

"I know something of that. I can note melodies after the form of Saint Gregory. I have not done it in some time. The new choirmaster doesn't want my help. The old choirmaster did, and I helped him when I first came here."

"Show me," he ordered, sliding a quill, a small inkpot, and a piece of rough paper with some numbers on it across the table. The codex was too precious for a demonstration.

I drew four lines crudely and quickly across the paper. I thought for a moment, the quill tickling my tongue, and then dipped the tip in ink and drew six large blots on the lines. I turned the paper and slid it toward my abbot.

"What is that?" he asked.

"It is the *Te Deum Laudamaus,* Lord Abbot."

"Good, good. You're sure that a musician can read that? Can turn it back into music?"

I nodded. "I can read it. You can ask the choirmaster, but I'm sure he can. His predecessor taught me how to write the square notes."

"You see, the donor of this book was enamored of certain songs that he knew in his youth. Many of these songs were sung among the vile heretics. I think perhaps our donor was a heretic himself who has returned to the gentle arms of the Church."

"Thanks be to God," I offered.

"Yes, thanks be to God. This old man fears that these songs will be lost forever. Not the words," the abbot said, producing a sheaf of papers from somewhere. "Here are the words to many of those songs. These are the ones that he means to save." He waved the papers vaguely. "But he needs to find the melodies, the tunes. He is afraid the music will be lost forever. As you know, for the last century the North has been infected by the perfidious heresy called Catharism, or Albigensianism, as the Church would have it. The Church, in her wisdom and mercy, did all that it could to snuff it out and bring the people back into her arms. All that the Church could do meant a Crusade to save the souls of these benighted sinners."

"I have heard something of it, Fra Abbot."

"Everyone has. The North was wracked by war for almost half a century, and still there are pockets of people who don't have the good sense to believe what the Church has to say to them. The war was long and terrible, and the vengeance of the Pope was more terrible still. Whole cities were put to the torch. Castles were destroyed. At Montségur, over two hundred hardened heretics were sent to the flames. To this day our brothers serve as Inquisitors, rooting out the last of these unrepentant unbelievers."

"I know about them. You don't expect me to become an—"

"Of course not, boy, of course not."

"Because I have no training in Canon Law. I do not know what questions I should ask. I haven't yet taken orders as a deacon, let alone a priest. I am only a literati. I recite my prayers, my psalter, my office…"

"I know, I know, my boy. No, I have a different task for you. I want you to go over the mountains. To go to the North. I want you to find people who know the melodies to these songs." He waved the sheets of paper at me again. "Before this generation passes, there may be people who remember how they were sung. You must find these people, and you must write down the music so it is not lost. That is the condition of the donor of the book. It is a great gift to our humble cloister. It will be a great addition to our poor library. Take your guitarra latina and find the singers. Can you do that?"

"I am not such a scholar, Fra Abbot, I am just a monk."

"A monk who knows languages and music."

"I am not terribly strong. I have never made such a journey before." I'm not sure why I was making excuses, but I was.

"Nonsense, boy, you came here to Aragon from Basque country. That's a journey."

"I came in a caravan, Fra, I was not alone."

"You won't be alone on this journey. God will provide companions."

"Shouldn't another monk come with me? Aren't there brigands and dangers in the wilds? I have not been outside the cloister in a very long time."

"I don't think that's a good idea. People will not trust two monks traveling together. But," he stopped and thought a moment, "where do you work, Fra Itzal?"

"I work in the fields now, Fra Abbot," I answered. "I oversee the peons in the vineyards and at the haymaking."

"I'd best see your hand," he said, sliding the scrap of paper back toward me. "Write something."

I thought again and then started scratching out the opening phrase of the *Pater Noster*. I pushed the page back across the table.

"What does that say?" he asked, squinting. Before I could answer he was coughing again, with that same dry, scratching sound. I waited. The cough subsided into a sucking for air, and after three or four minutes he was ready to continue.

"It is the *Pater Noster*, Lord Abbot," I replied, embarrassed for him.

"I would not know that from seeing it," he said. "Tell me, why did you choose that prayer?"

"It was the first that came to me, Fra Abbot."

He looked at me long down his flat nose. He seemed about to say something, then thought better of it and nodded toward the paper and then toward me.

"Perhaps you *should* take a companion. One of the copying monks. We will want the words on the bottom of the pages where you mark the notes of the music."

"If I find it," I reminded him.

"If you find it," he agreed. "Still, perhaps the boy who brought you to me, Fra Pedro. He has a good hand as I recall. He copied a lovely gospel. And his Augustine is very legible."

"I wouldn't know, Lord Abbot. But I'm not sure that he can read."

"No, he can't, but he can copy. Show him your hand so he grows used to it. You will have time as you travel. Yes, take him, I think. No one will ever mistake the two of you for Inquisitors. You must never let them think that. You want these sinful northerners to trust you, to believe that you are only seeking music. Whatever you do, do not stand on your dignity as a preaching friar, as a Dominican. They will never sing you any songs if they think you can burn them. Travel humbly. Be open as a book to what the road offers you. Fall in with the companions the road provides. They may lead you to the people who know these songs. I think you should start in the South, along the plains. Go along the coast to Béziers first, I think, and then double back to Narbonne, perhaps. After that, turn back again, west and north, into the mountains. The closer you get to Toulouse, the more careful you will need to be. Be circumspect in the Pyrénées. That is where the last of the hideous God-deniers will live. That is probably where you will find most of your songs."

"How will we hear Mass, Fra Abbot?" I asked, good little monk that I was then.

"There are monasteries, shrines, cathedrals even. There are churches in every village. There are cathedrals in the cities. Have you ever visited a large city?"

"No, Fra Abbot."

"They will make you grow. There will be plenty of Masses. Carry your office book with you. You and Fra Pedro can recite your prayers as you travel. Should you neglect some due to the vagaries of the road, I absolve you in advance." He sketched a sign of the cross in the air.

"If it is your will that I do this, then I shall do this. I will miss the cloister."

"The cloister will miss you as well," he said, although he was not convincing. "You do us all a service, Fra Itzal, and in a way, you do God's service. You will not be gone forever. Come back after Christmas when the snows start to fall on the mountains. That gives you six months for the task."

"But…" I started when he broke into another fit of coughs. He waved one hand at me in both blessing and dismissal. I took up the papers and the codex and left him there. I returned to my cell to gather my few things for my journey.

***

I found Fra Pedro at the door of the kitchen. Fra Quartermaster was filling panniers for us.

"So you already know," I started.

"Yes, Fra Itzal," he answered. "I was waiting outside the abbot's door. I don't know why you didn't see me as you left. He called me in right after he stopped coughing. We leave tomorrow, right after Matins."

"You have pens and ink?" I asked firmly.

"Yes, don't worry about that. We get to take a mule." He seemed as excited as a child. "Fra Quartermaster is being most generous. We have two hams, good Serrano hams, and bacon, and hard bread and soft bread. And two small barrels of wine. Fra Abbot says we are free of dietary restrictions on our journey."

"That will make things simpler, especially when we seek hospitality from among the populace."

"Yes, and he gave me two purses of coins. I have never seen so much shiny metal. Fra Abbot told me to look after the money."

"That's fine, Fra Pedro. You do that. You seem to have all our preparations well in hand."

"I do, Fra Itzal, I do. This will be an adventure."

"I suppose it will," I answered. "I'll leave it to you then. We'll leave in the morning."

I walked back to my cell, the heavy codex under my arm wrapped in oilcloth. Once there, I set it carefully on my bed, knelt before the small statue of our founder, and prayed for strength. I don't know how long I prayed, although I seemed to have missed the midday meal. I didn't mind.

When I rose from my knees, I crossed my narrow cell and unwrapped my guitar. I strummed it softly so as not to disturb the monks who were no doubt taking their afternoon siestas, and I worked the eight strings into tune. Then I opened the beautiful codex and looked at page after page covered with four naked lines that were waiting for me to discover their music. I plucked the guitar strings with a horn plectrum, slowly at first, then faster and then faster and faster, playing the sort of furious, sensual music that my father used to play on feast days when I was little in the Basque country. The notes almost burned my soul. I was ready to travel.

2
Incipit

It was still dark after Matins on the feast of William the Abbot as we led our mule down the path through the priory vineyard. Fra Pedro reached out and plucked a bunch of green grapes and I slapped them from his hand.

"It's June, brother," I said sharply. "Those grapes aren't ripe enough to eat."

"They look so cool—" he started.

"They're green, brother. We can't have you stopping to run off to the side of the road every mile or so. Patience. There will be plenty to eat."

Our abbot was waiting by a gate in the wall. We would leave through the fields and avoid a crowded push through the heart of the town on a market day.

"Blessings go with you, my sons," he offered, sketching a cross in the blue-green air.

"And also with you," we both responded automatically in Latin.

Fra Pedro started to lead the mule through the gate.

"Your vows are loosed," the abbot added.

I nodded and slapped the animal's rump to get him started. Fra Pedro pulled at the lead rope and limped ahead.

"Fra Itzal," the abbot added with a quiet wheeze, "hold a moment."

"Yes, Lord Abbot."

"I saw you strike the boy just there."

"Fra Abbot, I merely slapped green grapes out of his hand."

"I know, I know. The spirit was charity. I know that. Still, that was a good thing. There is something in that boy, something that might need taming. Keep him in good check, Fra Itzal, that's all."

"I will, Fra Abbot," I answered, turning to go.

"And bring back songs," the abbot added as I followed the monk into the fields.

"We will," I called back, and he was swallowed by the morning darkness.

***

We made a broad turn through the wheat fields that were held by our cloister and then came to the river just as it entered the town gates. We held to the north bank of the stream all through the morning, walking, not speaking. I was reciting my assigned psalms, muttering St. Jerome's Latin phrases crisply but softly. I have no idea what, if anything, occupied the mind of my younger brother. His head bobbed as we left the area of cultivated fields, and he turned his eyes this way and that.

The sun rose, growing warmer and warmer as it will in June, wherever you are, but especially in Aragon. The rays beat down on our black traveling cowls. Fra Pedro soon tossed his back onto his shoulders, leaving the small circle of his tonsure to reflect bright yellow light into my eyes.

We made better progress than I expected. Fra Pedro's limp was pronounced, but it didn't seem to slow him down. The mule was strong, even burdened with our overflowing panniers. Just before the hour of Sext, the river began to widen out into a delta, and the ground became tussocky with tough grass holding on for dear life in sandy soil. There was a tang of salt to the air.

"Halt. Stop, brother," I called to the younger man who'd gotten a bit ahead of me. He pulled up, tugging the rope backward against the animal's forward motion.

"It's too hot to go on," I said. "Let's eat, pray, and take our siesta here."

Fra Pedro threw himself onto the ground and spread his arms and legs out in a broad X.

"Mind the mule," I cautioned. "Do you know how to hobble a beast, to keep it from wandering off?"

"No, Fra Itzal. I've never worked with animals. I live indoors, copying."

"I'll see to it. You might want to see what you have to offer to nature," I suggested. "I'll follow when you return."

He sat, looked at me curiously, then jumped to his feet and ran up a small rise.

I tied the mule's legs together and wiped my brow. I was hot. Between the white cassock and the black cowl, I wondered if this was what the heretics felt as the flames rose toward them and instantly knew better. All they would feel is terror and, one prayed, repentance. Heat was their friend, for it would steal their reason.

Pedro returned and I slapped the back of his head.

"What was that for, brother?"

"We have a long road ahead of us, Fra Pedro. You should learn the customs of traveling."

"I have journeyed before. Long ago."

"I'm sure you have; we are all of us only travelers. Still, you should know that you want to attend to your physical needs downhill from where we sit and eat, not above us. We'll move along a furlong or two." He looked embarrassed as I bent to loose the mule's feet. I flicked at its behind so it walked ahead of us and we followed beside the broad, slow water. We came to a spot with a nice group of three rocks that offered some shade. I stopped the animal and tied its two feet loosely back together.

"Downhill, Fra Pedro," I said lightly and illustrated my point by example as the boy laughed. When I returned, he'd set out a ham and some bread and was filling two wooden cups with wine.

"Here's a feast!" I exclaimed and bowed my head to say a blessing before the meal. He followed me, muttering something under his breath that sounded like Latin. Then we fell to the food. After a thin slice of ham and half a cup of wine, I rose and searched the panniers. I found paper and picked up a stick from the dusty path.

"Do you know what we are doing on this journey, Fra Pedro?"

"Collecting songs. It seems silly, really."

"It probably is, but it is what we are commanded by our order. It will serve the library, no doubt. Now—where are you from?" I asked suddenly.

"The mountains," he answered quickly, waving vaguely north and west.

"What tongue were you born to?"

"Catalan. And Occitan. We spoke both; they mixed freely."

No surprise there. We were both speaking in Catalan. It was the everyday tongue of our cloister.

"Now, can you read?"

The boy stiffened and looked at me with fierce pride. "I can copy," he answered.

"That wasn't the question. I take it you can't read. That's all right. Don't let it worry you. Now," I continued, "look at this paper." I opened the sheaf of song lyrics. "Copy these lines." I pointed to the center of the page.

"On what?" he asked.

"On the earth, boy." I handed him the stick. "We can't waste paper on practice. I have to be certain that you can make out the letters written here and that I can make out your letters. Otherwise, we'll have to find another system."

He looked at me and then at the page, then back at me, but said nothing. He began to scratch in the dust. After a moment, I looked over his shoulder.

"Ai las tan cuidava saber d'amore tan petit en sai," I recited. "Good. That's good."

"What does it say?"

"I thought you spoke Occitan?" I said, looking aslant at him. "It says, 'Alas, I've grown so wise, but of love, I know so little.' It's a song. The important thing is that you had no trouble copying it."

"I suppose. It seems true, too. I've learned much from our brothers in the cloth, but nothing of love. At least not real love."

"Of God's love, that's real enough. And you must have learned something of the love of the Virgin and the saints."

"Yes, yes, but there doesn't seem to be much juice in that kind of love, does there?" He seemed to have poured himself a second cup of wine.

"What are you talking about, boy?"

"The abbot said our vows are loosed," he started.

"Loosed, not absolved, not vanished. Relaxed might be a better word," I replied, finally choosing a word common to both Catalan and Occitan. "It means we can eat this ham and wash it down with this wine while our brothers in the cloister must make do with bread and water from the river. That's all."

"Perhaps that's what you heard," he said softly, not thinking I heard him, but he nodded almost respectfully and wrapped the ham in its cloth.

"Wash the cup in the river," I told him. "We'll take a nap until the cool of the afternoon." I was enjoying having this power over someone else.

***

At the hour of Nones I was kneeling, reciting the afternoon prayers. A hawk with broad wings circled slowly overhead. I was still sleepy from the heat and the wine, but I knew it was time to move on. Fra Pedro snored between the rocks. I walked down to the river, shaking my limbs awake as I moved, and filled one of the cups with cool water. I walked back up the gentle slope and dashed the water into the face of my sleeping companion.

"Thanks be to God!" he shouted, shaking himself. He was well-trained.

"Rise, my brother, it is time we traveled on," I admonished gently. "You can recite your prayers as we walk."

He looked at me oddly with something dark shadowing his eyes, but he stood up and dusted himself off. I'd replaced the songs in our panniers before we slept; now I just shook out the last drops from the cup and bent to untie our mule. I made a small clicking sound between my teeth and the beast began to move.

We followed the river as it made its sluggish way down to the central sea. Our first view of the blue Mediterranean came as we topped a rise a few hundred yards from where we'd rested. Fra Pedro gasped.

"The first time you've seen it?" I asked.

"*Oc. Si.* Yes," he said, searching for some language.

"You should see the ocean someday. It's on the other side." I gestured behind us. "It's much bigger and grayer. And, I think, more powerful."

"There's power enough for me here."

"No doubt, brother. And it is beautiful, isn't it?"

"No doubt, brother."

We turned north and followed the curve of the shore for the rest of the afternoon. I recited psalms in my head just to be sure I didn't lose the trick of discipline while we traveled. I doubt if anything occupied young Pedro's mind. I was beginning to think that there wasn't much in his brain at all.

The long day stayed warm as we walked, even with the cooler breeze off the water. Vespers would come late, I knew. It was the height of summer, and days tended to stretch.

"Have you ever seen anyone burn, Fra Itzal?" Pedro said after we'd been walking for some hours.

"What prompts the question, brother?"

"Just making conversation, brother. Passing the time. It will be a long journey if we don't speak."

"True enough, but it is a gruesome question."

"I guess. Can you answer it?" He sounded a touch petulant.

"I can. I'm not old enough to have smelled the smoke from Montségur. Or I could have, but I would have been just a boy," I began. "Still, they tell me its shadow lingers over that country that is waiting ahead of us."

"I didn't think you were that old, Fra Itzal, and it wasn't the question."

"No, it wasn't. Yes, I saw one burn. Just once back in my village, before I came east to join our order. She was burned as a witch and that's not common, you know."

"I've never seen a witch's fire," he replied. "Was she wicked?"

"Wicked enough to be accused, at least. She was no witch, of course. She was just a pretty girl who slept with the wrong woman's husband at the wrong time of year. An Inquisitor was making the rounds just then, between Ascension Thursday and Pentecost. Since there were no heretics in our village, the wronged wife denounced the poor girl as a witch. The Inquisitor was itching to light a fire, we could all tell. He pronounced the anathema and she was led to the edge of the village, tied to a stake, and set aflame." I stopped and muttered a quick prayer at the memory. "At least she was half strangled. She didn't feel the flames too much. Or so they said. I was a boy, barely fourteen. I'll never forget it. I suppose I was drawn to the power of the white-robed monks then." I grew silent, brooding, kicking a sea-smoothed stone ahead of me. "What of you, Pedro? Have you seen God's work etched in fire?"

"Yes. Four were burned when I was there. It was odd, really. They were arrested in the foothills, at the bottom of the mountains. They were a family. I watched the arrest and I followed them down into the city. They took them to Girona.

Everyone thought that it was strange. We were a crowd following by then. Usually, heretics were sent up to Pamiers or Carcassonne on the other side of the mountains, where the heresy was born."

"It wasn't born there," I started, but he interrupted my interruption.

"They said there was a new bishop in Girona. Perhaps he felt he had something to prove to his superiors or to the Pope. I don't know. The four—a husband, a wife, and two daughters—were led in chains to the plaza. A stake was set up in the center, in front of the cathedral—you know the plaza?" I nodded. "Their arms were stretched over their heads. They were chained to face the four cardinal points of the compass. They couldn't look at each other. They were shown no mercy, or perhaps it was a mercy to the mother. Of course they didn't renounce their heresy, nor did they name any names to the Inquisition. The wood was very dry. It was late summer. The girls screamed and cried when the torch touched the wood and the flames licked their way toward them. The mother, though, the mother, she just looked to heaven and her face glowed, and it was not from the flames. It was horrible, but it didn't take long."

We fell silent. There was not much to be said after such a tale, really. We plodded along, making our way east and north with the coast, watching the small waves. The tide started to pull out. Evening began to fall. The sky went that off blue that is almost green as the sun went down behind us. I took the hemp reins on our mule and coaxed him around a finger of black rock. There, up ahead of us, stood a vision.

3

Confessional

It was green and glowing. That's all we could tell at first. It was pale green and it glowed from within. It seemed to be outlined by a halo of flames that licked just above its crown. We could hear the crackling of the fire above the sound of gentle waves from the receding tide. It was real enough but it looked ghostly and frightening in the deepening twilight. I could almost hear Pedro trembling.

"It's a tent!" I said, laughing after my eyes finally sorted things out. "It's just a tent. It's not a demon. Or some sea creature throwing itself on the beach—I have heard of such things, brother—it's only a tent."

"I've never seen one like that," Fra Pedro answered, but fear was ebbing from his voice.

He was right; it was like nothing either of us had ever seen. It was constructed from some rich fabric, not silk, but there was shiny stitching around its roof that caught the glow of the fire. It was large. Enormous. Easily twice as big as my cell back at our priory, probably larger than that. It must have been glowing because of lamps within it. It was set with the flaps facing inland and supported by staves that looked like they might have been made of ebony, almost priceless wood.

"It must belong to some nobleman," I said needlessly as we began to approach the thing. We were able to take in more as we drew closer. There was some emblem sewn into the tent walls at regular intervals that I couldn't quite make out. It wasn't until we were within a few yards that we could see what they were.

"Yellow crosses!" Pedro hissed. "A heretic!"

"Perhaps, Fra Pedro, but penitent if he shows the cross," I admonished. Still, it didn't make sense. The Inquisition could sentence people to wear the yellow cross, of course, but it was a mark of shame. Whoever owned this tent was showing it off like a badge of honor, something he wanted to add to his coat of arms.

As we moved closer, a small man led a horse from the other side of the apparition towards the meager grass at the edge of the strand. He saw us and spat on the ground and then called over his shoulder in Occitan, "Visitors. Preaching friars by the look of them. Look sharp!"

"Hail, Christians," I called out. "No fear, no fear, we are not Inquisitors." I assumed that's what the fellow thought. "We are just a pair of traveling monks, nothing more."

A tall man strode out through the tent flaps. He was backlit and all we could make out was his size and general shape. He appeared to be dressed as a noble, his cloth hauberk falling to his knees. He was hatless at the moment.

"Who's this?" he called out in Occitan, his accent freighted with the dignity of the fighting class.

"Monks," I called back, "traveling to Beziers."

"You'll stop here," the shadow said, his voice telling us that we would not refuse. "You'll share my meal. Then you'll hear my confession."

"But we're not priests," I said, trying to object.

"You'll hear my confession," he stated flatly.

"If you insist, sire," I replied, trying to muster some dignity for the sake of my habit. "First, we will set up our camp and say our Vespers. You are welcome to join us."

"Take the space on the other side of the fire over there." The voice ordered. We circled between the tent and the retreating water and led our mule through the circle of light that the fire cast onto the gold sand.

***

We'd unrolled our spare cloaks on the beach to serve as beds. I gestured to Pedro to kneel and we recited a perfunctory Vespers. We rose and brushed the sand from the knees of our cassocks.

I pulled my guitarra out of our panniers. Fra Pedro looked at me, squinting through the darkness, causing the craters in his face to close down to thin fissures.

"Why that?" he asked.

"We might need to sing for our supper," I answered. "Besides, it's a long evening. Music may help pass the time. Let's not bring out the book but keep it near the top of our baggage."

"If you say so, brother."

We walked across the soft sand to the halo of light. A folding table had been erected and three campstools arrayed around it. The small man who'd led the horse away was setting out cups and food. Our host sat enthroned on one of the stools, waiting for us.

"Sit. Sit and eat. There's no point in waiting." He waved his arms expansively. Our cups were quickly filled. I surveyed the table. It was a feast.

There was a roasted joint of meat throwing off steam; it had obviously just come off the fire. There were dishes of salted freshwater fish, olives, figs, and quince arrayed around it. A bowl held a steaming heap of green peas mixed with onions and garlic. Ostentatiously there was a cellar full of coarsely ground pepper in the center of the board.

"It is a good thing our vows have been loosed, Fra Itzal," Pedro said softly.

"Accept what God gives," I cautioned him. I bowed to our host. "Thank you for this bounty."

"Nothing, it's nothing. Eat. Drink." He didn't stand on ceremony. He tore into the meat and drained a cup in one gulp. The smaller man ran up to refill it. I never saw him take anything for himself except a bit of fish.

We ate; thoroughly enjoying the food, so much richer than the cloister has to offer, even on feast days. Nothing was said during the meal. The wine kept flowing and the food was demolished. I was surprised at how much Pedro managed to stuff into his thin frame. From somewhere a loaf of sweet bread flavored with cinnamon appeared. It soon vanished as well.

"I thank you again," I said, uncomfortably full and verging on tipsy. I looked at our benefactor and finally took him in. He was a large man, well-muscled as far as we could see. He was dressed in a green tunic sewn with a yellow cross over the left breast. He seemed impossibly old to me, he must have been fifty if he was a day, probably older. His mustache was gray and wild, as was his hair, although both must once have been the color of late summer wheat. His eyes were deep violet, reflecting the firelight.

"It's just food, brother, just food. All of us must eat."

"True. But we are poor monks and seldom eat so well."

"Or so much," Fra Pedro chimed.

"Or so much," I agree. "To whom do—"

"We couldn't help noticing the yellow crosses on your tent. And your dress," Pedro leapt in before I could finish my question. "Most people don't wear them so boldly."

"Those!" he roared. "Those are a pitiful penance imposed by the vile Inquisition.

Damned Dominicans!"

"Sir—"

"Impose the yellow cross on me! Force me on a pilgrimage! They can make me wear them, but they won't mark me with shame. Raimon of Rousillon will not be humbled before any white-frocked, Pope-serving, Latin-spouting priest!"

"Sir!" I started again, somewhat shocked.

"Never mind, never mind me." He waved at me dismissively. "I don't mean you. You're not Inquisitors, are you?"

"No, we're not," Pedro answered.

"All right, then. They imposed this on me. They took my lands. And why? WHY?" he bellowed into the darkness.

"Tell us," was all I could think to say.

"I will, I will." He waved his cup towards the small servant. The man ran over and refilled the lord's cup and both of ours, though I wasn't sure that was wise. "They are sending me to Compestola, stealing my land, stealing my castle. Me a cousin of the Trenceval, the late count. And they force this silly little patch on me and all my goods, all of that. Why, you ask? Because I wouldn't let my aunt and her holy men die in the cold of a mountain winter. I let them stay in my castle. I sheltered heretics! My mother's sister. Bah! I sheltered family."

"But you know the law…" Pedro started.

"There's law, then there's blood. Blood matters more. I kept her warm. And her holy men with her. The church kept them warmer."

"You mean?" I asked.

"Burnt. The lot of them." He drained the cup again and stared into its empty depths.

There was certainly nothing to be said. I could defend the Church, but that would offend someone who had just shown me opulent hospitality. We remained silent.

"Enough brooding," he said as the waves tickled the soft sand behind us. "Let's get on with my confession. Later, we might have songs." He nodded at my guitarra leaning against the table.

"I warn you again, I am only a reader. I'm not a priest."

"You wear the habit. You wear the cowl. You'll do."

"Let's take the stools down towards the water," I suggested. "There might be more privacy. Sin is better suited to darkness, don't you think?"

***

"Bless me Father for I have sinned…" he started. We sat on the stools; he faced the land and I faced the water.

"I told you, I'm not a priest…" He waved away my protest.

"Bless me Father for I have sinned," he began again. "And not the sin you think. I bear no shame for sheltering blood. I feel more remorse for letting them all die. I should have taken a troop and ridden through the blasted monks and their minions. I should have rescued those poor souls. No one deserves to burn. Not my sweet aunt. Not her men. No, I want to tell you of another sin."

I sketched a blessing in the evening air with my right hand and nodded. I don't know if he saw me. He went on.

"It was years ago. I was a married man once. She was lovely. A small girl with auburn hair and green eyes. I saw that she never had to do any rough work. We had servants aplenty then. The castle was warm. I kept her close. But then one came.

"You may have heard of these… these rabble that called themselves troubadours. Finders of tunes. Of course, none of them can sing. That's why they always travel with another to sing their songs for them prettily. A joglar, this type of servant is called.

"One came. He was called Guillem. And he made songs. Some of them were pretty. Some were rousing, war songs, songs of battle. Some he made to ridicule my enemies. I enjoyed those. And his little joglar had a sweet voice.

"But the songs got too sweet. I could tell. There were so many addressed to some mysterious lady, a senhal he called her. He called her his lark. I don't know why. I didn't know who she was at first. Some serving maid, I thought, if I thought at all. I didn't know the rules of those men, not then.

"Months went by and I was noticing the looks that passed between my wife and this poet. Too often I came to my bed and found the clothes warmer than they should be from one. Eventually from his songs and her sighs, I knew.

"It was winter. It was hunting time. I was outside my castle, and this Guillem happened along. He looked so smug, so satisfied as if he had just left the arms of some girl. And he may very well have. It was only later that the milk girl came running up the path. By then it was too late. My hunting spear had pierced him through. She saw the blood on the snow and she ran. Wise girl.

"I took my knife, and I cut his heart out. I carried it to the castle and gave it to the cook. I told him to use only the best spices, the rarest from the East. And pepper, lots of pepper.

"That evening, my wife and I supped along in our chamber in the east tower. She ate the dish placed in front of her with relish, licking her fingers and smacking her lips.

"I looked across the board at her. 'Did you enjoy your meal?' I asked her.

'It was lovely, my lord,' she answered me.

'Know that you have just eaten the heart of your lover. Your Guillem!' I snarled at her.

You'll hear stories about this. There are those who say she fainted. But she did not faint. She looked at me, her green eyes cold and hard.

'Thank you, my lord,' she said. She stood up and walked to the window of the tower. 'Never have I eaten so well. I will not eat again.'

She stepped through the arrow slit; she was small. She stepped through the arrow slit and into the thin, cold air and she breathed it no more."

We sat, quiet for a while, the small waves whispering on the sand.

"So you are confessing to two murders…" I ventured.

"Murder? Murder?!" He jumped up and the stool tipped onto the ground behind him. "No one could prove a murder on me. That was justice! He was a wife stealer, and the poor slattern was too susceptible to songs," he bellowed.

"Then what is the sin, my son?"

"I'm not your son, I'm old enough to be your father, your grandfather even. But no, murder is not the sin."

"Then where is the fault?"

"Prodigality! Prolificacy! I wasted spices, a ransom in spices, a kingdom in pepper on that worthless heart! What waste! What indulgence!"

I sat there speechless for a moment.

"But, Sir Raimon," I started, "what about this evening's meal? Wasn't that just as prodigal as any poet's heart?"

"Yes, you're right boy, father, brother, whatever you are called," he answered, righting his stool. "But you see, I will not eat for very much longer. I will enjoy what I have. This is under the seal, isn't it?"

"If you say so, as much as I have seal to grant. I keep telling you I'm not a priest."

"It doesn't matter. You see, I will make this pilgrimage that the Church has forced on me. I will wear these yellow crosses until I reach the shrine of Saint Iago. I'll blazon everything with them. When I reach there, I will remove them all. Then my man—you saw him, he is no simple servant. My man and I will find a private place and he will pronounce the *consolamentum* over me and I will submit to the *endura*. I will eat no more. I will die a good heretic."

4
Exits

♪En sovensa
Ten la car'et dous vis,
Vostra valensa
E-l belhcors blanc e lis... ♪

I strummed my guitarra and sang the words of the love song lightly to myself, thinking idly of sweet smiles and comely forms, my back propped against our panniers. I had made the old knight sing it three times over the night before. That was the only penance I assigned him. If he was determined to die a heretic, God would take care of any other punishment.

He sang the song in his tired, creaking voice. I leaned into the darkness and scratched four lines into the damp sand. I listened carefully, memorizing the words as quickly as I could while I scratched the music into the beach.

He didn't show much emotion the first time he sang through the verses, he just intoned them in a flat gray tone. The second time through his voice climbed up a notch, he gave the words more force and I thought I noticed his shoulders starting to quake. The final time, he dug into his chest and found a pure tenor that even his body had forgotten and he sang into the night with force and feeling. It was that last time that I saw the tears streaming down his cheeks, soaking his gray mustache and dropping down into the sand like sea foam.

"Your sins are forgiven," I pronounced in Latin. He didn't reply at first and then he said something softly. "What?" I asked him.

"I said don't be silly, boy. Only God can forgive sins."

"So you believe," I answered him. "Then what do you regret so?"

"The lost beauty," he said softly, wiping his mustache dry. "There was so much beauty. My wife, she was beautiful, she shone in the night she was so beautiful. And I killed her."

"You said she jumped—"

"I killed her and you know it. And that stupid, depraved poet. I killed him, too. They were young together. That's all. They were young and I was too old to see them. I should have let them be. He would have written more songs. She would have liked them. Then he would have left us and my wife would have come back into my arms. I know that now. Now that I'm truly an old man."

"It was a beautiful song, wasn't it?" he asked me.

"Yes, it was, Sir Raimon," I replied softly.

He shook his shoulders and rose from the stool.

"I'm just tired and full of music and wine. It's nothing. I'll go to sleep now."

He folded his campstool and walked back to the circle of light that was his tent. I watched his large back turn into nothing but a dark shadow against the fire and I waited for a few minutes, muttering whatever prayers of absolution I could remember, hoping they might do the old soldier's soul some kind of good. When what I considered a decent interval had passed, I jumped up, ran to our blankets, and roused Fra Pedro.

"Quickly," I said. "Bring some paper and grab a couple of sticks out of the fire. Don't burn yourself but bring me some with charcoal on their tips. Quick, hurry."

He didn't move as fast as I would like, but he did finally follow the orders I'd given. We raced back to where I'd listened to the old man's confession. At first I thought I might try to find the song among our pages, but I knew there wasn't time. I would just have to remember the poem. I used the back of the sheaf of papers and the small, charred stick that Fra Pedro snatched out of the fire and I scratched the staff and the notes of the song on the page as fast as I could, just managing to keep everything clear. I heard the water grow louder and I knew the tide was coming in.

***

The tent was gone in the morning, almost as if it had been wiped away by the rising tide. The old man was military and knew how to break a camp better than two rather inept monks. We rolled up our blankets, recited our Matins prayers together, and breakfasted quickly on some bread dipped in wine. Even so, the sun was high by the time we started eastward.

"We'll leave the beaches today," I told Pedro. "There's a Roman road up there that will take us into Perpignan. We ought to reach it by this evening if we choose to stop there. Perhaps we shouldn't."

"Why not?"

"The abbot only wanted us to go to certain towns before we turned into the mountains," I answered. "I don't know why, but he must have had his reasons."

"I think we should go into the mountains today. I think our true mission is in the heights and valleys up there." He waved to his left.

"We will go to the cities we have been told to visit. We will go there first. We owe obedience to the discipline of the habits we wear."

"I haven't taken that vow," Pedro replied with some bitterness but went silent after that, limping ahead of me, leading our mule.

We moved in silence through the morning and into the heat of the early afternoon. We took advantage of a low point in the cliffs to turn away from the sea and climb to the ancient Roman route. As soon as we crested the rocks, we could see the vast rolling plain of Langue d'Oc spread out in front of us, dotted with farms and vineyards. We were still above it, but it was a vision. We stopped, out of breath, to take our midday meal and siesta.

"Let's look at those songs," I suggested after we had eaten a bit of ham and washed it down with wine, not forgetting our prayers before the meal.

Pedro withdrew the satchel that held the sheaf of papers and the beautiful codex from our panniers. I walked over and removed the panniers themselves from the poor beast's back and extracted my guitarra.

I sat down against the baskets and started to sort through the pages in front of us, with the scrap of paper holding my notes from the knight's confession.

"I don't think it's here," I said after almost a half hour of looking. "I think this song is missing altogether. If I write out the words for you, can you copy them neatly into the book?"

If you write large and clear, I can." He dug around in the panniers and produced a pen and a jar of ink. He shook the jar to mix the black with the liquid. I sketched out the words with the charcoal stick I'd kept from the night before.

While Pedro concentrated on the task before him, looking very boyish, his tongue thrusting out from a corner of his scarred face, I tuned my guitarra and started to sing the song over and over.

♪*S'ieu per crezensa*
Estes das Dieu tans fis
Vius ses falhensa
Inter 'em paradis…

If, in my faith
I were as true to God
I would enter Paradise
Alive and without faith… ♪

I sang, thinking back to the old man and his sorrows.

"Why wasn't Sir Raimon on the Roman road?" Pedro asked, looking up from the vellum. "Isn't that the way most pilgrims travel to Compestola? He could have had company."

"I don't think he wanted company," I replied. "For all that bluff and bravado he showed us, I think he's a little ashamed of those yellow crosses he has to wear. Answering us is one thing because we are just two and so far beneath him as to be barely noticeable. If he were on the pilgrim's road, he would meet members of his own class and he would have to answer to them, over and over again as some joined the path and others left it."

"He didn't seem ashamed of his crosses."

"No, he didn't. But that is the best face he could put on things, at least for us. That's what I think. And then there's something else."

"What? Oh, you can write the music in now, just let the ink dry below your strange lines." Pedro passed the book and pen over to me. I rested my guitarra against the baskets.

"Well, he sent at least two people to hell. This poet and his own wife. A third if you count himself. He killed the poet before he could receive the sacraments, so he died with all his sins on his soul. His wife killed herself and we know what God thinks of that," I said. "Of course, he'll go to hell himself, but that's his choice. I don't think he minds too much."

"But he does believe rightly now, doesn't he? Perhaps the poet and the wife were both heretics, too."

"Maybe. That wouldn't matter, at least not to him. If they were of that faith, he still sent them to hell since they couldn't receive their own warped sacraments. If they were of that faith, it might weigh on him even more."

"Poor old man," Pedro offered. "But—"

"Stop," I cut him off. "I want to make sure I write this melody down as truly as I heard it.

♪Jafer ni fos so druitz
Per las vostras salutz…♪

I was singing under my breath, drawing the four-sided notes on the four lines of the staff. I kept at it for a few more minutes.

"There," I said, finally satisfied. "Let's nap a bit."

***

We started off again in the middle of the afternoon, the sun tilted behind us, casting our shadows much longer than we really stood. We walked in silence for the most part. Pedro kept looking off to his left, where broken mountains thrust like damaged teeth into the blue-white sky. I kept my eyes on the paving stones that were laid here before our Savior walked on this earth.

As the sun sank behind us, we saw the city of Perpignan below us with its bright walls and church towers and barges bobbing on its river.

"We could sleep under a roof for an hour or so more of walking," I said. "There's bound to be a Dominican house in the town."

"It's nice to be away from our brothers for a bit," Pedro suggested. "I mean, we still say our prayers and we are keeping our vows—except for the food, I suppose. But we don't have the bell ringing and certain times for everything to be done; we don't have all the other monks—Fra Miguel, for example, or Father Alfonso—to take up space and bother us with their disgusting habits."

"I haven't noticed them."

"Well, they have them. Miguel is just dirty, but he pretends he's so holy. I can't stand that man at all. And Father Alfonso, well, that should be between him and his confessor, I suppose. But if you ask me, he has a lot to confess."

"If you say so. Of course, you work in the scriptorium copying, and I'm out in the fields most of the day. I only see the brothers at meals and services. Still, I take your point. With just two of us, this is almost private, and that's a nice change." I looked around. There was a dry ravine that wound up into the mountains a few yards ahead of us, a flattish grassy slope above the road with a lovely view of the sea, the city, and the plain. "We can stop here and make our camp."

So we did, hobbling the mule, unloading the blankets and the satchel that held the songs and the book. We didn't bother with a fire since it was a warm evening. We ate bread and ham, quietly thanking God for the food. Afterward, while the light remained, I read through more of the poems and looked over our work from the morning. We had made a very handsome start in our task, I thought.

♪Qu'una not porta benda
Qu'ieu.n prezes per esmenda
Jafer ni fos so druitz
Per las vostras salutz...♪

I found myself singing. "No other woman who covers her head with whom I'd rather sleep, whose lover I'd rather be, whose greeting I'd rather have."

"Have you ever loved a woman, Fra Itzal?" Pedro asked, breaking my reverie.

"What? My mother, I suppose, and my sister. Like any boy, I had my mad yearnings for village girls."

"Not like that. Have you ever—before you entered the cloister, I mean—have you ever—"

He broke off, embarrassed. He looked so young then.

"I know what you're trying to ask," I said, offering mercy. "Yes, three times. Three times only."

"Who? How? Was your heart broken? Did that drive you into orders?"

"You're like a little girl. No, it was a story out of songs; it was just something that happened. I was the victim of a conspiracy, if you really want to know.

"I have an older brother. We lived away in the West, Navarre. Basque country. You knew I was Basque, didn't you?"

"I knew by your talk," Pedro answered.

"We all lived together in one small house. My older brother, Agri—his name means light, so mine means shadow—married a woman, Eskarne—"

"What's that mean?" Pedro interrupted.

"It means mercy. Still, he married her and brought her into our small house. She was a little woman, brown and round where she should be. There was my mother, my sister, my brother and his new wife. My father had made the journey to heaven long ago. I don't know if you've ever lived in a small house like that. It gets very crowded and close. And a small house with two young people who have just been married, well, it gets quite noisy, as you might expect." I stopped a moment and sipped a little wine.

"After a few months, Eskarne was pregnant of course, as it should be. A few months further, and she gave birth to a beautiful little boy who they decided to call Gitxi because he was so small. Eskarne nursed the child and he grew larger quickly, like my brother had, but the name stayed with him. She had him weaned by the summer that they burned that witch in my village.

"After the child was eating solid food and Eskarne's time was not as taken with him, something odd happened. I saw my mother talking with my brother's wife a little more often and there seemed to be some secret laughter passing between them, but I didn't think much of it. I was studying my letters, learning to read Latin and any other languages that were at hand. The priest in our village would stop by, bringing paper and his Vulgate bible. He would send me outside to practice changing Latin into Basque while he conferred with my mother. I guess I was something of a dreamy boy.

"Then, one night in August, the house was asleep and I felt something very soft next to me in my bed. And then things started happening beneath the covers. I won't say that I didn't understand them—or enjoy them—but they puzzled me. I knew, of course, that it was Eskarne. She never let me say anything and never said anything herself; she just passed the night with me."

"And two others?"

"And two others, all in that same month," I confirmed, nodding. "And after that, her belly started to swell again. That was when my mother took me aside.

She told me it was time for me to leave our village, to go to some cloister where I belonged, and that I should go to one far away. It would be a good place for me to read and write and sing and I could pray for her. I had done my duty by my sister-in-law, she told me. I didn't understand at first. My mother was determined that both my brother and I should leave heirs to carry on the family. But she knew my brother should raise both children as his own—he didn't mind, she told me—and that I should not stay.

"So I left my village with all the clothes I owned, the bread my mother baked for me, and a letter from our priest. I came to the east and I became a monk," I finished.

The night had grown too dark for us to see each other. I slipped the book back into the satchel. I opened my psalter to try and read Vespers and realized I couldn't see those pages either. I recited my office from memory, setting the book on top of my guitarra. I knelt and could make out Pedro doing the same, although I had the sense he was watching me under his heavy-lidded eyes. After Vespers, I placed the satchel under my head as a pillow, pulled my blanket over my nose, and slept deeply until the sun's rays falling from the east woke me.

Fra Pedro was nowhere to be seen, and our mule had gone with him.

5
Entrance

I jumped up and ran down the slope towards the city and the plain, not bothering with my sandals. The old road was completely empty. I ran back to where I'd slept, catching my foot on a sharp pebble. I hopped to my belongings, flopped on the ground, saw that my sole was undamaged and pulled my sandal on over it. I went back the way we'd come the day before and saw no one in that direction. I was alone. There was no question.

I went back and rolled up my blanket, threw the satchel over my shoulder, secured my psalter to my cincture, and picked up my guitarra. I walked a few steps towards Perpignan but could still see no sign of my missing monk. The Roman paving stones gave nothing away, and the earth that wasn't covered in grass was summer hard and offered no trace of man nor mule. I looked up the ravine that led into the mountains. There was a path along the west side that rose steeply as the cut grew deeper. I couldn't tell by looking if anyone had trod on it recently.

I hadn't any idea what I should do. That mule had our supplies, our money, the letter from our abbot that would grant us hospitality at sister houses as we traveled. If I went ahead into the city I would be destitute. If I turned back, well, I felt I'd be abandoning the mission too easily. So I did what monks do. I prayed.

Venite, exsultemus Domino, jubilemus Deo, salutary nostro…

"Come, let us sing unto the Lord and let us rejoice in our salvation…."

I knelt on the ground where the ravine opened to the road and sang my Matins prayers out loud; perhaps hoping that Pedro would hear them and come back. I held my hands out, palms upturned. I did not miss breakfast. I was practiced at the art of fasting. I wouldn't miss any meals for at least a day. I knelt there all day and all through the night.

I recited rosaries, contemplated the sorrows of Our Lady, contemplated the works and gifts of our founder. I recited the appointed prayers at the little hours of Terce, Nones, and Sext. I sang out loud, kneeling next to the oddly empty thoroughfare. I chanted Vespers, I stayed awake through Compline. I recited rosary after rosary in between the appointed hours.

I did not feel filled to overflowing with religious ecstasy, the way some brothers have described from the pulpit. I was not taken up in a fiery chariot. I did not see any vision of the celestial rose. I was granted no Pauline heaven. I did not feel enfolded in the warm, firm wings of an angel of the Lord. Not really. No, I felt sore knees, especially my left one that seemed to have found an especially rocky patch of ground. I shifted it from time to time, but the small stones still managed to dig into the joint. I felt my hands grow heavier as I held them out to pray. The back of my left thigh started to itch uncontrollably shortly after Nones. Hours passed. I felt my throat dry and my bladder fill. I rose to take care of both. After finding a thin trickle of fresh water near the gully and leaving some water behind on the lower side of the road, I returned to my knees. I was devoted to God but God never seemed to spare me any physical discomforts.

I offered up the suffering for the suffering of the world. That was my job. I was a monk doing my duty, performing my daily office. Monks pray. We pray for the people who work, who do not have the time or strength to offer thanks to God. We pray for the poor peasant, so weary and sore after a day's work in the fields that they can't manage to raise their eyes or thoughts to the mysteries of salvation. We never pray for ourselves. Our prayers help to hold the world together. At least that's what we're taught. Some work, some fight, we pray.

The night was dark but not cold. After Compline, I slept the light, uneasy sleep I was used to from the cloister. My body knew how much time it had to recover from a day and when it had to wake. When the first beams of the sun found their way from Jerusalem, past Rome and streaked my face, I was up on my knees, singing Matins again, with all my ticks and discomforts in place. I had no more idea of what I ought to do than I did the day before.

***

The sun rose, throwing light onto the gray stones of the old road. It got hot early and the sun shone directly in my eyes. I had just finished another rosary, trying to think of the joyful mysteries through my pains. I was about to start the psalms that went with the hour of Terce. My eyes were closed but then I heard something. It was a snatch of a song in a language that I felt I knew but couldn't quite understand.

♪Un muro de malo sueños
Me separa de los meurtos...♪

The voice was thin and high and seemed to come from the back of the singer's throat. I opened my eyes. At first, I couldn't see anything. My sight adjusted slowly, and I saw something moving ahead of me.

It took me a moment but then it became as clear and sharp as a puppet show. There, emerging from the ravine up ahead was the shape of a mule in sharp, black silhouette, outlined against the bright sun. It appeared, miracle of miracles, that someone was riding on its back, his shadow as clear as the animal's.

I leapt from my knees to my feet, forgetting my sandals.

"Fra Pedro!" I called. "Fra Pedro, where have you been?"

The rider and the mule came fully out of the ravine and started to turn down the road towards Perpignan, ignoring me completely.

I ran towards them.

"Pedro!" I shouted again, trying to muster some authority. The shadows gave way to images and I could see that the gray mule was unsaddled and carried no panniers. I could also see that the rider was not a monk at all. He was a small man with dark hair, dressed in a brown tunic that came just below his knees. He wore no cowl or hat, but there was a white cloth wrapped around his neck.

My momentum carried me forward and although I could feel the sharp stones cutting my feet, I ran on.

"Wait. For the love of Christ, man, wait!"

The rider made a small noise to the animal. They stopped and he turned to look towards me, one leg hanging against the side of the mule, the other bent across its back, his chin held in a hand resting on his knee.

It was not Fra Pedro, of course. He was about the same height as my missing monk, but he seemed more compact, better fed, and a bit more wiry. His hair was dark and so was his skin. He wore a thin mustache that framed his thin-lipped mouth before curving into a neat beard that spoke of insolence and indolence, somehow. His eyes were hard and as dark as his hair, and he watched me as I slowed on my approach.

"Greetings, holy friar," he finally said in Catalan.

"Hello, good man," I panted in the same language, leaning against the mule, pressing a hand on its haunch. "Good morning. Where have you come from?"

The fellow unwrapped the cloth from around his throat and I saw the seashell badge of a pilgrim from Compestola.

"From the holy shrine, Father."

"But this doesn't seem like the direction you'd be coming....?"

"I made my pilgrimage, now I wander here and there," he replied.

"In your wanderings—your recent wanderings—have you seen a monk of my order? About your size? His face marked by the pox?"

A sly smile played between his mustache and beard. His teeth showed oddly even and oddly white.

"The reason I ask," I went on, "is because the last time I saw him, he had this mule in his charge."

He shook his head ruefully but said nothing.

"I am certain this mule comes from our priory," I said. "Because the brother farrier marks them all at the ear," I pointed, "and the haunch."

He shrugged.

"It seems pretty clear to me that this is the mule I was traveling with. It also seems clear to me that there was recently a monk with this mule. Have you seen him?"

"Perhaps," the man finally answered after a long, slightly impudent pause. "I can't be certain. I was walking down the ravine back there." He jerked his thumb over his shoulder. "I saw this mule wandering. It is very steep up there. It gets steep and deep and rocky very quickly when you go in that direction."

I just nodded.

"This mule was wandering, as I said. The path is narrow. Did I say the path was narrow?"

"No, you did not."

"Well, it is. I looked over the edge of this narrow path and there, at the bottom of the ravine was—I am sorry to tell you this—"

"Tell me what?" My voice was rising.

"I did see something there. It looked like it wore a white cassock and perhaps there was a black cowl. It might have been a monk. Once. There was a lot of red, too."

"You're telling me that Fra Pedro is dead?"

"I don't know any Fra Pedro. I did not see a person. I saw a form, a white cassock, a black cowl and much red far below me. It may have been your Fra Pedro. I cannot say with any certainty on such evidence."

I didn't really have much answer to that. "How far up?" I asked at last.

"Three miles, maybe four. It is very steep that way."

"Could I reach the body? To bury it?" I asked.

"Perhaps," he answered. "But then you could not reach this road again. You would be trapped down there."

I pondered the situation for a moment. Fra Pedro, if it was Pedro, was with God. There was nothing to be done for him.

"There were panniers—baskets—on this beast?"

"Oh, those. I left them just up the way. I led the mule down the path, but as it widened out I felt that I should ride rather than walk. The baskets wouldn't get weary. I glanced in them and saw nothing I could use. I prefer to travel light."

"Do you acknowledge that this is rightfully my mule?"

"You say so. I don't know that. You could be standing here waiting to claim any animal that came along as your own. I don't know what a brother farrier is and I don't know if the marks you pointed to are the works of man or God. Still, you knew about the baskets."

"I did."

"Perhaps it is yours then. Perhaps we should travel together."

"Don't you care where I'm going?"

"I have no home. No one is waiting for me. The world is a large place. I would see some of it. If it makes you feel better, I will ask you. Where are you going?"

"I'm wandering through the cities of the plain and into the mountains. I am collecting songs—music, I have the words."

"That sounds like a charming way to pass the time in summer. I shall come with you."

"Shall you now?" I asked him. "Do you wish to know who I am?"

"You are a monk who is collecting songs. You are Basque. You play the guitarra. What more do I need to know?"

"My name, perhaps. I am called Fra Itzal." I bowed slightly.

He bowed back at me and slid down from the mule's back.

"And you are?" I asked.

"In the Church my name is Sixtus. But I answer more readily to what I was called as a child, Zaid."

"Well, Zaid," the name felt strange on my tongue, "can you write?"

"I can write the letters of Latin and the letters of my fathers. I have a good hand, I'm told."

"Very well then. We shall travel together, though I'd like to get those baskets. You may not have need of what they hold, but I believe that I shall."

"Yes, yes, my holy friend, let's go get the baskets. Then we shall seek some songs."

6
Words along the Way

"My father would have fought you."

"What?" I asked.

"My father, he would have fought you for the mule. You were just a chance encounter on a road. You claim the mule by ownership; he would claim it by possession. He would have fought you. I thought I'd tell you."

We were climbing up the ravine where Fra Pedro had vanished. We'd already reclaimed the panniers. The sun was just below noon and the day was hot. Zaid was right, the ravine rose fast. The path was narrow and climbed high above the sharp stones below us. There was a trickle of water running down there somewhere, that was probably a torrent in the spring and treacherously slippery in winter. A few scrub pines clung to the brown and white walls that rose above and fell beneath us.

"There," Zaid said, pointing towards something on the ravine floor.

I stopped and looked down the steep slope. The scree on the path was marred here, and the edge looked crumbly and dangerous enough. I couldn't see anything at first.

"Where?"

"Right there. See, just on this side of the little stream. By that gray rock. The round one, not the sharp one."

I peered into the shadows having trouble because of the bright light where we were standing. I thought I saw something white down there. Maybe a little stain of black. Something that might have been red. I'm not sure what I saw, really.

"Are you sure that's a body?" I asked.

"No, holy one. I'm not sure at all. It is just that this is where the mule was wandering untended. You can see the break in the pathway. All I see is cloth and some red. But there was no one above this point on the path and I met no one until I came upon you. It seems likely that is where your companion ended up. But I would not swear to anything on such evidence."

I sighed and squatted by the side of the narrow trail. I stared down but still wasn't sure of anything. I looked around a bit and became certain that Zaid was right—I might be able to get down, but I could never get back up, and the floor of the ravine was littered with enough broken rock that trying to follow it back to the road would be a fool's errand. I rolled to my knees and crossed myself. Zaid stood behind me.

Requiem aeternam dona eis Domine: et lux perpetua luceat eis...

I intoned the words of the Mass for the Dead. I only knew the Introit by heart. We had buried enough brothers for that. Since I wasn't a priest, I wasn't used to performing this ritual. I finished the Introit and prayed a *Pater Noster* and then rose to my feet.

"That's as much good as I can do him. I wish we could bury him."

"It is not practical, Fra," Zaid reminded me. "There might be a way down, look." He said, squatting at the edge of the precipice. I bent over and followed his finger. "You could climb from rock to rock, perhaps support your weight with some of the scrub. It would be a stiff climb, but it could be done. Still, we could never get back up, especially not burdened with a body. If we had ropes, ladders, and a great deal of help, perhaps, but we do not."

"No, we don't," I agreed. "Let's take a bit of refreshment away from this sorrowful cliff, at least, and then move on. I'd like to be close to Narbonne before we halt for the day."

I pulled the mule towards the high side of the path and produced a ham, some bread, and wine from the panniers. I poured some wine down my throat and then offered the bottle to Zaid.

"No, thank you," he said, pushing it back towards me. "I don't partake of wine."

"I hope you have some water, then, because I don't," I informed him. I tore the bread, passed him a piece, and began to cut a few strips off the ham.

"I don't eat the flesh of pigs, either," Zaid told me rather stiffly.

"What? Are you a Jew? Or a Moor?"

"Do you see a yellow crescent on my shoulder? A yellow star? A yellow cross, even?" his voice rose in anger. "No, you see only the pure white of the scallop shell. I have made my pilgrimage." There was a cold fire in his eyes. They held mine for a moment and then he laughed.

"No, Fra Itzal, I am a good Catholic," Zaid said. "My parents, they were Moors, though, can't you tell by looking at me?"

I nodded. He was dark. So am I. So are many people in this part of the world.

"I was born in the south, in Granada. My parents worked their way north and found themselves in Aragon. Moors are not especially welcome there, so they converted. I was baptized when I was six and have prayed as you pray ever since."

"Then have some ham. Have some wine."

"No, Fra. It is not conviction, just habit. Neither pork nor wine were served in the house I knew as a child and the memory stays with me. That is why I left those baskets behind. I saw nothing that I could use. Although I should have looked further. I did not notice the purse.

"Pay me no mind. Eat and drink what you will. But eat quickly. I would like to get back to the road. I don't like this place much."

***

"It won't get much cooler, we might as well move on," I said after we had tried taking shelter in the little shade afforded by the ravine walls. The road rolled out to our left and right. The hour of Sext had passed as we climbed down from the heights, but the sun was white, bright and unrelenting.

"No, monk, it won't," Zaid responded. "We may as well walk and be done on all sides instead of being baked here."

So we chivvied the mule and headed down the ancient stones. They were still flat and almost even after more than a thousand years. Gray and white, with the occasional flag missing, it rolled gently downhill. We saw Perpignan ahead, tucked in its bend of river. Zaid, bored and hot, started to sing after a while.

He sang in a language I didn't know at all. I assumed it was a strange tongue of the South. Something Arabic, Saracen, or bastard Granadan for all I knew. He sang mostly through his nose, it seemed, and the music was odd but not altogether unfamiliar. He came to what was the end of a verse and words came out that I almost recognized as speech.

♪Tant' amare, tant' amare
Habib, tant' amare?
Enfermaron uelios gaios,
E dolen tan male...♪

"Wait," I said. "Stop singing for a moment. What were those last words?"

"What? Oh, it was in Spanish, sort of."

"What kind of language is that?" I asked.

"It is the one they speak in the South, at the edge of Aragon, south of Navarre. Where Catholics are few. And the words aren't exactly that language. It's just something they tack on."

"I don't understand. Not that I understood what you were singing before."

"It's an Arab kind of song, or a song from al Andalus, really. The verses—stanzas are in high Arabic, what I was singing when I started. Then the chorus, refrain, response—" he was searching for a word in a language that I would recognize. "The response has to be in a, well, what they call a vulgar tongue. They chose the tongue of the Christians as vulgar enough for the purpose."

"Oh," I said dumbly. "What did it mean?"

"The song was about love. All songs are about love, aren't they? Most, anyway. It is the song of a young girl whose lover has gone away. I don't really know why. I don't really speak much Arabic; I just learned the songs at my mother's knees as she sorted chickpeas. The girl is sad because her lover is gone. She misses the loving they had. That's the part in the other language—'so much loving, so much loving, beloved, so much loving. My eyes were happy but now they are sad and tired.' Something like that."

"So much loving? Doesn't she mean so much love?" I asked.

"I don't think so. Forgive me, your holiness, but I believe what she is missing is more physical, shall we say, than any emotion. This girl isn't high-minded. It's her bed that's empty, not her heart."

"Oh," I said. I didn't think I could add anything. "It doesn't seem very pure."

"All love is pure. Especially the physical."

"I wasn't speaking of that. I meant the language. The Arabic, the—Spanish, did you call it? The Spanish, and there were some other kinds of words in there, too."

"Maybe. I don't know. But tongues are like that. They get mixed and mingled. There are invasions. There are Crusades. There are ships and camels and mules, and one people who speak one tongue trade with another people, and words get left behind. You speak to me in, what? The tongue they call Catalan, right?"

"Right."

"Well, what is that besides the residue of the collision of the Visigoths with Roman legions, and perhaps some stray trading men from the other side of the central sea?"

I shrugged. I didn't know much of these things. We had reached the flatlands before the white brick town of Perpignan. We stayed south of the river and avoided the trading center altogether. We kept on down the rolling plain with vineyards stretching away to our left. We were both hot and weary. Dust was stirred by our feet and the little winds that came from the direction of the sea. Our lips got thick with it after some miles. We walked on mostly in silence. Every now and again, Zaid would sing another strange song, but I was too hot, dirty, and sticky for much conversation.

After some hours, after Nones certainly, but before sundown, we could see Narbonne in all its size and magnificence rising in front of us. It wasn't far. We could probably reach it before it got too dark. Still, I slowed.

"Keep moving, Fra," Zaid urged. "Don't you want shelter tonight?"

"What for? It's fine in the evenings. Still hot, but not so bad. Besides, my abbot, for his own reasons, wanted me to start the quest in Beziers before turning back towards Narbonne. I don't know why, but I am obedient."

"It's not my mission. I am just following you. I don't mind sleeping outside. How could I? I made my pilgrimage and there was not always shelter along the road. Certainly none to be had that was not ruinously priced unless you wanted a great deal of company, which I seldom do."

We walked on for another hour or so; the great city with its walls and river port grew larger and larger. We could see the old walls, some built by the Romans, some by the Visigoths. Walls that had been assaulted, breached and repaired, over and over again. A good part of me wanted to enter, but still, I felt bound by my instructions.

About a mile west of the city, we started to come upon the suburbs, the small house holdings that surround cities but are never quite part of them. We walked on a little further and I saw something on the sea side of the road. It was a small white building with a steeple of some sort.

"There's our shelter," I said to Zaid, pointing. We turned off the road and reached the building in just a few minutes. It was obviously a chapel but there was no cross at the tip of its low tower. A small hut stood nearby. I walked over and tapped on the wall. No one emerged. I waited.

Zaid had walked over to the chapel itself. He pushed open the door. There were cries of protest from what must have been old and stiff hinges.

"I don't think anyone is here," he said.

"You may be right," I answered. I ducked my head into the hut. There was a broken table, a small clay cup, and the remains of what might have been two palettes but no evidence of recent habitation. It looked dirty and had a foul smell as if something unclean had been burnt here. I walked over to the chapel.

"It looks abandoned."

I walked into the small, dark room. There was no altar or altarpiece that I could make out in the little light the door allowed in. There was no odor of sanctity, no remnant of years of burning incense left to the place. The windows were plain glass and one or two of them were broken. The walls were once whitewashed but showed the ravages of time. Pillars made of wood supported the ceiling, with the work of worms evident along their length. The sea had not been kind and there was sand and dust on the floor. There was no presence lamp or any hint of candles. It did not even smell as if beeswax had ever melted in that room.

"Well, if it is abandoned, no one will object if we stay here for the night. At least it will be a little cooler. We may as well bring the mule in with us. This may once have been a holy place, but it isn't any longer."

7
Approaching Beziers

We unrolled blankets in the hollow room. There was still light leaking in through the dusty windows and the east-facing doors. Zaid looked around while I removed bread and hard cheese from the panniers.

"This is an older building than you might think, Fra Itzal," Zaid said, running his hand along the doorframe. "See here, there is mosaic tile work that has been white-washed over. Probably Moorish. Their forces have been this far north before and they did leave a few things behind."

"If it was Moorish it hasn't been for some time. It does look like it was used as a chapel in recent memory, but if so, no relic has been forgotten here." I proffered the bread in his direction and he took it from my hand. He didn't say anything more but chewed thoughtfully.

The sky grew darker and the room grew dimmer. I finished eating and knelt, facing east, facing towards Rome and Jerusalem, to say Vespers. I intoned the Latin, chanting it since that's how my memory best held the words. Zaid didn't kneel or even bow his head. He just watched me with a cat-like curiosity.

Prayers finished, I took off my traveling cowl, rolled it into a pillow, and lay down on my palette. Zaid sat cross-legged, looking around the room as long as there was any light to see. At least, that was my impression as I drifted off to sleep.

Later in the night winds came off the sea and sang through gaps in the old plaster. I heard odd skittering sounds on the roof above us, vaguely, through my dreams. It sounded heavier than a rat, but perhaps some residue of the day haunted my sleep.

Late in the night, there was a loud bang, like a callused palm hitting a fat monk across the face, only multiplied in volume. I sat straight up, confused as to where I was. The room was black, but there was a lighter purple archway showing in the eastern wall, with pinpricks of light hanging within it and a bit of milky light illuminating the flags. I sighed. It was nothing. The winds had blown open the door. I rose and closed it, looking out at the night. I had a fleeting impression of movement out of the corner of my eyes but nothing more. Just dust in the wind, I thought. I lay back down on my palette and drifted back to sleep.

***

Morning came sooner than desired, as it tends to do. We rose and gathered our things. I dipped some bread in wine by way of breakfast, handing the loaf to Zaid. I said Matins while he set off to find something to serve as a privy. When he returned, I followed his example and found a disused outhouse behind the shack. Then we set back out on the road.

The morning was fine and bright and we managed to cover the miles to Narbonne before Prime. We didn't enter the city but skirted it, walking through the crowded bustle of the docks. Here we were able to buy some salted dried fish and some that had been smoked. I felt better knowing that Zaid would have something to eat for the next leg of our journey.

We turned inland from Narbonne, still following the old Roman road from the ancient capital of Gaul. The ground rose steadily. The grasses were already golden brown, almost burnt by the force of the summer sun, which was rising higher in the sky as we walked. We stopped at the hour of Terce for refreshment and, in my case, prayer. I was glad of my little book of offices, with its reminders of all the feasts. It was the feast of Saint Irenaeus and I tried to remember what I knew about him as we walked. I recalled several large volumes with his name on them in the priory's library and tried to recall their subject as the road wound upwards. Then, suddenly, I could see the title almost as if they were right in front of me, the Latin stamped in gold on calfskin—*Contra Heriticum*.

***

The road was no longer deserted. There was traffic between Narbonne and Beziers between Montpellier and Avignon. There was traffic and trade throughout this part of the world, not like the lonely coasts of Spain. We were slowed by a herd of sheep at one point, which must have confused the animals since they should have been in the mountains this time of year, but perhaps they were fated for tables instead of clothing. At one point, I remember seeing a knife grinder ahead of us, his stone wheel strapped to his back, a Gibraltar monkey traveling with him for no discernable reason. Behind us was a thin boy with a shock of white hair in a loose shift. He never seemed to get too far behind us or ever catch up to us. We were passed by others—fishermen and miller's assistants dusted white with flour, night soil gatherers with fragrant wagons pulled by more fragrant animals, turning off the road here and there towards the fields that needed manure. Some farmers had begun to make their hay already, although it was early in the season.

It was worldly of me, but I enjoyed the activity on the road. I took pleasure in the work that these people pursued, the everyday chores that circumscribed our lives. The hay being cut on the left-hand side of the road smelled fresh and bright and made me think of my brother and his wife, so far away to the west. I was sad when the grinder turned up a path towards a small clay house. I would miss his monkey, I knew.

There was chatter, too, on the road, something I hadn't been used to over the last few days. I'd had the company of Fra Pedro and now Zaid, but that was different from the undifferentiated noise of fellow travelers. Catalan blended into Occitan. The Lombard dialect seemed to be prevalent as well, as a troop of glass-workers came walking our way, one or two singing words I didn't understand in accents I found quite thick. I was able to make out something about a church in Narbonne, apparently some stained work was needed and only Italian craftsmen would do.

It was good to be on the road among people again. I had been kept safe in the cloister for so long, and then the first part of this journey seemed to cover such lonely paths. Had they been less lonely, Pedro might still have been with me.

Then the road took a wide, sweeping curve and crested a hill, and there it was, materializing ahead of us—Beziers.

***

The River Orb took a bow-like bend right there, and the old city loomed above it like a scar on the landscape. On the southern side, there were new buildings and newer construction underway, but the walls of the old stronghold of the Trenceval looked like broken teeth in front of us.

It has been almost two generations, but the world must still know what happened there when the invaders came from the North with the Pope's blessing at the Pope's request. They came to save souls, they said. The heretics were everywhere; they held sway, they would seduce good Catholics to their evil ways, and the Devil would have more souls to play with. It had nothing to do with the rich vineyards and the rolling plains. It didn't matter that there were good ports nearby. It was because they loved God differently that these people had to be stopped. That was what the chronicles said, that is what they told us in the cloister back in Aragon.

And I believed what I was told. I was wearing the white robe and black cowl of the Dominican order as I approached the city. I was a member of the Order of the Inquisition. I believed that purest Catholicism was the only road to God. I believed those people had to be saved from themselves.

"That's quite a ruin," Zaid observed as we turned towards the city.

"The first casualty of the Crusade," I replied. The walls still showed soot from the fires of all those years ago. You could see that there was work going on around the cathedral of Saint Nazaire where those fateful orders had been given. I tried not even to think of them.

"What happened here?" Zaid asked.

So much for avoiding it.

"The Pope declared a Crusade. One of his legates had been murdered up near Avignon." I waved towards the north. "There were heretics, Cathars they called themselves, and they were part of the culture here. They were ministers and millers, knights and ladies, many people were Cathars. And they were not rooted out by their local lords. The Pope could not have that. They were a threat to the Church. A threat to the Church is a threat to everyone's salvation."

"So you say. I will agree. I am a good Catholic."

"The armies came from the North. Many of them were noblemen trying to serve God. Many more were seeking the indulgence that came with the cross, and they could do it without the risk of crossing the sea. Raymond of Toulouse, their own lord, joined the crusaders, though it is said that he did it to protect his people."

"If the lord is in the Crusade, then his lands are inviolate, correct?"

"Correct, or so it should have been. This was the first city besieged. Look at it. Look at those walls or remnants of walls."

I waved my hand in a grand gesture towards the old town above the river. We had stopped on a small hillock, a perfect podium for my lecture.

"It should have been a good, long siege. It should have lasted the forty days of everyone's vows. After ten days, rations would grow smaller, after twenty days, smaller still. Towards the end of thirty, there would be hunger enough to serve as a penance for the sins of the city. The sinners within and the soldiers without would have had their sins forgiven, too. Or they might have capitulated, given up a few souls to the flames. Either way, the quarantine would have been over, the army would have dispersed to the North. Raymond of Toulouse would promise to root out the heresy. He might have even meant it. That is what should have happened."

"You are going to tell me that is not what happened," Zaid prompted.

"No, it's not. This is what I have heard, though I may have heard it wrong.

"Before camp had been set, before the noble knights had a chance to break out their gold plates and their fine wines, the rabble that follows an army wandered too close to the walls. It looks like it must have been over there." I waved my hand towards a broken bridgehead below the bright new bridge across the Orb. "Apparently, the inmates of Beziers decided to pick a few of them off. They were stragglers—workmen, poor pike bearers, women of no virtue at all. They were nothing, they held no rank. But they were human and they were foreign. They were attacked and they turned on their attackers.

"The defenders of Beziers, so brave moments before, ran back towards the walled city. However, they were slow to close the gates, and a strong party of these camp followers followed them in through the walls. Even so, they should have been killed right away. The damage should not have been done, but the people who knew their business were elsewhere, trying to shore up the defenses for the battle that was sure to be joined in the morning. No one remembered to close the gate. They threw stones at the rabble. One or two were stabbed, but enough made it back to the gate to raise an alarm, and then the rest of the camp followers and some of the foot soldiers came pouring into the city. The knights followed. They killed everyone in their path. Everyone, sparing not a woman, not a child, not a cripple or a priest—because the keepers of the Catholic Church refused to leave their countrymen, who they felt had done no wrong—they killed them all. The streets ran slick with blood.

"There was a panic. Of course there was a panic. People screaming and running upwards towards the top of the citadel, but it was too late. Those inner walls had been breached by then. Those who could take refuge in the Cathedral of Saint Nazaire—right there, still being rebuilt." I pointed needlessly for Zaid's benefit, but I didn't care, I was caught up in the story. "All of the remaining populace, Catholic and Cathar, the believers and the heretics. The knights, their ladies, the tradesmen and their wives, and all of their children. Hundreds, the chronicle says five thousand, but even I know that's more than the city held. The true military men followed their own camp followers into the city. They were furious. The poor vagabonds had already grabbed as much of the loot as they could carry, and what they hadn't taken, they burned or broke. The city was on fire. All the houses, all the rugs and tapestries, all the wine and candlesticks, all the wealth of Beziers was burning.

"The army, the official army of noblemen, along with the papal legate, Almheric, who was supposed to be the commander, followed this rabble. They climbed the streets, their horse's hooves slipping on the blood-rich cobbles, holding their hauberks in front of their faces against the smoke and the heat. They reached the square in front of the cathedral. The entire population of Beziers, all those that still lived. Every last one of them was inside the house of God, the house of Christ.

"One of the knights turned to the legate to ask him what should be done. There was no way to tell who was in the church. There were both Catholics and heretics. How could they possibly be able to spare the faithful and destroy the infidel, he asked this man of God. The answer he received will live forever."

"Well," Zaid asked, impatient. "What did he say?"

"This holy man uttered these words—'Kill them all. God will know his own.' And then the torches were thrown. No one left the cathedral alive."

8
The Broken City

"Do you suppose they remember any songs?" Zaid asked after a moment.

"I don't know. This is where I was told to start though, so it's here my search must begin."

"But you already began," Zaid said. "There is a song in your book."

"How do you know that?"

"I read it by moonlight while you slept," he answered coolly. "I was kept awake by the winds."

"Never mind. We may as well move along." I tugged at the mule's reins and we started down the busy road towards the town.

The south side of the river was covered with new construction. New houses built with more timber than I was used to seeing. As we entered the unwalled town, the language began to confuse me. They weren't speaking Occitan or Catalan or even Lombard. It wasn't some dialect from Provence. It was a tongue that felt familiar but didn't sound it. The accents were harsher, more guttural than I expected. As we walked on it came to me that this was French, a tongue I had only read on the page. The people building these houses did not come from around this part of the land at all; they had come down from the North with the invaders. Beziers was getting a whole new population.

As we walked down what seemed to be a main street lined with shops that sold wine and oil, the people bowed to me, tugging at their forelocks, caps, or hoods. "Bonjour, Pere," they all murmured almost too softly, too deferentially to be heard.

I looked around but saw no sign of any church except the cathedral across the river. I did see a pair of Dominican brothers coming my way, walking stiffly erect, the people parting to make way for them.

"Brethren," I called out in Occitan. They didn't seem to understand me at first. "Brothers," I tried in Catalan and they stopped.

"Greetings brother," the taller of them said in oddly accented Catalan. The habits that both men wore were blindingly white, almost crisp and there was not a bit of dust on their black cowls.

"We are visitors. I come from Aragon," I explained. "My prior has sent me here on a mission. Does our order have a chapter house here?" "In the shadow of the cathedral," the one who spoken already told me. He waved across the river. "You will lodge there tonight."

"And my companion?" I asked.

The two brothers looked at Zaid and apparently did not like what they saw. They surveyed him thoroughly, put their heads together, and conferred softly in the northern tongue. The one who had yet to speak turned towards me and said, "You servant can sleep in the stables with the workmen. You will share meals with us." He nodded stiffly as if everything were settled and the two brothers walked away, stiff and erect as boards.

**

"I apologize," I said as we crossed the Pont Neuf, leaving the new town behind us.

"For what, Fra?" Zaid asked softly.

"For the servant remark. They didn't know that you are my traveling companion and not a serving man. That you are free."

"I am free enough to be thought your servant if that makes things easier. I think the fewer explanations we give to monks like those the better. Besides, if I am taken for a servant I may be able to speak to people who would not speak to you. You noticed the people of the town almost cowered before your brothers, even though they spoke the same language. You must spend your time with those monks, but I don't think they are singers of songs."

"You are kind. And you are probably right."

We walked through the gates of the old citadel. The streets wound uphill towards the cathedral. All the buildings were either painfully new or burnt ruins. There weren't many of the new buildings and what there were all seemed to belong to the Church. There was a house for the Friars Minor standing alone on a street that had nothing else but blackened holes in the ground marking the sites of forgotten shops. All the commerce was below in the new town. There were a few knights in evidence, speaking their northern tongue loudly and forcefully, but mostly this part of the city was populated by monks and priests of various orders.

We reached the top of the hill and the street widened out into a square in front of the cathedral. At least, it must have been meant as a square. At the moment it had the look of a quarry. There were rocks of various sizes and shapes scattered across the flags. A small army of men worked on them with chisels and stone saws. Most were stripped to the waist, and there was a pile of their loose jerkins, most of them emblazoned with yellow crosses. The cursing in the air was mostly in Occitan. Here was the local peasantry, working off the penance for their parent's heresy.

We wound our way through this garden of stones across the great square, which was much larger than it looked when we entered. We saw before us a Dominican Chapter House on the north side of the square. This complex, at least, had been finished. A large group of buildings built out of yellow stone featured carvings of the saints and our founder, and marking the corners here and there were repentant heretics serving as gargoyles and rainspouts.

I walked to the great door and presented myself to the monk stationed there.

"Greetings, brother, I am a fellow of your order from Aragon. I have been sent here on a mission. I travel with a man and a beast," I said, waving towards Zaid and our mule.

"Welcome, brother," he said. At least, I think that's what he said. It is very difficult to get your ear around a tongue that you have only read on a page. "I'll take you to our prior. A man will see to your servant." I was led into the bowels of the great building.

***

The prior's study was deep inside the complex. We had passed through two rectangular cloisters before entering into a long hallway that seemed to go on for miles. The floors looked like marble, the walls were paneled in dark wood, and the monk's habit was as crisp and clean as those of the two I'd met below. The fabric seemed softer than my robe's, but I was only looking.

We came, this monk and I, to a large wooden door. The monk knocked and the door was opened by another brother, older and more dignified than my escort. He left, and this taller brother led me into a dark and cool room lined with books.

There was an imposing desk in the center and a dark wooden prei dieu in the corner, facing a painting of some saint I didn't recognize. A large man sat at the desk, turning the pages of what looked to be a ledger.

"That's fine, brother," the man said, closing the book and sliding it across the polished expanse of his desk to the other monk. "Who is our visitor?"

"From Aragon, I do not know his name." The fellow took the ledger, bowed, and backed out of the room, leaving me with the person I presumed to be the leader of this community.

"Fra Itzal," I said, bowing a bit as the heavy door closed behind me. "I am from a chapter in Girona. My abbot has sent me. This letter will explain." I pulled the bundle of papers that my superior had entrusted to me out of my satchel and slid them across the slick surface of the desk. The presumed abbot said nothing but picked them up and examined them. He refolded the pages and slid them back to me.

"Welcome, Fra Itzal," he said, smiling. He spoke in Catalan and I was relieved. It was heavily accented, but it was still a tongue I knew. "I am not sure that I approve of the mission that you have been assigned, but that is not my place. You are welcome to our hospitality as long as you would like it. It is now past Nones. Take the evening meal with us. Join us for Vespers and Compline. Tomorrow you should rest from your journey and join us in prayer. A novice will guide you to a guest cell."

This seemed to be a dismissal. I went to the door and opened it and found a very young monk who guided me back through the maze of halls and cloisters, finally leading me into a room that seemed large to me, with a bed, a prei dieu, and a basin.

"I will return to lead you to our refectory when it is time," he said deferentially, and then he vanished.

***

I spent the next twenty-four hours, the feast of Saints Peter and Paul, immersing myself in the rituals that I knew, that I had come to depend on. I ate with fellow members of my order in their vast refectory. The meal was silent, as it should be, but sumptuous. There was more meat than there should have been, certainly, for any day other than a great feast. The wine was poured more liberally than had been the habit in Aragon. There was a monk reading from the Acts of the Apostles in good, if to my ear, highly accented Latin. After the meal I joined in Vespers in a chapel so new that it smarted from fresh wood and fresher varnish. The prior wore a gold-embroidered chasuble and much incense was splashed around the room. Too much for such a minor feast, I thought, then asked God for forgiveness for my ingratitude.

I slept in the large cell on a softer bed than was my custom, softer than any bed I had made on the road. Around what must have been midnight, I felt a hand slip around my shoulder then beneath my habit. I started awake. It was the novice who'd shown me the way through the halls.

"What?" I asked groggily, probably in Basque.

"I'm only waking you for Compline," this pretty boy said.

I pushed him off the palette and he landed on the floor with a light thud. I was startled and unused to being touched by anyone.

"Very well," I said. "I'm awake. Lead me to the chapel." The boy seemed unabashed. He picked up his candle and led me out into the cool, dark halls.

Hundreds of solitary flames glowed against the new stone as monk after monk, many of them in pairs, made their way to the nighttime chapel service. We all chanted the Latin in good voice, the ancient words echoing roundly off the tapestries that lined the wall. We were deep-voiced and deep-throated, although I heard a hint of soprano here and there. After the services, the young monk led me back to my cell. He lingered for a long moment at the door and then turned away.

I spent all of the following day going through the sacramental motions with my fellows in the order. After the nakedness of the open road, it was good to be clothed in liturgy again. I didn't venture out of the confines of the chapter house at all.

Still, it was odd. I had no duties here. I was treated as a welcome guest. I was taken to the baths and cleaned and then escorted to the brother barber to have my tonsure reshaved, my hair cut, and several days' growth of beard removed from my chin.

I tried to engage the barber, asking questions about any songs he might know that were local, peculiar to this town, but he seemed to speak only the French dialect that my ear couldn't penetrate. We communicated in a series of grunts and very vulgar Latin.

After the midday meal, another large one I thought, and after prayers at Sext, I visited the library. It was large and well stocked, and like everything else here, it was new. The room reeked of fresh leather and ink that you could almost taste in the air. The brothers in the library tried to be helpful, but I had trouble making myself understood, and the local lore and music seemed to hold no interest at all for these monks. I felt, after a day, that I had done all the work I could on my mission and decided we should move on the next day. That is, if I could find Zaid and if he wanted to continue as my companion.

After the evening meal, after Vespers, I asked my escort, a different novice, about the city.

"It's new and growing, Fra," he told me. "Most of the inhabitants are from the North. They have come from the estates of knights and their families, families like the de Montforts, great people, good Catholics. Here, they get to have land of their own, or shops, even. Almost no one who once lived here remains."

"What about those in the square?" I asked.

"Stonecutters. Local vermin. Yes, they come from families around here, families that strayed before we showed them the light. They have all been before the Inquisition—our prior is a great Inquisitor—they work off their heresy with their hands."

"And my...?" I couldn't recall what they had called Zaid.

"Your servant is fine. He is wandering among those in the square. He is fed. He has shelter."

"I must see him," I stated.

"In the morning, after Matins. In the meantime, we are here." He indicated my cell. "Here you stay. May I be your servant?" He smiled shyly.

I only shook my head and he sulked off, sandals scraping on stone flags.

***

The bright sun of the feast of the Blood of Christ bounced off the stones standing in the square, casting shadows across one another. The area was alive with activity and loud with the noise of hammers chipping at rock and the whine of two-man saws cutting through blocks of granite and sandstone. I bobbed my head here and there, peering around the various workmen, looking for Zaid.

"Well," a voice said over my left shoulder, "do those monks sing?"

I turned, face to face with Zaid. "No," I answered. "They chant well enough, but they don't sing. I don't think any of them come from south of the central mountains. Do any of these?"

"Most of them barely speak," he said. "They are sullen, angry men who feel like slaves. For good reason, I would agree. I was treated well, as nearly as I can tell, and I have seen dogs treated better."

"I am sorry. My brethren are usually better hosts than that. They treat guests better than they treat themselves. At least, that is the rule of our order. This place seems to have rules of its own."

"Every place has rules of its own," he observed. "However, I did hear one of these stone men sing. I don't know if they were any of the words in your book, but he did sing. If you want to hear him and hear what he has to say, perhaps you could get some wine and cheese or meat. He will sing more loudly if his belly is made quiet. Needless to note, these men are not well fed."

That made sense to me. We walked back across the bright, noisy square to the chapter house. I sent a young monk to the commissary for supplies. He came back with a large bottle of gray wine, a loaf of good white bread, some kind of cured sausage, and an onion. It was enough to make a poor man sick.

Zaid led me through the zigzag paths among the rocks. It felt like navigating a maze, with turns out of light into darkness then back into light again. Expressions of pain and disgust burst out around us. It seemed to take a long time, but Zaid eventually found his man.

♪*Sest joglar mi fant grant pavor*
E Deus mi gard de lor amor
Qu'il ne gardent ni driet ni tort
E qui est lor amix est mort...

These joglars give me such fright
God save me from their company
They see no right, see no wrong
And if you're their friend, you're a dead man...♪

The voice that sang those words was as gray as the stones in front of us. We came around a large triangular stone, and there was the man as gray as the voice, weakly pounding at a rock in slow time to the tune he sang.

"Pons," Zaid said. "Pons, this is Itzal." Zaid pointed at me with his thumb.

The old man took one look at me and threw his arms over his face, dropping his tools.

"No, Pons, he's not one of them," Zaid explained. "He's from Catalonia, from Aragon. See, he travels alone." Zaid stroked the man's back gently. I moved to pick up his hammer and chisel and hand them back to him. "See, he's kind. He brought you something to eat and drink."

The old man seemed to grow quieter as Zaid rubbed his hand up and down his back. I took him in. He was once tall but now bending towards the ground, as old men will. I could see why he had trouble maintaining a grip on his tools since he had been deprived of both his thumbs. Possibly an accident, I thought, but more likely some sentence for a minor infraction. His hair was longish, roughly chopped off below his ears. His eyes were as gray as his hair and a scar ran across his face from below his right eye, across his nose, to the lower left corner of his mouth.

"Greetings, Pons," I said. "Here, have some wine." I passed him the bottle and he drank swiftly and deeply.

"Gratis." He said, in some semblance of the common tongue.

"That song you were singing," I said, addressing him familiarly in Occitan, "I didn't hear much of it. It seems to be about joglars. Is that what you did?" I asked.

"Once," he answered in the same language, breathing more comfortably now that he was reasonably sure that I wasn't here to burn him.

"Joglar?" Zaid asked. "I don't know the word."

"The men who wrote the songs," I explained. "They could compose words and they could find the tunes. That is what is said of them. Many of them, though, were not made to sing the melodies they found. They would travel with men, sometimes women, called joglars. It was these who would perform the songs. Isn't that right, Pons?"

"Almost, master monk," this old relic croaked. "That is how it was for many of these troubars, as we called them. My master could sing very well, but he chose not to sing most of the time."

"Why is that?" I asked as gently as I could.

"Because he was always too angry. He chose me as his singer because I was so sad."

"And what makes you sad, old man?" I asked.

"I am sad because of what I saw."

"What did you see?" Zaid asked, impatient.

"I saw everything. I was there. I was at Montsegur."

9
The Stonecutter's Song

"You were at Montsegur? As a joglar?" I asked.

"Don't be silly, man, Fra, I'm sorry. But still, don't be silly. Why would there have been joglars at a massacre?"

"But you said you were there. You told us you were a joglar. And I don't even really know what the word means," Zaid continued for me.

"I was and I was. I mean I was both. I was a joglar and I was at Montsegur. Just not both at the same time."

"Were you in the siege? In the fortress?" I asked, hoping to get somewhere near clarity.

"*Allons, allons!* Back to work. No one commuted your sentence," a guttural voice filled with coarse consonants barked behind me.

A square, very stolid man blocked out the sun, completing the shadowed darkness that the stones began. He reached out towards Pons; whether to strike him or take him, I'll never know. Zaid tugged at my white sleeve and winked.

I straightened up, trying to invest my slender body with some kind of authority, and turned towards the man who'd interrupted us.

"*Pardon, Pere,*" he said quickly, bowing a little bit, or so I gathered. It was more like the bob of a head and a tug at where a forelock might have been had he not been so perfectly bald. "It is my task to keep these penitents working." At least, that's what it sounded like to me. I still was on shaky ground with the languages being used here in Beziers.

"*Ego absolvo te,*" I offered in Latin, hoping to be understood. "I have questions."

"*Oui, Pere, pardon.*" The rectangle of a fellow backed away, allowing the sun to shine on our little trio once again.

***

"I will protect you, Pons," I assured the gray man, using the familiar *tu*. "You don't need to fear these men today."

"That's a small comfort. He will punish me tomorrow for making him look bad in front of one of the white monks. It doesn't matter, I'm used to being punished. How did their mothers raise them, these northern barbarians? I'd rather be a priest!" He spat on the ground.

"You were speaking of Montsegur….?" Zaid prompted, almost licking his lips and thin mustache.

"No, no I wasn't. I only said that I was there and that is why I was so sad. That is why Peire Cardenal wanted me for his joglar."

"The name is familiar," I said, reaching over my shoulder for the satchel that held all our papers and our book. "But wait, I will find it. In the meantime, old man, you should eat and drink. You too, Zaid." I noticed the stonecutter started at the Moorish name. "I have been too well fed across the way there." I gestured to my thumb over my right shoulder.

The two men took me at my word. They tore the bread. Zaid cut slices of onion and then passed the knife and sausage to Pons, apparently too unsure as to what kind of meat it might be to trust eating it. He confined himself to his water bottle while Pons drank deeply of the murky wine in the tall flagon.

Meanwhile, I searched through the papers in the satchel, certain that I had seen the name of Peire Cardenal among the poets in the bundle. I had no luck. I kept the bundle in front of me, turning the pages over until I found a blank space so I could write down whatever may be recited or sung by this convicted heretic. I relieved Pons of the wine bottle and drank some myself, then passed it back to him. I leaned against the side of the blond, triangular stone and waited for my companions to finish eating.

***

It took less time than it takes to tell, really. These were two poor and hungry men, one a virtual prisoner, and this was good food that was usually reserved for their betters. Except for the onion, of course. I had only asked for one because I knew the old man would find it familiar.

"Ah," Pons pronounced, "that is a pleasure." I slid the bottle across the rough flags and he drank again. "We never get anything better than barley bread, and most of the time not even that. And did you know we have to pay for that privilege?"

I just shook my head.

"You said you were at—" Zaid started. I waved silently in his direction and he stopped.

"You were a joglar?" I asked.

"I was. I had two careers as a joglar," Pons answered. "One early, one late."

"Early?" I asked.

"As a young man, I had a pretty voice. It was high and strong. And I could remember any tune that I'd ever heard," he said with a kiss of pride. "I wasn't attached to any one man then. There was a castle just this side of Foix. The lord and his lady liked my voice. It was after the Crusade had started, but it hadn't really reached us in the foothills yet. That came later."

"Yes, I know." I prompted.

"At the castle, the troubars would call. I met many of them. Some were famous, and some never became known at all, mostly for good reason."

"What might be a good reason?" Zaid asked.

"They made bad tunes. Or bad poems to good tunes. Those would be a pair of good reasons. And, there were always those who thought they could sing their way into the lady's bed. Rather, they thought I could sing their way there for them. I would have none of that."

"Why? It seems that is what the troubars were for?" I asked.

"Why? Because I was trying to sing my own way into ladies' beds! Why should I help anyone else? I would sing their songs in front of the community, in the hall of the castle. Often, they would play on lute or guitarra. Sometimes I just sang alone, my voice echoing against the stone walls.

"I had a very comfortable life. My hands stayed soft. I didn't have this scar across my face and I was called handsome. I never did sleep with the lady of the castle, but I slept with some of her ladies. That was my youth. I knew there was a war going on, but I didn't think that it would reach into the mountains." He stopped and reached for the bottle. I passed it.

"And then it did," I suggested.

"And then it did. They came in such numbers. I wasn't used to that. I was used to skirmishes with the Count of Foix or his small army. Ten or twelve knights, a hundred or so of infantry. A little blood would be spilled. Mostly superficial wounds. People were rarely killed, although an infection could carry you off. A treaty would be quickly signed and some poor animal would be killed for the peacemaking feast. That was war to me. Then they came down out of the North like God's own vengeance. They weren't interested in peace or terms. They all came for blood and they burned almost anything in front of them. Because they had no souls, they won."

"No souls," Zaid echoed.

"I was alone in the world. I tried to fight with my people. I took a sword across my face and nearly died of it. I was no longer a handsome youth. I saw which way the wind was bending the grain. I joined with the French." He laid his head down on his arms and looked down at his feet for a long moment.

"It was then I was put to work. It wasn't bad, most of the time. I was a—I'm not sure of the word, a *scriptor?* A *literari?*"

"A scribe?" I suggested.

"A scribe," he agreed happily. "I copied records. I wrote down names—I wrote down names." He began to sob dryly, heavily. Zaid and I looked at each other, then at this old man in front of us, and silently agreed that it was best to let him tell his tale in his own time.

I carved a sliver of sausage, more to have a place to direct my sight than for any reason of hunger. Zaid took the sheaf of papers from my hands and, holding my place, flipped through the poems I was sure he couldn't read. After a bit, while the stonecutter sobbed, Zaid gestured me close to him.

"Peire Cardenal," he whispered, pointing towards a name in the middle of the page, buried deep in the text. So much for my guesses about who could read what.

I looked at the page but didn't see a poem, just a passing reference. Still, I nodded to Zaid and he smiled. Pons had quieted now.

"You wrote down names," I coached, almost cooing the Occitan words. "Whose names?"

"There was peace. Uneasy peace, but peace. You remember." He looked at me and then at Zaid. "No, you're too young, you wouldn't remember. Anyway, there was peace. The Pope had won. The Cathars were quiet, if not gone, and the French controlled our land. The war was over or so it seemed. Old Raymond of Toulouse died, humiliated. His son, Raymond-Roger held much of the land as long as the Pope said it was all right. Montfort was dead. Your white monks, your Inquisition, went from village to city and chose people—at random, it seemed to us—and burnt them. We all watched because if you didn't, you might burn next."

I had not realized how long we had been talking. The sun had reached its zenith and was shooting its beams straight down through the forest of half-dressed stone. It was hot and there was no shelter nearby. If we walked to the portico of the unfinished cathedral we would suffer as much as if we'd stayed put. So we sat. I sipped some wine idly. Pons reached out and I passed the bottle over. He wiped off his gray lips, stroking the lower end of his scar with one of his four remaining fingers, and then he went on.

"People were fed up. The Cathars lived. They held the mountain fastness of Montsegur, and they probably could have stayed there until Christ came back, for all anyone seemed to care. But the people were weary of the Inquisition and the high hands of you preaching friars—forgive me, Fra." I gestured a half sign of the cross. "Bless you. Well, there was a stupid, bloody murder. A papal party, Dominicans and Friars Minor were attacked and killed. It was a well-planned conspiracy, no random act, and the Pope and his bishops decided it was time to eradicate the Cathar fortress."

"Everyone knows all that," Zaid said. "Even I know that. It was over twenty years ago. What did you do?"

"I, well, I was a—scribe. I traveled with the Church. I took no orders; I was just in ecclesiastical employ. We arrived after the siege was almost complete, almost a year into the fighting. The fortress was doomed. We were there to take the surrender.

"The terms were unusual. All the fighting men and their women and children would be free to go. They would submit to penance at some later date. Of course, none of the heretics, that is none of the *parfait*, the good men and women would be allowed to live. The citadel accepted the terms. They were given two weeks to make ready—that was very odd—and we were given two weeks to take down the names of all of those who the church, in her great mercy, were going to burn."

"And that was your job?" I asked.

"That was my job. I sat there at a table in the ruins of a fortress that had been under siege for the better part of a year. I had a scroll of parchment and, one by one, these gentle people, the Cathar elders and priests, who had taken it upon themselves to shed no blood, these men and women came to me, and I wrote down their names. For some reason, the bishops, in their wisdom, felt it was important to know exactly who was going to die.

"While I was making my list, looking into the sunken eyes of these people, a vast pyre was built at the foot of the mountain. They built a fence almost a mile around and filled the ground with drying wood. The people in the fortress could see it. Everyone knew what was going to happen. There were just over two hundred *parfait* and other heretics who had taken the *consolamentum* within Montsegur. I know. I wrote down all their names. That was sad, that was tragic, but it was inevitable. It was widely known that the Church wouldn't let any heretics survive. No, that wasn't the truly odd thing."

The sun had tilted a little to the west. Shadows started to appear around us. We all three shifted to find some shade. Then he went on.

"No, that wasn't odd at all. What was strange was that over thirty more people came up to me and had me write down their names. These people didn't have to burn. They had been through the long siege. They had suffered enough. They could have walked free, like me, perhaps, just marked with the yellow cross. No, they chose to go up in smoke. They came and they begged me to write their names down. I was a scribe. I wrote.

"When the two weeks were over, the people were separated like sheep from goats. The soldiers and camp followers were allowed to walk out and everyone whose name was on my parchment would go to the flames. And go they did. They were solemn, silent at first, as they walked out of the gates of that ruined citadel. When they reached the flat and saw that vast pyre up close, some of them clutched each other. Some dug in their heels. Then, one began to sing, and they all started to sing. Weakly at first, but drawing strength from each other, more strongly. And even if that's not how it happened, that's how I remember them. They all rose up to the sky in a great cloud of smoke. The fire burned for days."

Zaid and I sat there, squirming in the inadequate shade; feeling like we'd invaded someone's heart.

Finally, Zaid said, "You became a joglar again because you were so sad."

The old man raised his eyes, first to Zaid and then he looked towards me. He didn't say another word but began to sing in his gray, weary voice:

♪*Una ciutaz fo, bo sai cals,*
On cazet una plueia tals
Que tug l'ome de la ciutat
Que toquet foron dessenat...♪

He sang for a long time.

10

Transactions

The voice was old but it grew more and more pure as he sang out his long tale. The melody was simple and the verses were short. He sang slowly, sadly, as if this were a dirge. His voice grew into the story.

"A village went mad, I can't say where. There was a shower of rain and whoever got wet lost all their sense. They were quite berserk and none escaped but one. He was taking a nap inside when the rains fell.

"As soon as the shower was over, so was this man's nap. He strolled among the people but they all seemed deranged.

"One dressed like a child, and one was nude, another spit straight up into the air. One threw rocks, another sticks. One tore at his own flesh.

"One was a beast, another a stone, one thought he was a king and stomped out a dance with hands on his hips.

"The one who'd held his sense marveled at his townsmen who seemed to have lost all of theirs. He looked right, he looked left.

"He was the only one wise, the only one sound. There was no one left like him. He stared, wondering at them, and they all looked back at him, even more amazed."

By now I had written the melody out on the blank side of one of my pages and was searching the words to see if this was a song we were looking for. Zaid just listened, wrapped up in the song.

"They saw him so calm, they thought he must be mad," Pons went on, his voice gaining strength as he sang. "He seemed so outlandish, and everyone thought themselves quite sound, so clearly, he must be insane.

"One slapped his face, one punched his mouth, another spun him around. He rose, then slipped, and then fell back to the ground.

"He lurched away and crawled into his house to hide, bruised, spattered with mud, but alive—and sane, he knew.

"This earth's the town I have in mind, and such madness isn't hard to find.

"A rain of madness fell on this world—covetousness and sin, pride and malice, always prey while we humans pray. And if one man's kept safe by God, it's quite clear that he must be mad.

"He knows something they don't share, they send him like smoke through the air. God's wisdom is called lunacy; he knows who is mad and who is sane.

"But people know the sane man's crazy since he refused the world's sanity."

When the voice stopped, the silence was almost palpable. It seemed as if all the work had come to a halt on the square, and all the stonecutters had paused with their chisels and saws in mid-stroke. It only lasted a moment before the northerners started shouting at these poor penitents to go back to work.

"Sins don't absolve themselves!" I thought I heard one of them shout.

Saws whined again, hammers cracked against chisels that rang into the gray and gold stones. The square came back to its loud life.

"What's going on here?" one of the guards shouted into our little circle. I stood up to my full height, dusting off my habit, and looked straight at the fellow, mustering all the authority I could manage and just stared at the man. "*Pardon, Pere,*" the man said and backed away.

Pons looked at me and smiled. "Thank you, Fra," he said in Occitan. "That was the first time I have been able to let a whole song go in a long time."

"Whose song was that?" Zaid asked.

"That was my old master, Peire Cardenal. He didn't write many *cansos*, love songs. Mostly, he wrote *sirventes*, satires, invective—is that the word?" He looked towards me and I nodded. "Last I heard he was alive somewhere in Catalonia or Aragon. If he is, then he is very old. Perhaps over one hundred years."

Zaid rocked back and forth on his heels, still bent over the pages in front of us. He took my pen and quickly wrote out line after line and I realized he was putting down the whole song while it was fresh in his mind.

"Where are you journeying? May I ask you? You don't seem like the preaching friars who are the only law here."

"I am of that order," I answered. "But I am from Aragon. We have come up here to collect songs like the one you just sang for us. We don't want the music to vanish. See," I said, showing him the crude staff lines and the notes I had drawn. He looked at the marks dumbly. "Those are the sounds you made when you sang."

He peered at the page for a while and then shook his head. "If you say so, Fra. It looks like blots on a page to me."

"It is a way of remembering," I said. "That's all. It's not the same as the song. We have many songs here and we would like to write down their tunes so that they are not lost."

"Where do you go from here?" he asked again.

"We will go down to Narbonne, then north to Toulouse. Then we will turn into the mountains."

His eyes lit up at the mention of mountains.

"Take me with you, Fra. The mountains are my home. I could guide you. The ways are not always clear in the Aude, the Sarbathes, even along the Tarn."

"I'm not sure. I don't know how much we have by way of provisions," I answered, not because I wanted to leave him behind but because I wasn't at all sure that I could free him.

"I was a joglar, good Fra," he started to plead. "I didn't sing the only song I knew. I know many, many melodies, *cansos, sirventes*, even *tensos*. I can help you. Perhaps I know some of the ones that you have in your book. Even if I don't, many different words were set to the same tune. I can help, I can be of service. I hate cutting stone. I am a poor, old thumbless man. Save me, Fra."

I looked at his pleading eyes and then at Zaid, still squatting, smiling up at me with some slyness playing below his mustache.

"How long have you been here, cultivating these rocks?" Zaid asked.

"It has been three years," he answered.

"Who sentenced you?" I asked at last.

"The abbot here. He is a fervent Inquisitor."

"I will go see him. I don't know if it will do any good. But I will ask if your penance can be assigned to me. What is your surname, Pons?"

"Tor, Fra," he replied, bobbing his head. "But it won't mean anything to the Abbot. Just call me the thumbless singer. That he should recognize."

"You'd better bring your purse," Zaid advised. "But don't show its weight."

I stepped between the stones that had been our shelter and picked my way across the square.

***

Once more I was led into the bowels of stone that housed the brothers of my order in that damaged town. The other monks and priests were about their various tasks, so the halls were deserted. Our sandals echoed more loudly, my guide's and mine, as we strode along the flags past the scriptorium where a small army scratched pens against parchment, past chapels and cells, through two colonnaded cloisters before I found myself standing in front of the abbot's study once again. My guide pushed the door open, waved me to wait, and then signaled me to enter.

"Our visitor," the abbot greeted me, rising from behind his vast desk. "Fra Itzal from Aragon?" He framed the question with his voice.

"*Si, oui, oc,* Fra Abbot," I answered in three languages, a bit nonplussed at his deference. "That is, you are right, that is my name."

"Have my monks treated you well?" he asked, taking my elbow lightly and guiding me to a chair that faced across his desk towards a high window that threw warm yellow light down onto the marble flags and the polished wood.

"They have been very kind, reverence. It has been good to be inside a chapel again and to recite my prayers with others."

"The community is good for prayer." He nodded and folded his long hands resting his chin on his fingertips. He stared at me with his dark eyes for almost as long as it took to say a *Pater Noster*. I wasn't sure if I should say anything. Finally, he asked, "Is there some way I can serve you?"

"Yes, Fra Abbot, there is. It concerns one of your stonecutters."

"One of the penitents, working away their sins by rebuilding the cathedral that their unbelief destroyed? One of those?" His voice held an audible sneer.

"One of those," I agreed. "There is one among them who might prove of use in my mission. I was hoping I could persuade you to transfer his penance to me. I could oversee it, and see that he does not slip back into his heretical ways."

He nodded at me, his eyes staring through my chest. With his left hand, he lifted a small silver bell from his desk. The high, delicate tinkle was startling, but a door in the left wall opened immediately and silently. A very tall monk with a scarred face and a gray complexion entered.

"Fra Abbot?"

"Fetch me the register of our Inquisitions," he told the monk and then gestured to hold him back and turned towards me. "Do you know how long ago this poor man was sentenced?"

"He told me he has been cutting rocks for three years, Fra Abbot," I replied. He nodded at the tall monk who vanished through the door and reappeared in just a few seconds carrying a very large, leather-bound codex.

The abbot looked me up and down. He seemed to be taking in every detail of my habit and cowl. The fabric I wore was once as white as his but woven of rougher, more homespun cloth. His and his fellow monks all seemed to be woven from linen or very fine wool as far as I could tell. I was embarrassed by the dirty state of my cassock as he examined me. He stopped looking at me and then opened the codex flatly on the desk in front of him. He turned the pages at random, scanning what I assumed to be the writing in front of him.

"The man's name is Pons Tor," I told him, thinking it might be helpful to his search. "He said he was from the mountains."

"They are all from the mountains," the tall brother said speaking for the first time. His voice was as hollow as his cheeks. "The mountains are thick with heretics still. They refuse to let us save their souls."

"True, true, Fra Lazaire," the abbot murmured, still turning the pages in front of him. The tall monk examined me almost as closely as his superior had.

"He said his name might not mean anything to you?" I started.

"If he was sentenced," the abbot said, "his name will be in here."

"He told me to tell you he was the thumbless singer."

"Oh," he nodded to me. I couldn't tell if it meant anything to him. I sat.

The tall monk leaned over his abbot's shoulder. He ran his finger down the page, turned it, searched further, and turned the page again. Finally, his finger stopped halfway down the length of the long book. He whispered in the abbot's ear.

"Here, yes, Pons Tor," the abbot pronounced, not looking at the page in front of him. "It seems he was not himself convicted of heresy. At least not directly. He is guilty of sheltering heretics. And of not reporting them to the Inquisition."

"That is," I observed, "to you."

"That's correct," the abbot answered coolly. "It is not as serious as some offenses, still, it is serious enough."

"Serious enough that three years of cutting rocks is not a sufficient penance?" I asked.

"I am not sure I like your tone, brother," the abbot said. "Still, you are right. He has served most of his term. There is just the question of his fine."

"Fine?"

"He must pay for masses so that we can pray for his soul and save him from the fires of Hell."

"He has narrowly avoided the fires of earth," the tall fellow added.

"All right," I said. "How much will it be? My abbot has granted me some funds and it does seem that this poor soul can be of some use to me."

The two men looked at each other. The taller leaned down again, whispering some more while pointing out something on the page and then taking one last appraising look at me.

"Two *livres,*" the abbot announced.

It was an obscene amount of money, but I'd had enough of these monks. They carried themselves gravely but with a high hand, and I was not at all sure they were as interested in the greater glory of God as they were in the wealth of the community and the adornments of their monastery. I turned as far away from them as I could and opened the purse that was left to me. I was surprised by all the coins it held but was still reluctant to part with so much of it at once. I pulled out two silver coins and slid them across the dark surface of the desk.

"Then it is done," the abbot said. "You may take—"

"Pons Tor," I prompted.

"Pons Tor with you when you leave. And that will be?"

"We will leave here in the morning. I thank you for your generous hospitality."

"Our brethren are always welcome," the abbot answered, scribbling an order on a scrap of paper and handing it to his tall companion who, in turn, handed it to me. He guided me to the door and handed me off to the younger monk who had led me there. We made our way back to daylight.

***

"It is done," I said as I found the triangular rock that sheltered Zaid and Pons. Both the wine and food had disappeared. I held up the paper for them to see, but it meant nothing to them.

"Bless you, Fra," Pons fell to his knees, almost weeping. "How soon can we leave this hellish city?"

"We will leave in the morning, at the hour of Prime. I would hear Matins in the chapel if I can," I said, suddenly full of dignity.

"Do you have any money left after that transaction?" Zaid asked.

"Enough, I hope. The purse held more than I thought."

"Can you spare a small coin for me? I think it would be good to take Pons to the lower town today—"

"The Faubourg," Pons said.

"What?" both Zaid and I asked together.

"The Faubourg, the false town. That's what we call it."

"Oh, still, we should stay there in case these kind monks change their minds. We should sleep in an inn."

I searched through the purse and found two copper coins. I held them out to Zaid. "Will that be enough?"

"Enough for food, lodging, and perhaps even a girl."

"For each of us?" Pons asked.

"For each of us," Zaid answered.

11
Tempi

I spent the hours between Vespers and Compline carefully copying Pons' melody into the book. Then I extracted the scrap of paper where Zaid had written the lyrics to the song. I read through the words again, clearly outlined in Zaid's firm hand. I saw that he had written another column of words in an alphabet that I didn't know. It was strange writing, it seemed to almost approach pictures without ever quite surrendering to representing anything real or imagined. I stared at the writing for a long time after I put my pen and ink away. Then I shook myself and rose to join the other monks for the nighttime prayers.

***

With morning came Matins and the breaking of my fast in the dining hall. I went to the stables and reclaimed my mule. The monks here may be rapacious towards the local folk but they were generous to me. The panniers had been replenished with another ham, some cured sausages, a small bag of onions, and another of dried peas. Three large bottles of wine, one gray and two red had been squeezed in as well. I thanked the brother farrier and asked him to convey my gratitude to the abbot. He assured me he would, I think, although it was still early and I had difficulty understanding his language.

I walked through the gate in the priory walls and led my mule on a snake-like path through the many half-cut stones that peppered the square. The workmen were hard at it, swearing by God and his saints as they tried to shape those rocks into a monument of piety.

The early morning light didn't penetrate into the streets because of the remnant of walls left behind by the attacking crusaders. I wound down the hill hearing echoes of chisels on stones and the steady footfall of my mule. It seemed like a world of shadows, with almost no life in it, and I was grateful to finally reach the ruins of the gate and pass into the sunlight. The yellow-white masonry of the Pont

Neuf stretched across the Orb in front of me, and I was glad to be crossing the river and leaving Beziers behind. Zaid and Pons stood on the southern end of the bridge looking rested, fed, and satisfied.

"Good day, Fra," Pons said, bowing low to me.

"Please don't," I told him, waving him upright. "We will be traveling companions for a while now and it is best that we be friends. However, before we go, I must ask you to swear that you will be true to me and that you will remain truly penitent for your sins. You are my charge now."

"Fra, I cannot swear an oath," he said to me. "But I will be your good man and true. And like any good Christian, I truly regret and repent my sins."

"But you can't swear an oath?"

"No, Fra, it would scandalize my mother."

"What do you mean?" I was starting to get a bit angry.

"Let it go, Itzal," Zaid whispered, leaning towards me. "No doubt it is some custom of the mountains we do not understand. Let us begin our journey."

I nodded and flicked the mule's reins gently. The four of us started down the main road of the new town. It was just beginning to rise with the morning. Women were walking past us to the river to fetch water. Fieldworkers, hoes and rakes slung over their shoulders, were falling into the road on their way to tend crops outside the city limits. A few sleepy children were trying to gather eggs from under the chickens that seemed to lodge in front of every house. The crowd formed a clot in the road and it seemed like nothing was moving at all.

"What's the delay?" I asked no one in particular, not expecting an answer.

"It is the custom, Fra," Pons said. "Though the town has no walls—since none are needed here. The heretics have been defeated and the town is loyal to the king in Paris. Still, there is a pike man at the edge of town and he does not let anyone pass out of the town until the hour of Prime is reached."

I didn't say anything. I just stood there, shuffling from one foot to the other, noticing the dust at the hem of my white habit. I was surprised by that. My habit should have been so dusty that I wouldn't even see the dust, but then I realized that someone had cleaned the white cloth during the night. The Dominicans of Beziers may not have been as austere as our rule proscribed, but they were good hosts.

The crowd piled up behind us. A thin, white-haired boy of about thirteen seemed to be everywhere, sliding in and out with the ease of a ferret. He was behind us, then I saw his head pop up a little way ahead of us among a knot of children and brandishing a brown egg in a dirty hand, and then he was beside us, separated by a few farmers. Watching the white hair go from here to there was like watching a bit of cork bounce on a rough stream. That's the only reason I noticed the boy.

Finally the people ahead of us began to move and breathing space was opening up. We shuffled along with everyone else and, at long last, passed the pike man who had held everyone at the town limit. The people began to break off into different groups, heading to the fields to tend the crops. The new road from town joined the old Roman pavement heading towards Narbonne, and by the time we were ten yards down that road we were almost alone.

The sun rose into the sky behind us and to our left. Our shadows were cast across the old stones, long in front of us. The air was light and there was a breeze coming from the distant sea. It was a cool fine morning; dew was still rising off the grasses. If we looked up to our right, off the road, we could see plump red grapes in a vineyard. The tragic city of Beziers was behind us now, and all three of us felt relief. I don't know if it affected our mule, but he did seem to pick up his pace.

It didn't take Pons long to start a song:

♪*L'autrie jost'un a sebissa*
Trobei pastora mestissa,
De joi e de sen massiss
Si cum filla de vilana...♪

He sang loudly and lightly. It was a very vulgar song about a shepherd girl and a chance meeting with a handsome man. It was happy and just dirty enough to be entertaining. The notes came quick and Pons' voice was much brighter than the day before. It took me back to my days in Basque country, tending sheep with my brother while he talked about all the girls he would get and all the mothers he would find a way around. I had always just listened to him boast, wide-eyed with younger brother admiration. Sometimes I would tease him, but not often. The time came when I kept watch for him while he took some of those girls into the tall grasses, and I would deflect their mothers with stories of a lamb that had wandered off. I wasn't straying too far from the truth.

We walked on, the sun rising higher and the day growing hotter. Pons finished his song and then Zaid started to sing. His voice wasn't nearly as pleasant. He sang from the back of his throat in a language neither Pons nor I could understand. We realized that it must be Moorish. Still, he finished each verse with something that at least sounded familiar:

♪*Que fare, mamma*
Meu-l-habib est' ad yana...♪

It wasn't quite Catalan and it wasn't quite Occitan. I stopped him after the first time and he translated:

"The girl is asking a question: 'What shall I do, Mother, my beloved is at the door?' It is another song about a girl who is doing something that she knows she shouldn't. But she will do it anyway."

Pons laughed and Zaid went on singing in his strange tongue as the day grew hotter and hotter.

***

By the hour of Nones it was too hot for any singing. We trudged quietly over the low rolling hills, the mule braying softly every now and then, the bridle rattling. Pons was still light-hearted with his freedom but silent.

We came to a roadside shrine. It was a small wooden shelter over a relief of Saint Martin cutting his cloak in two. The shallow eaves offered some shelter from the almost vertical rays of the sun, so we stopped to have a bite to eat and perhaps a siesta before moving any further.

Pons walked our mule around the back of the small structure and tied it to a post. With Zaid's help, he unloaded a bottle of wine, some bread, cheese, an onion, and the last of the ham I'd carried from Aragon. While they were unpacking, I knelt and said my hourly office before the image of the saint.

It was almost too hot to eat but we managed, as poor men will. Zaid stuck to water, cheese, and the onion, while Pons and I made a feast with wine and ham. The only sounds came from eating, the chirp of cicadas, and the soft chomping of the mule as he cropped the grass around the shrine. Finished, we left the few crumbs where they lay in front of us, leaned into the sparse shade, and fell asleep.

***

I woke to the sound of a gut string being struck and echoing in the body of my guitarra. This was followed immediately by swearing in Occitan. I shook myself and saw Pons holding my instrument. He was trying to tune it and having no luck at all.

"It's no good, Fra," he said seeing me look at him. "Without thumbs, I can no longer play. I can't even tune."

"You played guitarra?" I asked.

"No, no, I had a lute once. I played that when I was a joglar. Still, it is the same idea. This one has more strings and I have never seen the body of an instrument shaped like this. But it is strings and a sound box. I know how it works."

"But you can't play it any longer," I said. "Pass it over. I'll get it in tune."

I strummed the strings and then adjusted the tuning pegs before testing the strings again. While I was doing this, Zaid came to himself, grunted something, and walked down the hill to find some privacy for his bodily needs.

"There," I announced, pleased with myself for no good reason. My instrument was in tune, the sun was slanting lower, and a breeze was blowing gently from the south. I was fed, light-hearted, and rested. I struck a chord and then started playing a fast tune, a zejel, without singing any words to it—there were too many different words to the old song and I couldn't remember them all—it had been several days and my fingers rejoiced in the memory of music. Pons smiled at me and Zaid shook his head, laughing as he returned.

"You don't think of it, Fra," Pons started, "but there are many things that are difficult to do when you have no thumbs. I had trouble holding the girl last night."

I waved a benediction in the air. I didn't want to hear about girls. He stopped.

"And using the hammer on the stones, that was hard too. And, of course, I can no longer play a stringed instrument, probably not even a bagpipe. I doubt if I could hold a flute. Those bastards took away a lot when they took my thumbs."

"You never give them much thought," Zaid said, sitting on the dust next to us. "But you are surprised at their usefulness."

"Always, always," Pons agreed. Then he rose and in the direction from which Zaid had just returned.

I sat, strumming on the strings, leaning my back against the image of the saint. Zaid rocked on his heels.

"How did you use those useful thumbs of yours?" Zaid asked as Pons reappeared.

"The monks, the Dominicans. It was a judgment. It was all very legal. They had me in the priory court and witnesses were heard. I even got to say a few words myself. Of course, I don't think it did much good. I don't think the northerners really understand our tongue."

"Not very well," I assured Pons. "But what was your offense?"

"Officially, my sentence was for singing heretical songs. That's what the notary wrote down. It was the same song that I sang to you. I don't know if it is heretical or not, I just like the song. But my real offense was singing it late at night and keeping that abbot awake."

"Of course, you would wake someone with that song," Zaid chimed in. "It would keep anyone up because you didn't sing it truly yesterday, did you?"

"What do you mean?" Pons was offended. "I sang all the words. It sang the correct tune."

"Yes, yes," he said. "Of course you did. But you sang it very slowly and very softly. That is not how it was meant to be sung, now was it?"

"Well," Pons conceded, "that was not how I sang it when I performed for my master. And that was not how I sang it when I disturbed the abbot; you're right about that. Of course, I also had my lute and I played along."

"So that was the noise?" I asked.

"Yes."

"But," Zaid kept on with his point, "that song is not meant to be so slow, now is it? It's meant to make people laugh, to make them dance. You slowed it down."

"I did," Pons admitted. "I was cutting rocks and I was sad. Besides, I didn't think anyone in a white cassock would like it if that song seemed happy." He waved his four-fingered hands in the air. "My body has memories of that.

"You've probably seen them, you know, the judicial maimings. It is really quite awful, but I suppose it's meant to be. The good brothers don't do it themselves, no; they can't be tainted by carrying out their own orders. No, they turned me over to the secular arm, as they called it. After trying me in their church and condemning me there, they called for soldiers from the lower town. These Frenchmen, speaking barbarically, led me out of the old city to the block they had set up on the Pont Neuf. They were very thorough men. I wasn't their only victim that day. In fact, my sentence was one of the milder ones. The fellow before me lost both of his hands completely. He didn't live long after that.

"They washed his blood off the block. They stretched my forearms across the red-stained wood and then used staples to separate my thumbs. They wouldn't take an inch more than the law allowed. I couldn't turn to look, but I heard the axe being sharpened against a whetstone. Then—" He brought the blade of his hand down through the air, cutting through an imaginary thumb, "a whoosh, a chop, and no pain. None right then, anyway, and I saw one thumb fall away into the water. Before I could think or scream, the axe came down again and the other thumb tumbled over the edge of the bridge. They freed my hands very quickly and bound them in cloth. I didn't lose much blood. They were merciful, I guess."

I looked down at the strings on my guitarra while Zaid examined the old man's hands. Then he stood up and fetched the book off the back of the mule. He opened to the song of the insane village.

"Look, Itzal. Decide how to play this, to play it quickly and lightly. Then we can hear it the way it was meant to be heard."

I looked at the page for a long while and started to choose chords. I picked out the melody on the high strings and then started strumming faster and faster. Pons stood up, excited, and he began to sing:

♪*Una ciutatz fo, no sai cals*
On cazet una plueia tals...♪

He clapped his mutilated hands together and stomped a dance on the hard earth. Zaid clapped along, laughing. We three were all full of music, played properly in the right time. Pons sang the whole song through twice; he was so full, finally being allowed to sing out again, and then he fell to earth. I wasn't sure if he was laughing or weeping.

I stood and wrapped my guitarra in its cloth.

"We should be moving. The sun is getting lower. If we start now, we should reach Narbonne by the cool of the evening."

12

Among Women

We arrived at the eastern gate of Narbonne just before Vespers. I had been to Barcelona once, but I had never seen a city as large or ancient as the one we entered that evening. The sun was slanting low on the western horizon, its beams painting the white stones of the Church of Saint Paul a delicate pink. Streets and houses sprawled out before us, a vast maze, and I wasn't sure how we would set about finding anything, let alone a chapter house of my order.

"Let's just follow the Via Domitia," Zaid suggested.

"What?" I asked.

"The Via Domitia, I thought you knew. That is what the Romans called this road. It runs from Italy deep into Spain. I thought you knew what road you were traveling on."

"I only knew it as the Roman road," I answered, embarrassed.

"Still, in a city as old as this, it should run into the center of town. It should lead us to a place where someone can tell us where we should go."

So we wandered into the city following the pavement of the old road. Streets crisscrossed it everywhere as we walked. The city was alive with the activities of early evening. Women were visiting market stalls getting ready to prepare the evening meal. Children carried water from the fountains and pipes that descended from the Roman aqueducts. There was the usual confusion of odors that goes with a city—sewage and cooking meat, smoke and waste water, the chemical smells from the great wool-dying plants, and, of course, the miasma that rises off a large population of unwashed humanity.

The road opened into a large square in front of the great church of Saint Paul. I have since been told that it was built over an ancient charnel ground where early Christian martyrs were buried, but the building itself looked new. Near it, there was a building under construction, two towers, one smaller, one taller. Beside the construction was something that resembled a house for monks, so I walked up the steps and pounded on the door. After some time, a young monk with a large tonsure and a blind eye opened it. His habit showed that he was a Cistercian.

"Who's disturbing Vespers?"

"A traveling preaching friar," I answered. "With two companions."

"You can't stay here."

"I didn't ask. Is there a house of my order nearby?"

"There is," he replied curtly. "But you can't stay there, either."

"Why not?"

"The bishop has taken over all the extra rooms that belong to the orders. That palace over there will be his if he ever gets it finished." He waved in the direction of the construction.

"Is there somewhere we can stay?" I asked as calmly as I could.

"Stay with the women. There are good women across the river, outside of the walls and away from us. Beguines. Clarisses. They'll put you up. Cross the river and take the first turn. It's a large white building with a dark door. Stay there." Saying that he closed the door in my face.

***

The Roman bridge was in need of some repair but it got us across the river. Here the houses were newer, that is to say only a hundred years old instead of a thousand. The streets were broken up with small fields and bits of vineyards scattered among the dwellings. The road split in front of us, offering us the choice of north or south.

"He said the first turn," I said to my companions.

"There are only turns," Zaid observed. "Didn't he tell you which direction?"

"I don't think so. I don't remember, anyway. He said the first turn."

"His shoulders didn't twist? He made no gesture with one hand or the other? A nod? A wink?"

"He couldn't wink. He didn't indicate which way to go at all."

Pons just bounced on the balls of his feet, offering no suggestions. He would follow us.

"Let's turn left, south. We are looking for a larger building, I would guess, with a dark door."

"That should make things a little easier," Zaid said, waving his hands at the various houses around us. "Most of these are small, and look at the doors."

It was remarkable. All of the doors in this neighborhood had been washed with a bright yellow. It didn't look like paint, really, just yellow mustard seed crushed in oil and allowed to dry. Every door we saw as we wandered down the road looked exactly the same. Finally, we reached a building that was a story higher than the others, with a wing stretching off to the rear. It was getting difficult to see, but the door wasn't yellow at least. I left the other two behind me, walked up, and knocked.

After a very short moment, the door swung open. It was held by a young woman; she couldn't have been much more than sixteen. She was dressed in heavy, dark cloth with a white band across her forehead and a black head cloth. She took one look at me, screamed, and slammed the door in my face.

I stood wondering what to do. I returned to my companions and told them what happened.

"They fear the Inquisition," Pons said. "They may be holy women, but the Church distrusts women. The Inquisition can accuse anyone. If they see a white robe, any sane person starts to tremble."

"He has a point, Fra Itzal," Zaid agreed. "If we are going into the mountains you might want to change the color of your habit. People rarely sing when they fear the flames."

"Perhaps. I'll think about that. But what we need now is a place to stay for the evening," I observed.

"Let me ask them," Zaid proposed and left us standing next to the mule in the middle of the road.

We saw him knock at the door. The same young woman opened it, visibly terrified. I stood on the other side of the mule and Pons held the reins. Zaid disappeared into the building. We waited. The sky went from a dark blue to black. One by one, stars started to show themselves. Eventually, the door opened again and Zaid emerged and walked over to us.

"Take the mule around back, Pons," he instructed. "There is no stable, but there is a fenced courtyard. He will be safe enough. Fra Itzal, I would advise you to leave the black cowl in the panniers. It will just be easier."

I looked at him. He held my gaze steadily. I removed the cowl slowly.

"Come," he said.

Pons walked around toward the back of the building as we walked to the door. It swung wide at Zaid's tap.

"Pardon, Fra," the girl said. "I am new here. This man says that you are a good Christian and Na Carenza says I am just a silly girl and that I should not fear anyone. Please, you are our guest. Come, share our meal."

She led us into a hallway, very clean, with a scrubbed stone floor. There were no decorations of any kind in the hall, or in the one or two rooms we saw off to either side. She led us into a large, whitewashed room with a trestle table set in its center. Even though it was a warm night, a fire was burning. Three other women sat around the table.

"Na Carenza," the girl said to the old woman at the head of the table, bobbing in some kind of bow, "these are the visitors."

I bowed to the woman I presumed to be the abbess. She looked very old, her face framed by the same sort of white band and dark head cloth as the girl, was like a relief map of a river delta, eroded with wrinkles. She had deep, gray eyes that seemed to be home to wells of sorrow.

"We thank you for your hospitality, ma'am," I said.

She nodded to us. "Visitors are welcome. We are not used to seeing men here, but you may join us for our meal." She gestured to the table. Zaid and I sat as Pons came in carrying the panniers.

"Alais," the old woman said to the girl who'd led us in, "show him where to put that." The girl rose from the table and led Pons out the door. We heard their steps echo down the hall.

The table held a pitcher of water, a large bowl of pulse porridge, and a loaf of barley bread. There was a small jar of oil next to the bread. It was poor enough fare.

"Madam—" I began.

"Address me as Na, please," she said.

"Na," I continued. "Let me offer more food for this table. The baskets my servant carries hold a ham and some cheeses, onions, and wine."

The old woman looked at me as severely as if she were a granite mountain.

"I do not know the rules of your order, Fra, but we are not permitted wine here, nor the products of animals. We can use the onions. Tomorrow."

"Your rule is strict, Na, but you are welcome to them," I said as a woman of about thirty spooned some porridge into a wooden bowl and set it down in front of me.

"Only as strict as God requires. Eat," she ordered and all of us directed our attention to the bowls in front of us.

The youngest sister cleared the bowls and Pons followed her out into the courtyard, presumably to help her clean our dishes. Na Carenza stood up, bowed her head and the other women followed her lead. She began to pray in Occitan.

"Our Father, who art in heaven…" The rest of the women remained silent and Zaid and I remained silent, too, since that seemed to be the custom. It was odd to hear this venerable prayer in a woman's voice and pronounced in a tongue other than Latin. Still, it felt homely and the room was clean and cool. "Deliver us from evil." The abbess finished, and the other two women rose. I looked over at Na Carenza.

"Is there a chapel where I can recite my office? It is late for Vespers, but I would do my duty," I asked.

"Na Iselda will show you," she answered and left the room.

The woman who had served the porridge touched my elbow and I stood. She reminded me of my brother's wife. She was small and sturdy but round where she should be. The black fabric of her habit was fading towards gray and showing wear around the hem. She walked out of the dining hall as I thought of it and led me down a hall.

We turned into a large, empty room, as painfully clean as the one we'd just left. The walls were whitewashed and newly scrubbed. The ceiling was higher than the rest of the building, and I gathered that was the extra story we'd seen. There was a round window in the eastern wall but made of the clearest glass, with no stained saint's life or scene from scripture. I thought this might have more to do with poverty than with the severity of their rule. There were no benches or pre dieus of any kind, nor even an altar, crucifix, or lectern. I turned to Na Iselda.

"No altar?" I questioned. "Is there no relic here?" I thought I detected a slight shudder from her, although the room was warm.

"No, Fra," she answered.

"You hear Mass here?"

She looked at me curiously. I couldn't tell what she was thinking, if anything.

"There are not many of us here, Fra," she said. "This will do for us. We are just a few poor women. We have no priests."

She nodded towards me and then backed out of the room, leaving me to my prayers. It all seemed odd to me, but then I didn't need a presence lamp to perform my duty. I knelt down on the stone floor, pulled the breviary up from my belt, and read my office by the moonlight that streamed through the clear window.

♪*Non voilh voler voltage*
Que-m volv e-m vir mas voluntatz
Mas lai on mos vols e volatz...♪

"I wouldn't want love's payment nor be slave to a wayward will. It is false, it does not fulfill."

I heard Pons singing as I came back to the dining hall. He was pounding out a beat on the trestle table, entertaining the three ladies who had remained. Na Carenza had apparently retired for the evening. Alais was laughing and Iselda's face was ruddy. All three women clapped their hands along with Pons' beat and broke into applause when the song ended.

"That was a farewell to love by my master Peire Cardenal," Pons announced. "He may even have meant it. I have not seen him in many years and he was old enough to give up the game even then."

"You don't have to be old to give up love," Alais said, almost sighing, and then blushed deeply.

"You gave up only illusions to come here, child," the third woman said. She was tall and rail thin, but there was a kindness to her face and warmth in the sad smile she bestowed on the girl.

"You say that, Na Bieiris. You've been married. You've had children. You're not like me."

"I am just like you, I am a child of God. I give back to God what I have."

"That's very pious, Bieiris," the one called Iselda said. "But now give something to us. Tell us a story. It's too early for bed, and we will wake Na Carenza if we let this rascal keep up his singing."

"Yes, yes, tell us a story," the younger girl asked, clapping her hands. "Tell us a story of the old days. Tell us a story of La Loba."

"You are wanton," Na Bieiris answered the girl, but with a smile. "All right, I'll give you a tale. But first fetch your distaff, Alais, your spindle. We must not waste this time nor this good fire." The two women seemed to vanish and then return in an instant. They both settled by the fireside and Na Bieiris produced some needlework from somewhere. She looked to see that everyone had settled, and then she began.

"Time past, long past, before the French came down from the North, time past, in the mountains, a land so remote, so fast, so deep that it had no name, there lived a woman named Beatrice, but all knew her as La Loba, the she-wolf. She was a Comtesse and held her castle with no man nor husband.

"And she was beautiful," Alais chirped.

"And she was beautiful," the woman answered, looking a little disapprovingly at the girl. "Her hair was red as the sky at sunset in stormy weather. Her eyes flashed both green and black. She was lithe and strong and all men desired her. But she had no man. Her lands were fruitful and her people strong and they would always answer her call.

"One day the bishop of the plains sent a seneschal and a priest to call upon her. La Loba was haughty. She made them wait outside her castle for three days before she let them into her presence. Finally, she relented and they came into her great hall, damp and bedraggled, for it had rained off and on, as it will in the mountains.

'What is your will?' She asked them.

'The bishop summons you to his palace on the plains,' said the priest.

'I am not one to be summoned,' she answered.

'The bishop requests your presence,' said the seneschal.

'That is different,' she said. 'I will come.'

"She had her men make ready her snow-white mare. She had her ladies make ready her emerald green dress. She had her armourer make sure that her sword was sharp and took from him a shirt of light, silvery mail.

"They rode down the mountain for three days. She rode demur as any great lady, sidesaddle on her white mare, resplendent in her emerald green dress. The night before they were to arrive at the palace of the bishop of the plains. She stayed up all night, plucking at the stitching in that dress. In the morning, she arrived and was called before the bishop. There was a conference there. The lords of all of Provence and Rousillon and the Toulousian were there. And the bishop of the plains spoke.

'Dompna, you must take a husband,' he said.

"She stood, tall and haughty in front of them. 'I will not,' she said.

'These are the finest men of the South,' the bishop said. 'Choose one and wed.'

'I will choose, but not just one,' she said. 'I will choose who I choose, and I may choose a bed, but I will not wed.'

'Then you sin,' the bishop said.

'So say you,' she replied. 'But in the mountains, God is different. I am renewed with every moon. I am who I am, and I belong to no man.'

"She stood, tall and defiant. She reached under her left breast and pulled at the stitching she had plucked. The great green dress tore down the seams and fell to the floor. She stood in shining mail and green leggings. 'I am chaste,' she said. 'Still, I do not mind being chased.'

"She turned and strode out to the courtyard. She mounted her milk-white mare like a man and she kicked in her heels, galloping away, moonlight glinting off her silver mail.

"All the men of the South, the Counts from Avignon, from Pamiers, from Narbonne, from Toulouse, from Nimes, all the men stood there with their mouths gaping open. But Roger—"

"The Count of Foix!" Alais said, almost bouncing.

"Roger, the Count of Foix," Bieiris continued, looking sharply at the girl again, "ran out into the courtyard calling for his horse. He leapt onto the black warhorse, and the hooves struck sparks off the flags of the courtyard as he galloped after her.

"He followed her for three days and three nights. He did not stop once, Roger of Foix, and Beatrice La Loba galloped always just enough ahead. On the third evening, the snow-white mare splashed across a stream. The land rose into the mountains, and Roger of Foix splashed through the water after her.

"La Loba slowed. She was waiting for him; she was waiting for the moon. Her pure white mare came to a green meadow just as the sun vanished and the moon, white and full, rose and bathed the mailed woman and the grass of the meadow in silver light. And Roger of Foix found her there. And Roger of Foix loved her there.

"Roger loved her always. Roger made many love songs in honor of La Loba. But none of the *cansos* he made was any match for the music the two of them made that night, in the tall grass, beneath the light of the moon."

13
Metropolitan

I was distracted and disoriented the next morning. I rose from my knees after performing a solitary Matins in what passed for the chapel there. I was by now used to waking up in unfamiliar spaces after the days on the road, but the silence here was palpable. A monastery had a certain bustle to it most of the time, and a campsite, while quiet, was open to the elements. This place, with its four women, did not speak of a routine. The complete lack of decoration, the absence of any picture, statue, or piece of stained glass was new and puzzling.

I found my way back to the whitewashed cell where Zaid and I had slept. I extracted the satchel from our panniers and checked the contents. It held the codex, a pen, and some ink, as well as pages of scrap paper. It also held the letter from my prior to any of our order that I might meet. I didn't see Zaid or Pons anywhere. I extracted a piece of bread and doused it with wine from one of the bottles by way of a quick breakfast and then walked out into the hallway, not sure which way to turn, which way led to the street.

I heard a sound around a corner ahead of me, a damp rubbing of one thing on another, and then I heard low singing:

♪Na Carenza, penre marit m'agenza
Mas far enfanz cug qu'es grans penedenza
Que las tetinhas pendan aval jos
el ventrilhs es cargatz e enojos... ♪

The song was interrupted by pants and grunts of effort. I turned the corner, and there was little Alais on her knees, scrubbing the floor while singing about wanting a husband but not wanting her breasts to droop from the penance of carrying a child.

"Girl," I said. "Which way leads to the street, to your abbess?"

She looked up at me, startled. One strand of her hair had escaped her headscarf and she tried to blow it back. She seemed puzzled by my use of the word abbess. She tilted her head, a little pink of tongue showing between her teeth.

"This way, Fra Itzal," she answered, rising. She led me further down the hall that she was scrubbing. We turned once and there was the dark door opened to the bright street. There was a room just off to the left, and a crowd of poor people were lined up, waiting to go in.

"Where is Na Carenza?" I asked my guide. She didn't say anything but nodded to the doorway where the people waited. I hesitated.

"Go right in. They will wait," she told me and then turned back into the maze of halls that seemed to make up this house.

***

Na Carenza was seated on a plain wooden bench in another plain white room. There was a table next to her that held cloths, jars of dried leaves and herbs, and bottles of wet things in various colors. Zaid stood next to her, looking over her shoulder. Straddling the bench, facing the old woman, was an ancient man in gray homespun. He was missing one ear and his nose was bulbous and scabrous. Na Carenza was wrapping what appeared to be varicose veins in a damp cloth.

"Dompna," I said, bowing my head. She looked up from her charge and then continued to bind his leg. "Dompna," I went on, "I have work to do in Narbonne today. Would it be too much to beg your hospitality for another night?" "Go. Stay. You are welcome to return," she answered without lifting her eyes from her merciful task.

"Zaid?" I inquired. He looked up at me.

"Fra," he said, "you go and gather what songs you might. I will stay here. This woman has a gift for healing and I would learn something. And I have some little knowledge I might be able to share with her."

I looked at him for a moment and then knew that I had no real hold over him. I nodded and walked out of the room. I passed along the line of people and then reached the street. The poor people stretched down the street, beyond the corner of the house. All of them seemed to be suffering from one malady or another. I turned towards the old Roman road and headed into Narbonne.

***

It was early but the road was alive with people moving produce and animals and materials before the sun grew too hot for such work. The Roman bridge was packed and I was uncertain it could hold all of us. The local people had no doubts at all and hurried across as fast as they could. I tripped once, catching my sandal against a rough bit of stone that fell through the roadbed into the river. I leaned against the parapet for a moment, catching my breath, before hurrying into the city.

I followed the road into the square, breathing in the city. Along the way I didn't hear any songs, exactly, but the music of a metropolis. There were hawkers of fish chanting the morning's catch in singsong voices. There was the ring of hammers in a street of blacksmiths, the familiar sound of haggling at market stalls that lined the wide road. Wagon wheels creaked past me every now and then, full of early hay or, more often, bricks and stones that were making their way to the construction up ahead.

Most of the buildings in Narbonne were very old. People had been living here since before the time of Christ, and it had been an important city all that time. It was said that the bay was silting up and that the port would be lost someday, but that day did not seem like it would arrive soon. Where the road rose you could look down to the right and see the fishing boats and cargo ships bobbing in the harbor.

When the crusaders came, Narbonne had surrendered without a fight. They had seen what had happened elsewhere, and this population came from a long line of people who had seen armies come and seen them leave. Romans, Visigoths, Franks, Romans again, all had their day, but the city—and its commerce—went on as it always had. This city had never been a hotbed of heresy, just a trading port and a crossroads market. They had turned over a few people to the Inquisitors, mostly moneylenders who had been overzealous in their interest charges. The people of Narbonne knew that the crusaders needed victims and that they were not too curious as to actual guilt or innocence.

I pushed along with the crowd heading into the center of town. The air was alive with a cacophony of languages. I heard Italian, Lombard, French, Catalan, and a little Latin among other tongues. I'm sure there were shouts in Greek, but I didn't really know what that might sound like; there may have been Arab traders from across the sea, for all I knew. The road opened into the great square. Here the noise swelled, although the crowd became diffused. The hammers of stonecutters and masons echoed, along with the thud carpenters shaping and pounding wood. The archbishop had a small army building his new palace. Unlike in Beziers, these all seemed to be free workers; I saw no yellow crosses among the mob. Of course, many of these masons and carpenters were stripped to the waist and so their crosses would not be visible.

Standing in the square I realized that I didn't know where my order had its house. The one-eyed Cistercian had only told me that they had no place to put me, not where it might be located. I worked my way around the great square, trying to stay out of the way of the men at their work and avoid the wagons hauling stones to be shaped and taking away the shavings to be made into plaster. I spotted the Cistercian house again next to the half-built palace, but I had no desire to encounter anyone there again. I reached the southwestern corner without seeing anything promising at all. There was an open-air glazier set up there, staining glass for the Archbishop's chapel, I supposed. I tried to inquire.

"Good morning," I said to a small dark man with a crucible full of glowing lead in his hands. He ignored me. "Ave," I tried in Latin. The man expertly poured his lead into a mold and leaned the crucible next to it to cool.

"Que?" he asked, looking at me. His face had been marked by hundreds of tiny cuts, a consequence, I guessed, of his profession.

"Good morning," I said again in Occitan. He looked at me for a moment before comprehension dawned on his face. He smiled.

"Buongiorno, padre," he said and I realized he was from Lombardy.

"Is there a house of St. Dominic near here?" I asked. He didn't seem to understand me. I plucked at my habit. "White Friars? Bianchi? A *domus* near here?"

Another long moment while this sunk in, then he nodded, smiling. "Bianchi! Si, si," he said. He pointed across the square and gestured to indicate a left turn. There were words accompanying the gestures, but I did not really understand many of them.

"Grazie," I said and headed in the direction he'd steered me.

***

The Dominican chapter house was located on a narrow street behind the construction site. It was obscured by the scaffolding that surrounded the rising palace. The entry looked narrow but the building itself seemed to take up most of this street and perhaps the next one. This side of the palace was not as full of working men and I was grateful to have most of the street to myself. I dusted off my habit and stepped up to the door which was standing open.

A young monk was dozing on a stool. I assumed he was meant to serve as the porter so I roused him rather roughly, feeling my seniority in the order. He stood up quickly.

"*Bonjour, frere,*" he said, sketching something of a bow.

"Good morning," I replied in Occitan. He looked at me queerly for a moment but seemed to understand me. "Is your prior free? I have traveled a long way and I would like to speak with him if that's possible."

"*Oui,* perhaps," he answered. "I will go see. Wait here." He disappeared down a long stone hallway.

I waited, looking around idly. There was dust from crushed stones everywhere, but this building seemed complete enough. There was a statue of the Virgin resting in a niche in the wall, and the window over the door was stained glass, showing our founder praying his rosary. There was a small table next to the porter's stool that held a short glass and the remains of a loaf of bread.

The young monk came back in the company of a thin, older monk who was so bald that his tonsure was the purest formality.

"*Bonjour, frere,*" he greeted me.

"Good day, Fra," I replied. "I have traveled from Aragon on the instruction of my superiors. Are you the prior here?"

"No, no," he answered, trying to keep his words in Occitan. "I am the brother quartermaster. I will take you." He didn't seem comfortable, but he turned and strode down the hallway and I followed.

This monastery looked well off enough, though not as opulent as the house in Beziers. The walls were solid and insulated here and there with tapestries on religious themes. I saw a chapel forming another wing but couldn't see into it. We walked through the scriptorium where brothers were furiously copying some writings. They didn't look like books as much as inventories and bills of various kinds.

Beyond the scriptorium, we crossed a quiet cloister and entered another building. Another long hall, and then we met a heavy wood door. We walked through it into what was obviously the study of a very important person. The walls were lined with shelves, most of which held books, but the two nearest the desk held bundles of pages bound in red ribbons. My escort bowed me in and then left.

The man seated at the desk was compact but powerfully built and seemed impossibly old. His head had a broad tonsure, but it was evident that he had to work at keeping it shaved, with gray stubble showing through already this morning. His face bore a scar over the left eye that looked like it might have come from an arrow. He was hunched over his desk examining three different sheaves of paper that were spread out like a fan in front of him. After a long moment, he looked up at me. His eyes were milky gray and I could tell that reading was hard work for them.

"*Bonjour, frere,*" he said to me, indicating a chair nearby. I bowed and sat.

"Good morning, frere," I began, trying out the word.

"Pere," he corrected. Of course he was an ordained priest.

"Pere," I repeated after him. "I am Fra Itzal. I have come from Aragon on the instructions of my prior. This should explain it." I searched in the satchel for the letter from my superior and slid it across his broad desk.

He took the page from me, unfolded it, and held it up very close to his face. Not only were his eyes failing him, but he seemed to be having trouble with the language, which I thought was odd. I had assumed my prior had written in Latin for all to understand.

A tall, energetic monk came through the door holding yet another sheaf of papers. He strode up to the prior and interrupted his attempt to read the letter I'd given him. He shoved his papers in front of the priest who looked at them briefly, then scrawled something on the bottom of the page.

"Tell them the red brick is for the inner rooms. They'll be plastered over. The white brick is for the outer wall. I don't want to have to take that wall apart and start again."

"*Oui, mon pere,*" the monk answered and bowed his way out.

"I am sorry, Fra—?"

"Itzal," I supplied.

"Itzal. All of us in this city, all of us in orders, at any rate, are involved in building the new palace for the archbishop. That takes up most of our time. We don't have any energy left for anything else."

"I had heard about the project, pere," I answered. "I was told by a Cistercian that there was no room in any religious house."

"That's true. We must neglect hospitality. We are bursting with Italian architects and weavers from Flanders, even woodworkers all the way from Germany. I don't know why the archbishop needed to bring all these people here. I would have thought he could just send for the tapestries and carvings and drawings. Of course, there is good wool spun and dyed here. The burghers are very proud of their wool and should be. Still, local people could have done the weaving, don't you think? And the carving too?"

"He is an exacting taskmaster, this archbishop. He has to make sure the work is done precisely the way he wants it done, and he is the archbishop. It's almost as if he thought he wasn't going to die, that he would live here forever. But he is as close to a sovereign as the city has. He must be obeyed."

"There's no count? No lord?" I asked.

"No, Narbonne has been ruled by its people for centuries since the Romans left and the Visigoths retreated. It is nominally under the Count of Toulouse, of course, but the Count of Toulouse is at the mercy of the king and the Pope in this age. There is a council for municipal matters and the archbishop sees to everything else.

"The Cistercian told you correctly there is no place for you to stay. Still, I suppose he was rather rude about it. They consider us upstarts, you know."

"He was…terse," I answered.

"But you have found lodging?"

"In a house of Beguines, across the river," I replied.

The prior looked at me long and hard, or at least that's what I thought. He might just have had difficulty seeing me.

"That's good then. I see your mission is to gather music. How very odd. It must be nice to have time for such concerns. We barely eke out the hours for our duties here, let alone fulfilling someone's bequest." He sighed heavily and leaned back against his chair. "It's true. We say our office every day and Mass, of course.

But we don't have the energy for anything more than this infernal building project. I doubt if it will be finished before I go to God."

"Surely before that, Christ will protect you," I said politely.

He waved his hand dismissively. "We have a couple of Inquisitors, as is our mission, making the rounds of the parishes. There are a lot of parishes in this city. Still, they are not overzealous. We have never been home to many heretics, although I'm told they are here, they are everywhere. More often the archbishop has them root out Jews and moneylenders when his coffers are low. They are easily charged and they pay their fines promptly."

"But you must do your duty."

"We try. It is not easy. As you can tell, I am from the North, as are many of the brothers here. We are not terribly welcome, really. Besides, this is a port city. You have Greeks, who some might call heretics, and Moorish traders and fishermen from places only the Holy Spirit knows. We can't arrest everyone who thinks differently. As long as the bloody Cathars keep to themselves, we tend to leave them alone. They tend to the sick. They are very good at that. We should be serving in that way, of course, but we have a palace to build. So we let them alone as long as they preach no sermons.

"As to your mission, I can offer no real help. There may be singers of songs in this city, but I do not know of them. Certainly we have no record of any music in our library. It is given over to orders for stone from Lombardy and wood from the forests of the Auvergne.

"This is not how I meant to spend my life. I was a soldier. I came here with the crusade. I took this," he said stroking the scar on his forehead, "at the siege of Muret. You must know of that, coming from Aragon. That was where King Pedro was killed. A great king and a great Catholic. The lords of the South couldn't agree on a plan and insisted too much on the honor of combat. Monfort had no such scruples. He attacked when he saw the chance and he won. They burned four hundred heretics after that battle.

"That's when I decided the best way to help those who have gone astray was to preach and use the tools the Pope has granted us, the Inquisition, the secular powers. Raping the countryside was not the way to salvation. Killing beloved sovereigns won us no friends. So I left the world of wars and became a priest, a preaching friar. And I was a good preacher. I led many heretics back to the Church. Oh, not consoled heretics, but the ones we called *credentes*. And some Waldensians I led back as well. Of course, they hadn't strayed as far. I had to impose penances—a thumb here, a yellow cross there. I tried not to be too severe.

"But now, now all I do is oversee carpenters and stoneworkers. I envy you, your mission, but I cannot help you. You might explore the taverns. I have heard that the workmen sing. Otherwise, all I can say, Fra Itzal, is to be grateful to your prior. Go with God and pray for me."

The interview was over.

14
The Taverns

I found my way to the street door without help. The same young monk was sitting just inside the vestibule. He wasn't dozing this time, but he did not look overly alert. I had the feeling he was a younger son, given to the Church because he wasn't bright enough to run the family wool business. I tapped him on the shoulder.

"Fra?" I inquired.

He looked at me dumbly.

"Frere?" I tried.

He straightened and smiled at me. His two front teeth were black, and he was missing three others.

"*Oui, frere?*"

"Your prior said he knew of no one in this city who knew any songs, but that I should ask your help." The boy looked puzzled. "No, not that you might know such people, or that you might know any songs at all. He merely suggested that you might be able to direct me to that part of the city where the taverns are, where people who have no better way to spend their time than trading in the singing of songs might congregate."

He looked at me more baffled than when I'd addressed him in his own language. I realized my vocabulary was more than he could understand.

"Where do the working men go when they want to drink and to buy a girl?" I asked. "What quarter of the city is home to the wine shops?"

He smiled again and I tried not to look at his teeth. "There are wine shops all over, like anywhere. But around the back of the square," he offered, speaking Occitan happily, "behind all the new buildings. That's where there are rooms that sell all manner of depraved things. So my brother told me—my real brother, not one of these weaklings in white. I never went there myself. He wouldn't take me. Besides, now I'm holy and I can't go to such places, can I?"

"No, you certainly shouldn't, not if you're holy. I wouldn't seek such a place except that my superiors have sent me searching for some things that may only be found there." I tried to look very serious, very holy, and just dripping with the authority of my habit. "How do I get there?"

For a boy who had never visited such a place, he was both accommodating and knowledgeable. I left the monastery and followed the streets around the back of the new palace, past a church that looked like it dated back to the days of the martyrs themselves. I turned left and then right, and followed what looked like a blind alley. The alley led to a small square with a fountain in its center and a few olive trees providing a bit of shade. There were tables set around the square and it did not seem like many people were drinking from the fountain.

I wasn't sure what I should do. I was still looking for music, but I didn't feel I could just walk up to any city dweller and ask him to start singing, or her, for that matter. There were more women in evidence here than I'd seen in the rest of the city. They weren't dressed like the Beguines that sheltered us. Their blouses were bleached muslin, with collars that were much lower than their throats and loose enough to allow at least one fat monk to slip a hand through and touch what no monk should be touching.

The sun was high; it was past the hour of Nones. I was beginning to hunger. I knew my rule would require me to limit my meals, but my mission seemed to call on me to indulge.

I made my way to a table cooled by shade. This was where the fat monk fondled the girl. He was seated on a bench, wearing a filthy gray habit that told me nothing about the order to which he belonged. Across from him was another monk, a very thin man with a long face and a shiny, tonsured head. His robe told me that he was a mendicant follower of Francis. If that was the case, he was ignoring his vows on this bright afternoon.

The table held two pitchers and several wooden cups. The remains of a meal were scattered around—bones of a chicken, a few half-eaten bread trenchers, and a bowl that looked like it had once held some kind of porridge. The girl seemed to have been trying to clear this mess away before she was accosted.

"A preaching friar!" the fat man called out, laughing. He spoke in the Lombard dialect with an accent so thick I could barely understand him. "Come, sit with us. We shall drink and sing us some songs!"

I was there for songs, so I sat. The fat monk poured something into one of the cups and drank deeply. His face, already shiny from sweat and oil, blushed red. I don't know if it was embarrassment or just what he was drinking. He poured some of what he'd drunk and slid it across the table to me. It was yellowish and foaming and smelled slightly spicy. I took the cup in the spirit of fellowship and drank. Only then did I realize that it must be beer. It seemed an odd choice and tasted very bitter to me as I drained the cup.

"Good day, brethren," I said, wiping my mouth on my sleeve. "Is there wine somewhere?" The thin Franciscan lifted the other pitcher and turned it upside down. I was obviously dry. "Can we have more wine?" I asked the girl who had managed to slip out of the fat man's clumsy hold. "And bread and cheese?" I extracted a copper coin from my satchel taking care not to reveal that there was more where it had come from.

The girl bobbed what might have been a bow in my direction and then vanished into a nearby building. She was back quickly with a tray holding a ripe golden cheese and what looked to me good barley bread. She set it on the table in front of me and went back through the door, the fat monk's eyes following her every step. She returned with a very large pitcher and a fresh cup for me. She poured out the wine; it looked thick and almost dead black, and then she vanished again.

"Welcome brother," the fat man said, reaching towards the wine, then thinking better of it and pouring himself more beer. "Where do you call home?"

"Aragon, Spain," I answered.

"I am from farther than you, then," he laughed. "I come from over the Rhine, far to the north. And this fellow," he pointed a greasy finger at the thin man, "he is from Pisa, I think. He doesn't speak much, and I have trouble understanding him when he does. I am called Pieter."

"Fra Itzal," I said. "I am on a mission for my chapter house." I started.

"We are all on missions," Pieter interrupted. "Missions to save souls. Missions to educate. I believe my companion here is on a mission to heal the sick. But as I say, I am not sure."

"Healing the sick is a work of mercy," I smiled at the Franciscan. He nodded at me, but I'm not certain that he heard any of my words. "My mission is slighter than that. I am looking for melodies."

"Then you couldn't be in a better place!" The northerner roared. "We do nothing but sing here.

♪Orate Fratres
Ego sum abbas Cucaniensis
Et consilium est cum biblulis…♪

He sang out in a ringing baritone. A few heads turned, but not many. I got the idea that this was a regular occurrence. He went on singing about his role as the abbot of drinkers until he came to the end of the verse, then turned to grin at me. His teeth were yellow and his front two had been chipped recently. His small parody of the Mass bothered me, but I felt I should be a good companion.

"That was truly awful Latin," I said, laughing.

"True, my friend, true. I am a wandering scholar but my scholarship is not as good as it should be. I studied in Koln, but I have forgotten much of what I learned there. I keep hoping drinking will make me remember, but it does not." He made a comical face and poured himself another cup of beer, splashing a bit on the table. He reached across and filled my cup with wine and another cup for the Franciscan, who nodded animatedly, finally proving he was alive.

"Don't you belong to some monastery? Some house or community?" I asked him.

"I did once," he answered. "But they sent me away. I was—" He looked at once slightly embarrassed and like he was searching for a word in some common language that would explain his expulsion, "too friendly with the novices. Yes, too friendly."

"So you took to the road?"

"The road took to me. And now I am friendly with whatever smooth, round flesh is willing to be friendly to me, boy or girl; I am not fussy."

"And you have no home?" I ignored his implication.

"Nowhere to call home. I have been here in Narbonne for some months. I can make enough money to drink and eat sometimes, copying for the builders. If I get work for the archbishop, I can earn enough money for a place to sleep and someone to sleep with."

"And you?" I said, turning my attention to the Franciscan. He looked at me glassy-eyed for a long moment.

"I am on a mission. I have a home," he answered, showing some shame in the company he was keeping. "We have heard of some medicines that they make here. Not here in Narbonne, but in the country, that way." He waved vaguely west. "My abbot wants me to learn to make them. So I come. I study. It is hot today. It was too hot to seek out healers."

"So we are all serious men!" Pieter exclaimed, reaching for the pitcher and singing out in more fractured Latin:

♪*Bibit hera, bibit herus*
Bibit miles, bibit clerus
Bibit ille, bibit illa
Bibit servus cum ancilla...♪

He sang on and on about how everybody drank. I wasn't sure how much of this company I could stand. If he were singing in Occitan, perhaps, but his crude songs were not the ones I was seeking.

I scraped myself a slice of cheese and pulled at some of the bread, hoping to soak up the wine. I turned my attention to the Franciscan. He had reached for the bread as well and tore off a piece with his fingers; his nails were cracked and gray with dirt.

"You, Fra—?"

"Lorenzo, Fra Lorenzo." He smiled at me again.

"Lorenzo," I repeated, "have you heard any songs here? And that the local men sing in their own dialect?"

He looked at me blankly as he sorted my words into ones he knew. His face stayed blank for a while as he tried to frame his answer in words that I would understand.

"Songs? *Cansos?*"

"Oc," I answered. "*Cansos,* or *sirventes* or *planhs. Aubades* or *albas* even," I said, naming all the forms I could think of.

"Alba, si, that is the river near where I am from." He nodded, happy and enthusiastic.

"No, not a river. It is a sort of a song. A song about lovers in the morning. I am here to find the tunes to some words I have with me." I touched the satchel slung over my shoulder. This obviously made no sense to him.

"*La Lobita,*" he started, "I have heard something of her."

"*La Loba!*" Pieter shouted. "Her I too have heard of. A wild woman she was, so I have heard. I have heard stories. She was given to love under the moonlight." He winked at me grotesquely. His guttural accent was growing thicker with each draft of beer.

"No, no," Lorenzo insisted. "Not *La Loba*. Those stories are old, ancient. She lived long ago. No, I have been hearing stories of *La Lobita*. She is an…" he searched for the word, "a *banditti*, an outlaw. She roams the plains from here to Toulouse and back again. She is bold. She is fierce. She is passionate. She kills men and women and robs them, too. But if she likes the man, she toys with him first. Sinful. Disgraceful." He trailed off, staring into his wine cup. I refilled it for him, but he continued to ponder its depths.

"I have heard something of that," Pieter said. "Of someone who has the run of the Toulousian. Someone ferocious. I thought it was a man. Someone who preys mostly on the French. And on those in orders. That's why I have lingered here. It is too dangerous outside the cities. There is something strange about this person, too. I can't quite remember what it is."

"I, too, have heard there is something odd about *La Lobita,*" Lorenzo agreed. "But I don't know what it is. It is strange enough that she is a young woman and an outlaw. That is wonder enough for me."

"It is a marvel," I agreed. "But that is not what I am here seeking. Is there anywhere you have heard anyone sing old songs? I thought there might still be some joglars around here. From what I've heard of such, this is the sort of place they would make their home."

"No, I haven't seen any," Pieter answered thickly. "I have heard of such men, of course, but they stayed around great courts, and there is no court here. Then the courts were destroyed in the crusade, so they scattered. I have heard there are some in Lombardy now and Catalonia."

Wonderful, I thought to myself. I could wander to Italy or go back home and ask our neighbors for this music. What a stupid mission I had been given.

"You may be right. I have found no singers here. There is nothing for it but for my friends and I to move on. Perhaps in Toulouse or Carcassone—"

I saw Lorenzo cross himself at the mention of the fortress city.

"Still, we should leave."

"You travel to Toulouse?" Pieter asked. "And there is more than just you?"

"Another man or two, that's all," I replied.

"Still, I have wanted to see Toulouse. They are building a university there. Where there are schools there are the young, the fresh scholars, the toothsome…" His voice trailed off but I did not like the look in his eye.

"Since there are no songs here, I should leave," I said, standing up and pouring the last of the wine for Lorenzo.

"No songs!" Pieter bellowed, his consonants conquering his vowels. "Wherever I am, there are songs." And began to half-shout, half-sing in his baritone:

♪*Stella puella rufa tunica;*
Si quis eam tetigit, tunica crepuit,
Eia!♪

I left him singing about the joys of the girl in the red dress. I walked unsteadily and had just wit enough to dunk my head under the fountain before I began my return to the Beguines.

15

The Road to Toulouse

I found my way back across the bridge and into the streets above the river. I was still a bit fuddled from the wine but I spotted the house of the Beguines by the line of people that snaked out the door and down the street. The skills of Na Carenza were apparently in great demand. I looked through the door where the sick were being treated and managed to catch Zaid's eye. He nodded in my direction but didn't rise.

The sun was still high and it was warm, if not as hot as it had been, and I'd been worn out with too much wine and too little food. I turned down the hallway and passed the kitchen. Na Iselda was doing something near the fire. Whatever work she was doing, it gave off a wonderful aroma. She looked over at me and smiled kindly. She waved at me as if she were shooing away a pigeon. To show that she knew what I needed she put her two long hands together and tilted her head onto them. Then she waved me away again. She was right. I needed a nap.

When I awoke, the sky outside my little sleeping cell had turned greenish blue and there were pink streaks in the distance. I rose and shook my head clear, then stepped into my sandals. I padded down the hallway to the bare chapel to make my solitary Vespers. As I passed the kitchen I heard several voices speaking in unison. It took me a moment to realize what these voices were doing. They were praying. They were praying the *Pater Noster*, but not in Latin.

I glanced into the kitchen to see Na Carenza, Na Iselda, Na Bieiris, Na Alais, and Pons with their heads bent down. They were just finishing up the prayer in Occitan "…forgive us our trespasses as we forgive those who trespass against us. Lead us not into temptation but deliver us from evil." I saw Zaid sitting off to one side, looking amused. It felt rude, somehow, to watch, so I moved on, found the chapel, and completed my evening office.

When I returned, everyone was sitting around the trestle table, everyone but Na Carenza, who had absented herself again. The onions I'd donated had been baked with cinnamon and a very light touch of pepper, perhaps in deference to our status as guests. Na Iselda put a piece of flat bread on the table, then topped it with soft onions, a mixture of greens, and last year's pickled turnips. There was a pitcher of cool, clear water on the table and everything seemed to be just what I needed.

Young Alais scooted over next to me, coltish and active. She seemed very much a child in those moments. She started to snatch little pieces of onion off my trencher. She dangled them playfully from her tongue and then sucked them into her mouth greedily. Na Iselda tried to look disapproving, but while her gray eyes worked to hold a stern look, the corners of her mouth were fighting their way upward.

When the older woman turned her back to tend the fire, Alais grabbed my arm and darted her face close to my ear. "Take me with you," she said.

"What?"

"Take me with you. Take me to Toulouse. Take me back to the mountains where I was born. I know pathways. My brother was a shepherd. I know secret ways where you'll be safe. Take me away."

"But why? Aren't you well cared for here? Aren't you doing God's work?"

"I don't know. I am cared for, but I miss the spring lamb. I don't know anything about God's work. I just know that I am not one of these women. I am not like them at all and I want to go away."

Zaid slid over to my left side and I felt trapped.

"She has been asking me that all day. Every time she came in with bandages or some poultice. I told her it would be up to you."

"Please, please, please take me away from here," she pleaded like a little girl begging for a ride on a pony.

"You are here against your will? And you've taken no vows?"

"My parents sent me here. It is all right most of the time. But it is so dull. I grow weary. I have taken no vows. They are forbidden. I haven't been consoled, either."

I didn't know what that meant, but I nodded.

"You will have to buy her," Zaid said into my left ear. "You cannot take away a valuable member of the community without offering compensation."

"I won't cost much, really I won't. One coin. Not even gold. Silver perhaps, but a little one. Na Carenza never really liked me anyway. She'll be happy to let me go."

By this time, I realized that everyone in the room knew what was going on and they were all waiting for my answer. I looked from Zaid to Pons, who was just staring over his food. I looked to Na Bieiris and she turned away. I looked most critically at Na Iselda. I held her eyes for a long moment and she gave me the slightest of nods.

"We will take you with us, Na Alais. You shall see Toulouse and guide us in the mountains. Pons will lead, but you will trace our secret paths."

The girl clapped her hand and then kissed me quickly, just below my right ear. Then she jumped up and ran out of the kitchen.

***

Our little troupe set out the next morning just as the sun was rising. I had said a quick Matins after an even quicker interview with Na Carenza. She showed no disappointment in Alais' defection. It seemed to me she expected it. She took the silver coin I offered without comment and wished me well.

We no longer followed the Roman road but a lesser track along the river Aude. We were making our way towards the hill country before turning north towards Toulouse. The day was bright and warm but a breeze from the sea kept the air pleasant enough. Young Alais was so full of joy and bounce and at being set free from her convent that it was contagious.

We had just reached the outskirts of the town; the world was opening to fields of lavender in bloom and vineyards where the grapes hung heavy. I was just thinking sadly of Fra Pedro and the green grapes I had slapped from his hand just a few weeks ago. We saw two men sitting on a stone by the side of the road.

"Hail brother!" one of them called out in a guttural tone. It only took me a moment to recognize Brother Pieter and Fra Lorenzo from the day before. The fat man rested on the round stone while the skinny Franciscan leaned against a staff.

"Pieter?" I inquired, stopping our party. "I thought you were making Narbonne your home?"

"I was, I was Fra—?"

"Itzal," I supplied.

"Itzal, but you spoke of traveling to Toulouse, and it sounded like such a fine idea. The morning was so fresh that it seemed like a good day to take to the road. I remarked to Lorenzo here that we could leave, that there were doctors in Toulouse who probably knew as much about medicines as anyone, and he could fulfill his mission. I told him it would be safe enough if we traveled with others. It was Lorenzo who reminded me that you were traveling in a party. We thought we might join you as far as the city."

It wasn't exactly a request and it couldn't exactly be turned down.

"Join us if you like," I said. "We won't reach the city today. It is pleasant and I would like to sleep under the stars again. You must keep up with us, though. We won't wait for you."

"*Danke,*" the fat monk answered. "Thank you. We will do our best not to slow you down."

They did, of course. Pieter just couldn't move his bulk as fast as we younger and lighter folk could. Even the mule made better time than he did. Still, he was less repulsive company out on the road away from his drink.

Early in the day, Zaid pulled me aside and said, "I'm not fond of this man. I don't think he's quite safe."

"He's just a renegade monk," I answered. "He'll only go as far as Toulouse. He was just too timid to make the trip alone. We couldn't deny him."

"You couldn't, perhaps. I would have and I think you should have." He dropped back a pace to walk beside Pons and the mule.

It was a truly fine day and the country was lovely. The lavender was in bloom and the air smelled alive. We hurried past an apiary where the hum of bees lit up the air and the beekeepers kept their faces hidden behind yellow wicker. Every now and again Pieter would sing out one of his obscene Latin songs. I knew that only the three of us in orders could tell what he was singing. Still, I gave him more than one sharp look throughout the day, and he grew less boisterous.

Of course, for most of the day, I wasn't looking at the men. My eyes were on Alais. I have known monks, scholars, travelers, even penitents in my life, but it had been a long time since I looked at a girl who was just joyful being in the sun. She had shed the dark headdress and let her hair loose. It turned out to be a color like wheat in late summer, that curious cross between bronze and gold. It reflected the bright yellow sunlight and picked up some purple notes from the fields of lavender that we walked through. Her long dress was getting in her way, so she tucked it up to walk more freely, and her ankles showed white, and if she jumped a step (which she did almost every third step, it seemed), her knees flashed, then vanished.

I did turn my attention to the others from time to time, but not too often. I saw Zaid talking with Lorenzo, or trying to. They worked out some kind of language out of sound and gesture and they seemed to have a lot to discuss. Pons was taciturn for most of the day, but every now and then, he would raise his voice in song. I couldn't tell if they were songs I was looking for, but at least they were more pure than Pieter's.

We didn't stop for a midday meal but shared bread on the road, washed down with a little watered wine or just water, in Zaid's case. Pieter was not satisfied with this, but since he'd brought no supplies of his own, he had to suffer.

As the sky went from pale blue to deep blue, we could see the fortified city of Carcassone ahead of us, an almost palpable threat. No one wanted to spend the night in the city, still considered to be cursed by the murder of its rightful lord, so we found a sheltered spot between two small hills and made our camp. We had left the Aude and were heading towards the Garonne, but there was a tributary stream nearby and a few thickets that offered dry wood for a fire that was completely unneeded, given the warmth of the evening.

***

It was a lively night. I produced the last of the ham I'd brought from Spain and I was rewarded by the look of delight on Alais' face.

"Meat! Meat!" she sang out clapping her hands and circling the yellow flame, throwing a long shadow into the purple night. "It has been so long."

"The rule you lived under was strict," I observed.

"Too strict. I want to please God. I do, truly," and she turned towards me with a look that was half mischief, half piety, "but I want to be a girl first. Is it wrong to want that, Fra Itzal?"

"Not wrong child; it's as right as could be." This was from Pieter. I liked the man less and less.

Pons came from the mule holding cups and two of the bottles of wine. The night became a feast. Pieter did his best to empty both bottles with help from Lorenzo. I wasn't shy but I did pace myself. Alais was as jubilant at the taste of wine as she had been at the reminder of meat. She started singing wordlessly, tossing her skirts around her legs as she circled the fire. She kept holding her cup out for more wine and then she would dance over to me, offering me tastes from her cup as often as she could. Pieter scowled and Zaid just grinned at us, sipping from his water bag.

"Oh, how I missed the midsummer bonfires!" Alais cried out, tossing her hair back and looking up at the moon, just off the full. Her face shone in the white light.

Someone, either Pons or Zaid, fetched my guitarra from the panniers. I pulled the strings into tune and began to play. I strummed chords softly at first, and then they built. Before long I was playing Pons' ballad of the strange town. He sang the words and we ran through it at a fast pace. Then I sang the old knight's song, sad and sweet. Zaid took the instrument from me, loosened the tuning a bit, and sang one of his strange Moorish tunes. This set Alais to dancing again, swaying her body to the unfamiliar music and swinging her hips in the firelight.

She swung around one more time and fell onto the ground just beyond my feet. She pulled herself up onto my knees and looked into my eyes warmly. I suppose that's the best way to put it.

"Take her away," Pons told me. "You paid for her."

I froze. That's not what I meant. The girl wanted to leave. She was too young to be so confined. She wanted to go back to her family in the mountains. The house of the Beguines was no place for her, anyone could see that. I had no intentions towards her; I was just trying to set her free.

Still, there she was, her head on my knee, her golden hair reflecting the firelight like a tapestry. She was breathing heavily from her dancing and her bosom was animated. I drained my wine cup and she stood up. She reached down towards me and led me to my feet. She picked up the half-empty wine bottles and danced me away from the fire, around a small rise, behind a thicket.

***

I was clay in her hands. She took me behind the trees and pulled my cassock over my head. I stood naked in the moonlight in front of her. She splashed me with wine and then licked me from my head to my chest. Then she lifted her dress over her head and let it fall behind her. She was as white as ivory in the moonlight. She poured wine between her breasts and pulled my head to her.

"You were sent to me," she pronounced with the seriousness only a young girl could muster. "You were sent to save me from them. I have never been one of them. I could not lead that Cathar life—no food, no men—"

I was startled; I pulled my head away for a moment. A Cathar life? That was a house of Cathar women? How did I not know? The white rooms, the absence of statues or pictures. The severity of the diet. I just thought they were good women serving God.

I wasn't occupied with these thoughts long. They flashed through my brain, but Alais pulled my face back to her breasts and was doing something to the other parts of my body that banished all thoughts, and we sank to the ground. This was nothing like the games I'd played under the blankets with my sister-in-law—this was fire, this was desire burning fierce and white. This was a young woman feeling all her powers and using them for our pleasure. It's a wonder I didn't burst into flames at that moment.

Later, she toyed me back to life. Then she grew serious and oddly ferocious. She turned over, rose on her hands and knees, looking over her shoulder at me.

"Take me like La Loba," she growled. "Under the moonlight, like a wolf. Like La Loba, like La Lobita." And those were the last human words I heard for a long time.

***

Morning came, I guess. I did not wake with my monkish hours in mind. The sunlight fell down onto my face, coaxing me awake. I rolled over and reached for Alais. She wasn't there. I rolled onto my back and absorbed sunlight for a few moments before I realized that there should be other people around. There should be the sounds of a camp being broken, a mule being laden with panniers, the creaking and stretching of men as they got ready for the day. There was silence except for the buzz of flies and the hum of a stray bee.

I got to my feet and shook myself. I was naked and I couldn't see my cassock anywhere. I thought they were all having a joke on the wayward monk. I walked out from behind the copse and looked at our campsite. It was deserted.

I stood there in the morning light, alone, as naked as I was born, on the sun-drenched road to Toulouse.

# Part Two

The Wall

1
Awakenings

I just stood there. I had no idea what to do. What I could do? There was no place for me to go, there was no one to help me. I looked west and north. The road was empty. I looked east and south. The sun was blinding and the road was just as empty. I looked at the ground. I was not completely bereft. My sandals rested by a small gorse bush. I did the only thing I could. I put them on.

I could see the remains of our camp. The ashes from the fire were still warm when I knelt to touch them. Grasses were still bent from where Pons and Zaid had unrolled their blankets. I decided to shout.

"Pons!" I called out. "Zaid! Alais!"

The only answer was the buzz of cicadas.

"Pieter!" I tried more tentatively. Still silence. "Lorenzo?" No answer.

I started to circle the campsite. I don't know why. I walked one ring around it and then another, widening out a little. There was no sign of anyone. The mule was gone. The panniers were gone. Whatever money I had was gone. The book, the beautiful book, was gone. At that thought I sat down on the ground hard and held my head in my hands.

I thought about the leather covers. The beautiful, creamy paper with lines just waiting for my hand to write down notes, to capture music that might be lost otherwise. Some music I had already captured. It was gone now. Would anyone ever see it, ever play it? Who had taken it? Who had taken everything?

My soul ached with the loss, but there was nothing I could do in this place, on this low rise along the road to Toulouse. I had other troubles. The breeze was warm against my skin and I remembered that I was naked. I was naked, I was lost, I was in a foreign country. I shook myself and stood up again. I resumed my circles for want of anything better to do.

I'm glad of it now. It seemed hopeless, but I kept on. The sixth circle, the widest I walked, took me to the edge of the water. The stream moved slowly, sluggish through reeds. At least I had water, I thought to myself as I kicked at a tussock. I kicked too hard and measured my length in the moist grass. I stretched my arm to lift myself and I felt something. Rather, I felt someone. It was a warm ankle with dark hair. I pulled at it as I stood up and I heard a grunt. It was Zaid.

He lay there, hard to see in the long grass since he was covered with a green cloth that I had never seen before. His shirt showed white at the top of his body. His hand was stretched out as if reaching for something and there was a dark clot of blood on the back of his head. I got to his shoulder and rolled him over. His body turned and there was a woof of air expelled from his lungs. He didn't say anything or open his eyes. Still, his chest rose and fell. I could tell that he lived and that was good news. At least I wasn't alone anymore.

I pulled the green cloth off his body. His shirt covered him and he still had breeches on. Whoever had stripped me had left him mostly dressed, and someone had covered him. I hurried to the water and soaked one edge of the cloth. I ran back to Zaid, rolled him back onto his belly, and washed the wound on the back of his head with cool water. I turned him back over to face the heavens.

I went back to the stream and soaked the cloth once more. I returned and used it to wash his face, and then I left the damp cloth resting on his forehead, thinking it might soothe him when he woke. If he woke.

I stood up and looked around again. The road was a few yards away. The memory of our camp was nearer. The road was still deserted. There were no people out on the low hills. To my left, downstream, there were thick shrubs hugging the shore next to the water. I thought that birds might make their home there. I thought there might be eggs.

Nettles stung my ankles and my calves. Some of the grasses were very sharp and cut at me as I fought through them to the water's edge. I was right. I discovered a small bird's nest with four blue eggs resting in it. I plucked out three of them and ran back to Zaid. I set them down next to him and made my way back, hoping to spot another nest so I wouldn't rob one mother of all her children. Cattails swayed in the warm breeze. The wind sighed softly across the water, rippling the sluggish surface. I could tell that it was shallow only near this edge and that the channel grew deep quickly. I knew that though the current looked slow, it was strong.

I beat at the bushes, hoping to surprise another bird into the air so that I could rob its nest. I felt sad and guilty about it, but our need was greater. God had given us dominion over the animals, I told myself. Perhaps my guilt blinded me, but I saw no other signs of life. I made enough racket, that was certain, pushing through the bushes and reeds, kicking at the soft earth. Once my sandal was almost sucked away as I sank into black mud. I pulled my foot free but my sandal stayed behind. I'm fairly certain I took the Lord's name in vain at that moment. The names of more than a few saints, too.

I was on my hands and knees, elbow-deep in river mud, reaching for my sandal, when I heard the voice. It was faint at first. I wasn't sure I was hearing anything at all. I thought it might be the wind. I pulled my errant sandal free and fell onto my backside. I sat still, the grass cool against my naked buttocks.

There it was again. It was a tune. It wasn't coming from Zaid but from a little way downstream. I sat up straighter but couldn't see anyone or anything at first. I concentrated on the tune. Then on the words. I was sure I could make out words by now, and that they were almost familiar.

♪Ab un baissar anz d'annou
Mi auci, e si enferna...♪

I'd read them somewhere—in my missing book? I wasn't sure. The words got lost in the breeze among the reeds but the tune persisted. Complicated but jaunty. I stood up and walked towards the sound. I knew that this kissing was going to land the singer in hell, or so he sang, but I missed more and more of the song.

Suddenly a figure leapt up in the middle of a yellow bush. His hands were raised as if to chase me away, but his voice stayed mild and he continued to sing. His face was pockmarked and his left ear was missing. He was dressed in a long green tunic, belted with a rope. As he stood just a few feet from me, he untied his girdle and threw it in my face. Then he pulled the tunic over his head, and raised his voice higher, singing:

♪Ieu sui Arnautz, q'amas l'aura
E chatz la lebre ab lo bou,
E nadi contra suberna...♪

He threw the green garment at me, this Arnaut who so loved the wind. He leapt at the end of his song and threw himself into the stream. He tried, like his song said, to swim against the current, but he couldn't. He reached the center of the channel, swimming strongly, at first, to the north, but the waters quickly turned him around and he was swept away.

I'd seen madness before, of course. People driven out of their wits by loss or hunger, by watching families die and homes disappear. I have no idea what had set this man off. I don't know if he would have stayed there, singing by the riverbank had I not blundered through the bushes and roused him. All I knew was that he was gone now. Gone to God, no doubt, who would take better care of him than the world had. Meanwhile, I became aware that I had a green tunic in my hands. There didn't seem to be anything else to do but pull it over my head, and then search the ground until I found the rope to bind it close to me.

***

I pulled the sandal back onto my foot, muddy as it was, and squished my way back to where Zaid lay. He was still unconscious, but he breathed steadily and I thought that was a good sign. Whenever I took hurt at our priory, I just made my way to the brother physician. I had almost no knowledge of the medical arts.

I knelt down next to my companion and found a small stone. I tilted his head up against my knee and cracked the little egg against the rock. I dumped the contents of the shell straight into Zaid's mouth and tilted his head farther back. The yolk slid right down his throat. I cracked the second egg and started to pour it into his mouth. I seemed to have missed my mark because he began to cough and sputter, but my clumsy blocking of his airway brought him to wakefulness.

His body shook and his head rocked back and forth on my knee. He tried to sit up and then slid back against me. He said something in a language I didn't understand before he opened his eyes and looked at me.

"Itzal?" he said softly.

"Yes, Zaid," I answered as gently as I could.

"I'm alive? You're alive?"

"Yes, Zaid," I replied again. "We both live."

"What happened?" He started to sit up again and made it this time, although it wasn't without the sounds of pain. A grimace crossed his dark face.

"I hoped you could tell me," I said. "All I know is that I woke alone and naked. I only just found you."

"Is there water?"

"The stream is close. I have nothing to carry water in. Take my arm. I'll lead you."

I lifted him from the ground as carefully as I could and then pulled his arm around my shoulder. He had to reach up to take it, but it supported him. We then limped down to the water's edge. We were on a firmer bank here; there weren't as many reeds and the ground was solid. Zaid stretched out flat and dunked his head into the water. He pulled it out, shook drops from his hair and beard, and then plunged it underwater again. I saw bubbles rising from his nose and mouth. He pulled his head out, shook it again, and then rolled over onto his back, breathing heavily.

"That's better," he said at last. "I don't think I'm badly hurt."

"That's good news, friend," I said, feeling a great tenderness towards this near stranger.

"I remember what happened now."

"Tell me. Don't tell me. I am content that both of us are well."

"I'll tell, I'll tell, just give me a moment." He rolled back onto his stomach and pulled himself to the edge of the water again. He looked at his distorted reflection for a moment before he lowered his lips and took a long drink. He sat up at last and pulled his shirt to his knees then wrapped his arms around the cloth.

"The fat monk—" he began.

"I knew it!" I said sharply.

Zaid waved at me to be quiet so I held my tongue, but visions of various forms of damnation flitted through my head, all of them featuring fat Pieter.

"Of course you did. He is a loathsome person. He claimed to travel with us out of fear of violence on the roads when he was the threat all along. Still, he seemed jolly enough, if vulgar. Particularly after young Alais pulled you away from us. She's not quiet, that one, is she?" He cocked an eyebrow at me as he smiled. I blushed and lowered my eyes, but I was glad of his smile.

He shook his head and went on. "There were crude jokes, of course. Pons had drunk too much wine. I, as usual, confined myself to water. Still, I entered into the spirit of the jests along with everyone else. We laughed too loudly to cover the music you and the girl were making. I don't remember why I turned towards Pons. I think I may have had another question about that massacre he witnessed. Anyway, I turned my back on fat Pieter and thin Lorenzo, and I knew no more. I assume I was struck on the back of the head. I don't think I was out for terribly long. I felt them remove my outer tunic. I heard Pieter say something that sounded vulgar about my backside in his barbaric language and I was afraid. Still, I heard them move off and I stood, running this direction, towards the water. Towards you, I thought. There was no sound from where you were and I gathered both you and the girl were worn out. I looked over my shoulder and I saw the two monks seize the bridle on your mule. Pons offered weak resistance. Then Lorenzo walked over to where you had vanished and reappeared carrying the girl over his shoulder like a sack of turnips. A sack of turnips that kicked and pummeled his back with tiny fists. He slung her over the back of the animal and bound her wrists with something. This ended any pretense of resistance from Pons. I think he hoped he could protect Alais. I don't know. I called out to them. Fra Lorenzo heard me but Pons didn't. The Italian threw a rock in my direction. It must have caught the back of my head, where I'd already been struck. I fell into the reeds and I was there until you found me."

"I should have known," I said. "I should have been more on my guard against that one. Those two."

"Perhaps," Zaid responded. "But you had a more tender temptation to negotiate. If you failed your God, at least you didn't fail the girl."

"Of course I did. I sinned with her. And I left her unprotected. I was weak."

"You were a man. Enough. The question is, what do we do now?"

"Let's search to see if they left us anything else that we can use. Then, I suppose our only plan will be to continue towards Toulouse and hope to find a Dominican house. Can you stand?"

"Yes, I can now. Before we search, there is a personal matter that I must see to," he said. It took me a moment.

"Do you need help?"

"Some things a man must do for himself," Zaid replied with a gentle laugh. He rose stiffly and walked downstream into the reeds. I waited a moment and then did likewise.

***

Afterward, we made circles around our spent campground. There wasn't much left to see. Matted grass, a little bit of ash, the mule's dung. Nothing else. After a few minutes, I heard Zaid shout something. I went over to him.

"Here's a book," he announced with triumph in his voice. I held out a moment's hope that it might be the music book, but it was simply my breviary.

It was odd because I hadn't missed it, at least not since I put the madman's garments on. There was something hard at my hip and my brain told me that it was my office. I didn't really remember that this wasn't my habit. I reached down and there was a cleverly hidden opening that led to a secret pocket. I slipped my hand in and pulled out a small book bound in green leather, a little smaller than my breviary. I had never seen it before.

"Where did you get that?" Zaid asked, indicating both the tunic and the book.

"I found it. They left me naked. I saw a poor soul living wild and mad. He tore this off and threw himself into the water. There was nothing I could do for him but pray. I was naked and I had more need of this than he did."

I turned the book over in my palms and opened it. I couldn't tell what it was at first. It wasn't written in Latin but it looked religious somehow. Slowly, the language began to make sense to me. I saw that it was in Occitan. I realized then it was a copy of the Gospel of John in the vulgar tongue. It was something only heretics carried. I didn't throw it away but slipped it back into the clothes where I found it. I might have given it more thought but just then, there was a sound to the south, and both Zaid and I turned our heads.

It could not have been better had they been angels. They rode on milk white horses and they wore the white robes and black cowls of Dominicans. There were two of them followed by another party, also on horseback, but I paid those very little attention. Here were my brethren, traveling along the road to Toulouse. We were saved.

2
To the Walled City

Zaid and I stood by the side of the road and waited for them to come up to us. As they approached, my eyes sorted out more people from the heat and the light. They seemed to be a larger group than I first thought. The two Dominicans were in the lead, their white habits glowing in the sunlight. They were woven from a fabric I'd never seen before. Their black traveling cowls were almost a relief to look at. They were followed by two men at arms on horses. After them trailed a ragged bunch of men and women in various states of tattered dress. They all looked poor and certainly miserable, with their hands bound in front of them and another rope tying all their bindings together. Finally, two more men at arms and one last monk rose on horseback; these last three horses were dappled gray. When they reached us, they came to a halt, the first monk holding up his hand and looking down his long nose at me.

"Greetings, brethren!" I cried in Occitan. This brought no sign of recognition, just an expression of distaste flashing across the monk's face. I tried bowing my head.

The monk said something but I couldn't make it out. The language seemed familiar but his accent was so thick, the words sounded so harsh in my ears that I couldn't for the life of me make out a single word.

"For the love of Saint Dominic!" I called out in Occitan or Catalan, I'm not sure which. I was frightened.

The second monk walked his horse over to where I stood, drew back his riding crop, and slashed me across the face. I fell to the ground with a long cut bleeding on my cheek.

"*Albigens chien!*" he spat in an accent just as thick as his companion's. I realized then that they were speaking in French but in the harsh accent of the distant city of Paris.

I tried to stand. I tried to say that I was a monk like them, but the blood was flowing from my cheek, staining my new green garment. My head was spinning from pain and heat. Before I knew what was happening, both Zaid and I had our hands bound and we were joined to the dismal procession that trailed behind these white-robed clerics.

***

I looked at my fellow prisoners as we stumbled along that road. The heat and light must have played tricks on my eyes because we were fewer than I had first thought, perhaps nine or ten. Most were men in homespun wool, but there were three women as well, two of them dressed in formless, once white dresses. They seemed to be the most stolidly resigned to their fates of all of us, or perhaps they were just wearier than the men. The man tied beside Zaid had a rough bandage across one eye and his bare feet were bleeding. I was anxious to speak to anyone, to get an explanation before we traveled much further. Before I could, one of the monks shouted something to one of the men at arms in their rough language. He came over to us and knocked us to our knees with his pike.

"*Nom!*" he yelled, producing a roll of crude paper and a stick of charcoal from somewhere. We didn't answer immediately. The halted gaggle of prisoners stared at us, open-mouthed.

"Tell him your names," hissed the man next to us.

"Fra Itzal," I muttered and was struck by the butt of the pike from my answer. "Fra Itzal!" I shouted loudly and quickly.

The man prodded Zaid.

"Za—" I kicked him, and he took my meaning. "Sixtus." He answered loudly.

The big Frenchman wrote something on his paper. Then two of the men at arms tugged at our bindings until we rose to our feet. The monks kicked the flanks of their horses and we moved on.

"Where are we going?" I asked the man with the bandage once I caught my breath.

He turned his good eye on me but he didn't say anything. He just held out his hand with fingers curled and then blew on them, opening his palm flat out.

"What? I don't understand." I muttered.

"He means we're going to the fire, Itzal. We're going to be burned," Zaid whispered from the other side.

"But I'm a monk!" I started.

"I don't think these people care," my friend went on. "I think all that matters is that we're not French, we're poor, and we're wearing home-woven green."

"What does the green have to do with anything?"

"I thought you would know in your order. This is the color the *Perfecti* wear, the confirmed heretics."

"But—"

"Save your words, Itzal. We'll need the breath for this march." Zaid turned his attention to his bare feet which were already flecked with blood. I felt a small wave of pity and stumbled along.

* * *

It was sometime between Prime and Terce when we joined the prisoners. We didn't stop until after Sext. The lead monks halted their horses near the riverbank where the ground seemed firm enough to support their beasts. The men at arms started pushing us to the ground and it took a moment before I realized that we were meant to rest. I sat on the ground with Zaid beside me. He was rubbing his feet, which were raw enough, but the bleeding had stopped. I tore some grass and passed it to him. He used it to cool his soles, although I'm not sure it helped much.

One of the pike men threw small pieces of hard-spelt bread towards us. There was a scramble among the prisoners as they reached for the food. The two women in white ignored both the bread and the other prisoners. They just sat, erect and dignified, leaning their backs against the other's, not saying a word. I picked up a crust and tried to chew a little bit but passed most of what I caught to Zaid. His need was greater, and I was used to fasting.

Two of the other men at arms had gone to the river and filled a canvas bucket. They passed among us, giving a ladle of water to each person. It was barely enough to slake a thirst, let alone wash down the rock-hard bread.

After everyone had been fed as much as we were going to be fed, I saw some of the prisoners stretch out on the ground. Of course, this meant whoever they were bound to had to lie down too, but no one seemed to mind. The others had a sense of how this was supposed to go but I was still in a state of confusion.

I truly felt that if I could only talk to the monks in their shiny white habits, I could prove to them I was one of their kind, another Dominican. The three clerics kept themselves separate from everyone, though. They knelt, rather ostentatiously, I thought, and recited the office for Sext together. At least that's what I assumed they were doing; they were too far off for me to make out any words. Then I saw them pull white bread, a creamy cheese, and a bottle of wine from their saddlebags. They were going to have a feast while we watched.

I looked at the man with the bandaged eye tied next to me. It took me a moment to realize that he was closer to being a boy than a man. He had few years, but they had been hard on him. He seemed slightly mad to me. At least, he was very detached from his surroundings. He sat with his arms grasping his knees, his head resting against them, and sang tunelessly. I thought it was nonsense at first, but I was finally able to make out a few words.

♪*Et eu vas dompn', ab braga bassada*
Ab maior viet de nuill as'en despan
E fotrai vos de tal arandonada...♪

It was an obscenity! A dirty song about a filthy man and what he would do with a filthier woman! Perhaps it was because of what I had done with pretty little Alais the night before—had that just been last night?—but I was shocked. I was more shocked when the younger woman in homespun seated nearby sang an answer:

♪*Pois tan m'aves de fotre menanzada*
Saber volria, Seigner, vostre van,
Car eu ai la mia port'armada...♪

She was taunting him with her sex! Were they all mad? I turned, rather red in the face, towards Zaid, but he just smiled his thin-lipped smile.

"It is what people do, Itzal, that's all. What else do these have to hope for except that they might be left alone together for just a little while before they are given over to the flames? I'm not sure that those two care if they were alone."

"But do they know each other? Are they married?"

"Were you married last night?" he replied. "Does it matter, Itzal? It is human contact. Besides, it's a funny song." He clapped his hands lightly in time.

I never learned how the dialogue in the song turned out. The young man was singing a verse promising enough sex to make the girl fart and faint away from satisfaction when the monks mounted their horses, and the pike men walked among the prisoners, pulling us roughly to our feet. We were on the road once again.

***

We moved at a brisk clip. They didn't keep us running exactly, but we were pulled along just fast enough that no one was dragged. If someone slowed down one of the bound lines, they were quickly lashed back to speed by one of the men with pikes

We didn't have that far to go. When we rounded the small hill on which we'd stopped, we could see the city of Carcassone ahead of us. It rose, stony and forbidding on its height. Double walls encircled it. True, there were now small houses and makeshift streets laid out across the river, but the citadel looked much as it did two generations ago, or so I thought, at least.

"It is a rock," Zaid said, breathing heavily.

"Yes, it was built for sieges and it has never really been taken. Or so I've been told. At least not by siege. By treachery but not by force."

"That can't be true, Itzal," Zaid argued. "It belonged to the lords of the South, and now it is in the hands of French monks and Frenchmen by the look of things."

"Yes, the crusaders took the place. But it wasn't by force or not by force alone. After Beziers, it was here that Raymond-Roger Trenceval decided to make his stand. The people of Beziers had urged him to leave them. They had no picture in their minds of the fate that awaited them; they just thought their lord could better defeat the invaders from this—this rock, as you called it.

"The siege was laid. There were stores within the walls. Everyone knew they were in for a long waiting game. But it was high summer and it was hot. The river does not flow into the city. They rely on wells and cisterns for water. The wells were good, the water fresh and pure. The French had siege engines, though. Eventually, their stones blocked the wells so that there was no more water. Flies were thick in the air and children were dying of thirst and hunger. Raymond-Roger left his citadel under a flag of truce, under a safe conduct. He pleaded for his people and they were granted mercy. They could leave the city with only the clothes on their backs. The crusaders conceded only that. Raymond-Roger they took prisoner, in spite of their pledges of safe conduct. They let the people leave the city in poverty and they threw its lord into his own dungeon. The odious Simon de Montfort ruled from here. Within the year, Raymond-Roger, the flower of the South, was dead in his ancestral prison. Murdered, many think. Dysentery is the official story. The city has a bad name, even now, as if cursed by the treachery."

I panted after my long tale. I hadn't meant to go on about it, the story just rolled out of me as we neared the great gray walls.

"You know how the city got its name?" a voice to my other side asked.

I looked at the boy with the bandaged face. I was surprised at the sanity of his words. I had assumed him a half-wit at best.

"No," I wheezed.

"Centuries ago," he began, "there was another siege. This city is the key to the plains. All the invaders knew that. It was Moors, I think, or perhaps Visigoths. I do not know. Long ago, a time buried in the mists.

"There was a siege. A long siege. It went on for months and months. The food was running out. The city was ruled by a woman then, by Dame Carca. I do not know what they called the place back then, because this is how it got its name.

"When Dame Carca saw how things stood, that the citizens could not stand another week without food, she hatched a plot. She took all the remaining fodder they kept for horses, the wheat and the oats, and fed it to the only living pig in that city. She made that pig fat. She fed it and forced water down its throat so that it swelled up. It was an enormous pig after only a week. Then she cut its throat and bound the carcass to a catapult. She had the pig flung out of the city. When the besiegers saw the beast land and explode, they admitted defeat. If they could throw away a gross pig like that one, then they must have plenty of food. It must have been Moors since they are afraid of pigs anyway. They folded their tents and the city was saved. As they fled, Dame Carca rang all the bells in the city. So the city is named "*Carca sonne*" you see because the lady rang the bells."

I didn't say anything. My breath was gone. I nodded as politely as I could under the circumstances. We seemed to be moving faster. It was about the hour of Nones. The horses could smell their stable. We almost ran up the small slope and entered through the gates into the double-walled city that was named after a resourceful woman.

3
Inquisitorial

We half-ran, half-marched through the city gates into the citadel of Carcassone itself. The city was formidable from without but it was frightening from within. It was constructed entirely out of stone and was obviously built for defense. There were two sets of circling walls surrounding the center of the town. There were towers everywhere you turned and platforms for archers. The streets were flagged with stone and were deliberately too narrow for more than three to walk abreast.

Our procession squeezed through the narrow streets. Shopholders and merchants watched us as we trooped by. They tended to turn their backs on us. I thought at first that it was because they were saddened by whatever fate might be awaiting us, but as we went along, I began to hear comments from the people, and it seemed evident that it was contempt for the invaders that made them turn away. Some spit on the ground as soon as the monks in white passed by them, others made obscene gestures towards the backs of the men at arms.

The streets turned back in on themselves so often that I lost any sense of where we might be. Finally, we reached a double door reinforced with iron bars. The doors swung open and we were kicked and shoved through the gates. We found ourselves on the river side of the city in a space made between the two sets of defensive walls. It formed a courtyard and there were obviously cells of some sort, as well as other rooms, embedded in the outer walls and probably beneath them. There was a freestanding tower towards one end of the courtyard and a few men lay sunning themselves on its roof.

We were organized into a crude formation and made to face the doors we had just been pushed through. One of the Dominicans started to address us, but since he was speaking French, his words were relayed through an interpreter—a small man with mouse-gray hair dressed in the black of the Friars Minor.

"Do not fear," he said in a high, piping voice. "You are here at the mercy of God. You will stay in this courtyard tonight. You will be fed and there will be water. In the morning you will be examined by the Inquisitors. Then your fates will be decided. You will be free and unbound. Make no mistake. There is no way out of here except through repentance and penance that is recognized by the merciful Church."

As he ended, the men at arms walked among us, removed the ropes from our hands, and coiled them up. Many of the prisoners, myself among them, just collapsed to the flagstones where they stood. The two women in white wandered off to a corner of the courtyard by themselves.

"Here we are, Fra Itzal," Zaid said to me. "Prisoners of the most holy Catholic Church. Here we are in the most notorious prison in this part of the world. We are in the Wall."

"It won't be so bad, Zaid. I will clear everything up in the morning. They will know that I am one of their order and that you are my companion. There is nothing to fear."

"There is everything to fear, my friend," he said wearily and then lapsed into silence.

I stood up and dusted the back of my green tunic. As I stood two of the other prisoners came over and knelt before me. They bowed their heads and held their hands out, palms flat and upturned. I could not for the life of me determine why they did that. I offered a small prayer in Latin and waved my hand over them in blessing. They left me and walked over to the two solitary women and did the same thing.

"There is much to fear," Zaid repeated. "You have just been treated as one of the *parfaits*, one of the heretic *perfecti*, and don't think it went unseen. That tower has eyes."

"What? That's nonsense. I just blessed them," I replied.

"As you will. I still smell smoke," Zaid said. And he left me to seek a privy.

***

Like Zaid, like everyone, I took my turn answering nature's call and then wandered back into the courtyard. I sat down with my back against the cool stone of the river side of the yard. The young man with the bandage dropped down next to me but didn't offer anything by way of conversation. Zaid moped for some time before coming over and squatting down next to me. He rocked on his heels and stroked his once neat beard. A look of disgust crossed his face. I suspect that he didn't mind captivity as much as the constraints on his personal hygiene.

The little man in the Friar's Minor black looked to be making the rounds of the prison. At first, I thought he must be distributing food, but I saw no one eat after he had left them.

When he reached the three of us, he squatted in the manner of Zaid and he spoke softly, although his voice was still unpleasant.

"*Bonjour,*" he began in French. Seeing our faces unmoved he switched to heavily accented Occitan. "Greetings. Welcome to our prison—*my* prison, I should say. I am the jailer here, and I see to the day-to-day business of this place."

"That is very good for you," I replied. "May God go with you."

"God always goes with me. I keep the keys, like Saint Peter. You will be here either for a very long time or a very short time."

"It will be a very short time. I don't belong here."

"No one belongs here. God knows I don't belong here. Still, if you are here a short time you will be carried off by the wind. If you are here for some time, let me tell you that it doesn't have to be wholly unpleasant."

"I can pass my time in prayer. That will be pleasant enough," I answered curtly.

"Perhaps, but time on your knees can be wearing. Perhaps you would like someone to get on their knees with you?"

I couldn't fathom what he was talking about.

"You perhaps have some coins somewhere?" he wheedled.

I shook my head. All I had was whatever remained in the madman's clothes. A gospel in the vernacular, my breviary, and not much else.

"Perhaps you have relatives," he stated and waved his hand towards the east. "Relatives who are outside? Perhaps they could bring something that would make your life easier in here?"

"Something that we would turn over to you?" Zaid spat out.

"It would be for the best," this fellow answered genially.

Zaid heaved a heavy sigh and went back to contemplating his bare feet. Next to me, the boy unwound the ragged bandage from around his face. The filthy cloth unfolded itself and two copper coins fell onto the flags.

"Here," he said. "Take care of me. Don't let them kill me."

"As for that, there is little I can do. That is between you and the Inquisitors. However, even if you only have a short time to live, this will make it more comfortable."

Zaid reached up and grabbed the man by the collar of his black cowl.

"Be true to the boy. Even if I don't have much distance between me and the fire, I can make you suffer."

"I'm sure you can," the man bobbed his mouse-gray head. "No fears. I will look after the boy. You two," he waved his hand over Zaid and myself, " you two have nothing to bargain with, so you are on your own. Should anything come your way—wool, wine, money," the smile spread over his face like a stain, "bring it to me. I, Pierre Fournier will see that it works to your comfort." He stood up and moved along to another group of prisoners.

I sat there seething for a few moments. Then I noticed a certain commotion. Apparently, our meal was being served. We rose and pushed our way through, each receiving a chunk of barley bread and a dipper full of water for our trouble. We chewed them down as best we could and returned to our place by the wall. The boy seemed content. I'm not sure if he received more than the rest of us. Zaid remained sullen.

"Don't worry, Zaid," I told him. "Everything will be fine. I will tell the Inquisitors who I am in the morning. I will tell them to send word back to Girona. This will all be straightened out and we can go on with our mission."

"Trust your monks if you like. I do not think you have been much in the world these last few years."

"No, I haven't. I am going to pray my Vespers and then I will curl up against this wall of good stone and try to sleep until Matins."

"Pray for all of us, Itzal," Zaid said, turning his back on me.

I fell to my knees and offered prayers for all the souls in the prison and all the souls on earth. A few people looked at me, unsure of the language that I was using in prayer, but everyone let me alone. As darkness began to fall, I pulled myself into a ball, making sure the green tunic covered me and sank into a fitful sleep.

***

Even before the first light found its way between those walls, I was woken by scraping sounds. A few men of the prison were arranging long benches on the flags. I shook myself awake and set myself to my morning prayers, trying to remember which saint the day was meant to honor. It seemed to me that it must be past St. Leo's day, but if so, I had missed honoring that saint who fought heretics and set the psalms to music, so I held him in my mind during my solitary Matins.

I prayed fast since everyone was being roused roughly by the men at arms. Each was handed a piece of bread and a ladle of water and then pushed towards the benches. A table had been set up in front of them and two Dominicans were seated there, shuffling papers. These were different monks from the ones who had brought us into the prison. One was plump and round, with a broad tonsure and a kind-looking face. The other was tall and severe with a scar running down his left cheek. As I saw him, my hand went to the wound on my own face. It was sticky in some places but seemed to be clotting and healing. I have no idea how I looked.

The fat monk rose and chanted a benediction in Latin. The prisoners may not have understood what the words meant, but they knew enough to bow their heads.

"You are all accused of heresy!" the fat monk announced calmly in French.

"You are all accused of Heresy!" Pierre Fournier bawled out in Occitan. I hadn't even noticed him standing next to the table.

"You will now answer the charge. Dompna Heloise d'Ariege, come forward!"

One of the women in white rose and took two steps away from her bench. Her companion stirred but stayed seated. There obviously had been some subtle sign from Dompna Heloise.

"You are a relapsed heretic," the tall monk said in French. Fournier repeated it in Occitan.

"I am a good Christian woman."

"You swear you are not a heretic?" The woman stood in silence.

"That's enough, brother," the round monk said. "Bind her over to the secular powers." He wrote something in a book that was on the table.

"Dompna Sybille Bailley," Fournier shouted. The other woman in white rose.

"I go where she goes," she said quietly before either monk could ask anything.

"It is not too late," the round monk started, his voice mild. "Renounce your heresy, offer testimony against Dompna Heloise, and you will be spared."

"I go where she goes," the woman repeated.

"Then you go to the flames, daughter," the monk said, still looking kind. He wrote in his book again. The two women were led away into the depths of the prison.

"Arnaud Leclerge!" Fournier called out and the once-bandaged boy stood up.

"You are accused as a heretic, that you believe other than what the Church teaches," the tall monk began and Fournier continued to translate.

"Lord, I am innocent. I have never had any faith but what I've been taught."

"Taught by whom, my son?" the rounder monk asked gently.

"By the good men," the boy answered.

"These men you call good—" the tall monk began, but the shorter man interrupted.

"Will you swear that you believe only what the Church teaches?"

"Do you order me to swear?"

"I do not order you. If you are not a heretic then you are free to swear an oath. If you are, then you will not. It is simple."

The boy raised his hand and spoke, "God help me that I believe rightly, that I am good and that I pray only as I have been taught."

The two monks put their heads together and then looked at the boy again.

"You will be held. You will be examined again. While you are here, you will wear a yellow cross, and your confinement will be close. You will wear no chains," the tall monk pronounced after a glance at Fournier. The boy was led away.

"Itzal, calling himself Fra," Fournier almost bellowed. I stood.

"You are accused—" the tall one began, but I stopped him. I stood on my dignity and I spoke in Latin. It was hard for me to think in that language, but I had spent part of my less than restful night practicing.

"My good brethren, a mistake had been made. I am a member of your order. I come from Aragon, from the priory of Our Lady of the Sorrows in Girona. Myself and my servant, Sixtus, were set upon on the road while performing a service for my community. We were taken by mistake."

"You are dressed like one of the heretics," the shorter monk answered in Latin.

"As I said, we were set upon by brigands along the road. We were left without anything. My servant had his shirt. I was left naked but for my sandals. This garment came to me by chance. A madman cast it off and I picked it up."

"Was this madman taken along with you?" the tall man asked fiercely.

"The madman is dead. God rest his soul. He drowned in the river after casting this in my direction. There is no reason to hold us, but if you feel you must, we will wait here while you send to Girona and inquire of my superiors about the truth of my tale."

Again the two monks put their heads together. They looked over to Fournier, then back to their book, and then back at me.

"You will be held," the bald man said. "We will send to your priory, although that may take some time, and you are not our only duty. There is no way to tell the truth of your story except through the members of your order. There is nothing about you that says you belong to our order. You are clothed like one of them. You carry a heretical book. You may keep it until we burn it, and perhaps you along with it." So the gospel hadn't been missed. "You will be held. Your confinement will be close but it will not be hard."

He looked at Fournier whose smile was as oily as it had been the previous day. The man nodded.

"Manacles," he said. "No shackles. He is to be treated with kindness. He is to be fed well."

"As well as I can, Friar," Fournier replied. "With the little money the Church allows me."

"As well as you can," he agreed. He wrote something in his book. He was through with us.

We were led to a corridor within one of the walls. A man at arms, a large man with a nose like a beet, led us to a blacksmith's forge. Our hands were placed in manacles, loosely but not so loose that we could shake them off. We were taken up another flight of stairs and led into a cell larger than the one I had left in Spain.

"Well, Itzal," Zaid said, stretching out on not quite clean straw that would serve as our bed, "this is home."

"For now, Zaid, for now," I answered.

4
In the Wall

There was no door on the cell, no way to keep us in. I sat on the straw until I heard a bell chime somewhere in town. I knew it must be Terce so I knelt down and recited my small office. Zaid was brooding, ignoring me. He seemed convinced that this was the last room he would ever see. I felt less certain.

After rising from my knees I left him there to enjoy his sorrows and wandered down the corridor and out into the courtyard. The day was bright but not too hot within the walls. The great, gray stones seemed to hold some of the cool from the morning. The benches had been cleared away and the yard was rich with life. Men and women mingled together, taking pleasure in the bright sun and the cooler shade. They chatted in groups of two and three. I heard snippets of conversations about politics, gossip, and crops but almost nothing about religion.

The bandaged boy, Arnaud Leclerge, sitting on his own in a corner, was pulling apart a bright orange peach. He waved me over.

"This is not bad," he began, "is it father?"

"Not bad," I agreed. "But I am not a priest, so don't call me father. I am a monk, Fra will do."

"Still, not bad. I will be taken care of here."

"You're not afraid? They said they would examine you again. You certainly sounded like you were ducking the questions the inquisitors asked."

"Of course I dodged them," he said, smiling through gapped and broken teeth. "Nothing I could say would be safe. It is better to be clever." He unwound the bandage from around his face. There was a scar below his left eye, but the eye itself was intact. He looked like a healthy boy of fifteen or so, perhaps a little more.

"I suppose. How is it that you have no chains to carry? I'm just being held, charged with nothing, and I was awarded these bracelets."

"Well, I gave Fournier some coins, didn't I? You gave him nothing. That's one reason."

"I had nothing to give. I'd been robbed," I replied, reasonably, I thought.

"He won't care about that. Poverty is no defense in here. It's perhaps your greatest danger."

"You said one reason. What's the other?"

"Well, Fournier and I are vaguely related."

"Isn't he French?"

"Yes, I suppose you could say that. He speaks French, certainly. But he is second generation, even to this prison. His father came with the crusaders. He was the last man to see Raymond-Roger Trenceval alive and so now the family has this prison to run. He makes a profit."

"I imagine he does."

"And his cousin is married to my mother's uncle. His wife's sister was my grandfather's mistress for some time before she married Dompna Heloise's second cousin. Of course, that won't be of any help to the good woman. She is doomed."

"You're all related? All of you who came in together?" I asked.

"Not all of us, not closely, at least. I don't think I'm related at all to that girl who sang her half of the *tenso*—"

I must have looked puzzled because he went on to explain.

"A *tenso*. A song for two people. A conversation."

"Oh, you mean that dirty so—"

"Yes, that. I'm not related to that girl. I think her name is Marguerite, but I could have that wrong. Since we're not even cousins we might become—friends. Still, most of us in the mountains have some connection to each other."

"You say that Dompna Heloise is lost? And Dompna Sybille?"

"Yes, they will burn. It is too bad; they are very good women, and they have healing gifts as well. But there is no question that they are *parfait, perfecti*. They have been as long as I've known of them, and they are pledged, each to the other, for life. They will have to burn them fast, though, because they have both undertaken their *endura*."

"They'll starve themselves to death?"

"If the church doesn't burn them first. I suppose we'll all have to go out and watch."

He finished wrangling the peach, passed half of it to me, and plunged his few teeth into the half that he held. Juice flowed down his dirty chin. I hesitated a moment and then took a big bite myself. It was cool and delicious.

***

I sat in the sunlight for some time. I was disconcerted by the lack of any routine, any form to the day. In the priory we had a time for prayer and a time for work. I had grown comfortable on the road, but even then, I had a job to do—to track down the music—and a plan for each day. At least I felt like I had a plan. Looking back, I suppose I just wandered as the road took me. Here, though, inside The Wall, there was nothing but the passing sun to tell one minute from the next. There was no work for me to do. Nobody seemed to pray together except, perhaps, the doomed women, but they were locked away, out of everyone's sight.

I must have dozed off because I heard a bell ring from a church for Sext. I roused myself and knelt facing the sound, then recited another psalm. I shook myself and looked around. Another of the prisoners came over to me, dropped to one knee, and held his palms out upward. I didn't know what to do, so I sketched a blessing in the air, just a wave of my hand, really, and pronounced *dominus vobiscum* over him. He seemed satisfied enough to rise and wander off to another group.

I realized that there were many people in the courtyard who were not prisoners. I looked to the gate and saw there was a small door cut through it and people came in off the street. Of course, they stopped and handed something to a guard stationed there, but I didn't watch the transactions too closely. Some of them were vendors, bringing food or blankets the prisoners could buy. Others were obviously family members; you could tell by the gentle familiarity they shared with those they embraced.

There was no one to see me, of course, and I had no coins to buy extra food. I was at the mercy of Pierre Fournier and the generosity of the Church, which seemed to be confined to coarse bread and sheep's cheese. I left the yard and went back to our cell where it might be a little cooler. Zaid wasn't there. I hadn't seen him out and about. I thought idly about him but went ahead and stretched in the straw for my siesta.

***

About the hour of Nones, I was awakened by a sound in the cell and I sat up. Two burly men at arms tossed Zaid into the cell like he'd been made of the straw that broke his fall. He was half unconscious, although I saw no marks on him. Then I pulled his sleeves back. His wrists were rubbed raw, much more than what might be caused by those loose manacles we wore. I knelt next to him and recited my office for the hour since it seemed kinder to let him rest, at least for the moment. He snorted heavily in his doze and from time to time a whimper escaped his lips. After a half hour or so I went down to the courtyard where I'd seen the barrel of water. I found a bowl on the ground nearby. I rinsed it and filled it with cool water, ferrying it back to the cell. I soaked my sleeves and used the damp cloth to soothe Zaid's wrists.

I kept at it a long time. So long that I didn't notice when he opened his eyes. I just turned to look at his face and was surprised to see him staring up at me with sardonic amusement. His heavy-lidded eyes focused on my labors.

"Where have you been? What's been done to you?" I asked.

He smiled and then winced.

"No, don't talk if you can't." I lifted his head and poured the rest of the bowl of water towards his mouth. He managed to swallow a little, but most of it just sluiced down his neck and shoulders and soaked the straw beneath him.

"They are not gentle, these preaching friars. They will save me if it kills me," he said lightly, but still wincing.

"What do you mean? What have they done?"

"They put me to the pain, Itzal. I expected it. Didn't you?"

"Why should they? I'm a monk, you are my servant. I know that's not true, I don't employ you, but it was the easiest explanation. Why should they make you suffer? We are just waiting for word from my people in Spain."

"I doubt if your prior will ever know that you are here, my friend. I know that you think your brothers would send a fast messenger off with letters to ask about you. I don't think they believe you are what you say."

"If they don't believe me, why don't they question me? Why you?"

"I think they fear you, Itzal. They think you are a heretic. They think you are a greater heretic than those two brave women. But they think you might have some heretical magic at your command. They are afraid of spells and philters. So they torture the—the *servant* to get to the master. They think I will betray you."

"But there's nothing to betray. I am a Dominican monk. I am looking for melodies. I was sent out to fulfill a bequest."

"I know that, but they don't believe it. They see you dressed in the dark green, woven in a home. They find the Gospel in Occitan. You must be a heretic, you see?"

"I'll put a stop to this. I'll go to those friars. They will listen to me."

"No, Itzal, they won't. Right now there is nothing you can do that won't make it worse. They will continue to use me as they wish. It is very light torture, really. They don't want to break my body, just my spirit. Today it was the rack. Tomorrow, it will probably be water. I can bear those. I cannot bear the flames, though, and that is where they want to send both of us."

"It will not be, Zaid. It cannot be. If I can't stop the pain, can you bear it? I will try to take care of you."

"I know you will, although I'm not sure why. I can bear the pain, for a while at least. Let us hope something happens that allows us to get away from here. Now my wounds want more sleep." He smiled up at me and then closed his eyes.

That's how we lived within The Wall for the next three days. On the fourth day, we had a visitor.

***

It was after Terce. I had said my office in a corner of the courtyard and was now leaning against the stone wall, looking up at the stone tower. The bishop's tower, they called it. I don't know why. Young Arnaud was sitting with me, breaking off pieces of a white sheep's milk cheese and popping them into his mouth. He seemed amused by the way I prayed but was still unable to believe that I was a Catholic monk.

"See, this isn't so bad," he said languidly. "We aren't put to labor, we aren't put to the pain."

"We're not. My servant is. It's pointless. There's nothing he can tell anyone. We are travelers, I'm a monk. We're not heretics."

"No, but he's a Saracen, isn't he? Perhaps he's backsliding and bowing to the east again."

"He's a good Catholic. I've seen him take communion." That was a lie, but I felt like I should offer some proof on Zaid's behalf.

"Perhaps, perhaps not. It doesn't matter. It isn't the brother's doing. They're not here."

"The Dominicans have left? Did they send to my prior?"

"Of course not. They don't believe you either. They're just waiting. They'll be back. After Mass on Sunday, they'll preach a sermon and pass judgment. Some here will burn."

"Nothing will stop that, will it? It is meant to be good for the souls. We pray that they repent in the flames."

"Pray as you will, it will not happen." He stuffed his mouth with cheese.

I looked over at the gate of the prison and saw two people pass through the small door. One was a young woman in a dark blue dress with a white headscarf carrying a basket. The other was a thumbless man leading a mule that looked more than familiar. There were bundles of wood strapped to the mule's back, but I knew that it was mine and that Pons was leading him.

I stood up and half-ran over to them. As I got there the young woman looked into my face and smiled. It was Alais.

"Fra Itzal," Pons started but was interrupted as the girl reached out to embrace me.

"You are not harmed? What is wrong with your face? Did they hurt you? Have you been charged?" She kissed the wound on my face, brushed the hair away from my eyes, and stroked the stubble where my tonsure had been.

"No, not charged. They inquire. And I have not been hurt much. Does it look bad?"

"It looks hideous. How dare they do this to you!" Alais was enraged.

"It is dirty but healing, Fra," Pons offered.

"They are inquiring. I've asked that they send to Spain for news of me. I don't know that they have."

"They haven't." This was from Arnaud, who had slouched into our group. "Good day Alais," he said rather stiffly.

"Hello, Arnaud," she replied. "How is your mother, my aunt?"

"She was well before I left for the pastures in the mountains. I haven't seen her since I was taken here. No doubt I will be out soon enough."

"Fournier will see to that."

"Fournier will," he agreed.

"You know each other?" I asked foolishly.

"We're cousins," the girl answered. "Although our fathers are not on the best of terms."

"It's not his fault—" Arnaud started but Alais turned her back to him and addressed me.

"I would not have left you had I known you'd been taken. I thought you were dead, that the awful German had killed you. We had no choice but to go with them, you know. He would have killed us too, and raped me right then, right there. I put that off by going with him, promising more pleasure and more comfort. The Italian had eyes for this one." She gestured to Pons with her thumb. A little bit tactless, I thought.

"If I'm alive, it's not their fault. I was stripped and left for dead. You wearing me out probably saved my life." I smiled like a sheep at her and she blushed lightly under her scarf. "Did you know I was here, or is this just chance?"

"Nothing is chance, Fra Itzal," Pons answered. "We didn't know at first, but our saviors heard that two heretics were taken near the river. We reasoned—she reasoned—that it must be you and Zaid."

"You?" I asked, turning towards Alais.

"No, not me. Our rescuer, La Lobita."

"I don't understand."

"La Lobita, the brigand queen of the hills," Pons started proudly. "She is related to me on my mother's side, you know. She set upon Pieter and Lorenzo just as the dawn was breaking. You should have seen her; she was brave and fierce and her blade was sharp. Pieter was cut like the tub of butter he is. There is nothing more to fear from that one, he hasn't the equipment to bother either girls or boys anymore. I doubt if he survived her attack, there was enough blood everywhere that he should have died. We rode away, across the river and into the hills."

"A bandit rescued you?"

"And she will rescue you, Itzal," Alais said tenderly, stroking my face along the line of my wound again. "You will not be in here much longer. The manacles will be a problem, but we will get you out soon."

"How soon?" I asked.

"After the fire," Pons replied. I looked at the mule and its burden of wood.

"Is this for…?" I gestured.

"This, no, no, Fra, this is for the baker's fires." Pons waved his four-fingered left hand towards the opposite corner of the yard. There were chimneys with smoke pouring out of them. I had vaguely noticed it, but I didn't know what they were for. "That is where cheating bakers are punished. Those who give short weight when they contract to turn grain into bread. They are made to bake bread for the prisoners and the monks. And for Fournier, of course. I'm sure that he sells much of it, although that is against the law."

"We knew they would let us in if we brought wood and flour. Since we had no relatives within The Wall, we couldn't think of another way to visit. Of course, had I known that this one," she waved dismissively at Arnaud, "was inside with you, I would have been here much sooner."

Arnaud sniffed as if this meant nothing to him. I had no idea what sort of bad blood lay between them.

"We will get you out, Fra Itzal," Pons said. "That is what La Lobita wants and what she wants she can accomplish."

"Be patient, love," Alais said, and I was surprised by her words. "We will rescue you and take this steel from your wrists."

"Hurry if you can. Zaid is put to the pain every day. He has been racked and he has been forced to take in gallons of water. He said something about an anguish pear coming next, but I don't know what that is."

"Are there no Inquisitors in Spain, then?" Alais asked.

"I don't know, maybe. We had no Inquisitors in my community, no prisoners except for some monks who broke discipline."

"Well keep your discipline for now. Be patient. Don't attract attention. We'll get you out," Alais assured me.

"And me as well?" Arnaud asked.

"Since you've heard my words, you must come with us. Although I would leave you if I could," she replied coldly. Then she and Pons made their way over to the dark entrance of the prison bakery.

5
A Sunday in Ordinary Time

"You're in love with my cousin?" Arnaud asked me.

"I...I...I don't know what that means," I stammered.

"You fancy her. You like her and she likes you. You have taken off each other's clothes."

"We've done that. But love? What does that mean? I'm a monk. I'm not allowed to marry. What we did was pleasant and sinful; I imagine my prior will visit stiff penances on me once I confess. I'll not confess until I'm back in Spain."

"Perhaps you'll have a chance to sin again with her?" He smiled at me knowingly. I noticed that one of his remaining teeth was wobbling.

"No. I mean, perhaps that will happen, I don't know. I don't intend to sin with her."

"Why? Is she too ugly for you?" All of a sudden Arnaud was showing some sort of family pride.

"No, that's not it. She's lovely and sweet and, well, lively. But you don't need to know that. What is it that your father has done to her father?"

"It's nothing. It is a lawsuit from long ago, really. There was a matter of a sheepfold and some missing sheep. And my father took her father to court in Pamiers. Her father lost and he had to pay and he lost a pasture. The two haven't spoken to each other since, although the two sisters talk on market days."

"Families should not fight."

"Then who should we fight with? The French? They've already won. Family is less dangerous, although they seem to hold onto grudges longer."

I just laughed. I thought about my brother and his wife and wondered, idly, how the new child was doing. I left him there in the courtyard and wandered back to my cell to wait for Zaid.

***

He wasn't long in coming. He was thrown roughly through the door and landed on the straw. His eyes were open but he was massaging his jaw, working it back and forth.

"What did they do today?" I asked. He just gestured to me for water. He hadn't wanted water after the last two days, but they had changed his pain, apparently. I ran down with the bowl I'd appropriated for the task and returned with water that he proceeded to pour down his throat.

"Anguish pear," he said after he'd finished. "Mostly they just force your mouth open. You'd be amazed how much torment that can cause after just a little while."

"But then you can't talk, you can't confess and make them stop."

"You see the humor then," he smiled his sly smile at me. "Anyway, I think you are safe enough—*we* are safe enough from the flames, at least."

"Why shouldn't we be? I know they think I am some sort of heretical high priest with magical powers, but I'm not. They will see that soon enough."

"No, they won't. They're not terribly bright, these people, not even the French monks, as far as I can tell. One of them watched me today. They are back for the burning. Still, I heard the men talking, and your poverty will save you."

"What do you mean? If I *were* a heretic, nothing should save me."

"If there is nothing to be had from you, there is little point in wasting the vestments on you. Dompna Heloise, however, holds a large farm and vineyard that her husband left her. When she is burnt, it will go to the Church or to the people who denounced her."

"And Dompna Sybille?"

"A house in Narbonne, apparently, that she owns. It might even have been where we stayed, although I doubt that Cathars would still be there if they knew she was condemned. News travels fairly quickly in these parts."

"I've noticed. Everyone seems to be related to everyone else. But they can't condemn someone just because they own property."

"That's never the official reason, but there has to be something to gain, don't you see? And since you have nothing, well, it's not worthwhile to condemn you and certainly not economical to keep you."

"You think they'll let me out? We shouldn't have to wait even that long." I told him about my visitors and their talk of a rescue.

"I'm glad they got away," Zaid said after I'd finished. "I'm glad Pieter got what was coming to him. That he got it from a woman sweetens it."

***

The next morning I was kneeling, reciting my Matins, when two of the big men at arms came into the hall of cells. They whacked at the bars and rattled chains until everyone was roused.

"Outside! Services!" they shouted.

Anyone who had not been awake certainly was by now. Men were shaking their heads, clearing sleep from their minds. People stretched, yawned, and scratched themselves. We filed out into the courtyard. Apparently, it was Sunday. I had lost track of the days since the blow to my face.

The courtyard was lined with benches again and there was a platform set up where the monk's table had been. It was curious, but there was no altar.

The entire population of the prison seemed to be there, men and women. We were motioned to sit by the various guards and we all settled ourselves on the rough wood. When everyone was seated and the murmuring began to quiet down, two figures were led out of one of the passages from the deeper dungeons. They were both in chains and looked to be dressed in liturgical garments made out of crude paper. It was the two heretical women, of course, and they were led onto the platform. They shifted uncomfortably, stiffly, as if they'd forgotten how to move. The people on the benches began to murmur again.

After a short time, the rounder Dominican appeared from somewhere, accompanied by Fournier. He stood at the lip of the stage and the jailer stood a few feet behind him. The monk addressed the crowd in French, and Fournier bawled out an Occitan translation as he went.

"You are—all of you—excommunicate! There will be no sacrament today," the cleric announced loudly. Fournier turned it into the common tongue as quickly as he could.

"We would be remiss, however, if we ignored your spirits while keeping your bodies confined. We are here to heal the world of the disease called heresy. We are doctors, not evil men who are here to punish you. We wish to bring you back to the Church and to the light of salvation."

No one on the benches seemed convinced of his good intentions. They looked at one another and they looked at the ground. I noticed that young Arnaud had managed to find a seat among the female prisoners and was sitting next to that girl he'd shared the song with on the road.

"The text is from the Epistle of Paul to the Romans: 'Brethren,' says the apostle, 'I reckon that the sufferings of this present time are not worthy to be compared to the glory that will be revealed to us. For creation waits with eagerness for the revelation of God. For the creature is subject to vanity, not willingly, but by reason of him that made it subject to hope; because the creature also itself shall be delivered from the slavery of corruption, into the liberty and glory of the children of God.' Thus says the apostle. Heed his words." The monk had apparently memorized his text since he had no book in his hands. He paused, surveyed the crowd, then went on once he was sure he held our attention.

"God will welcome all his children. He will welcome even those in error if they confess their sin of unbelief, if they truly repent, and if they accept the penance that the Holy Church deems, in its mercy, right and just. These women—" he swept his hand towards Dompna Heloise and Dompna Sybille and they shuddered, almost as if they had been struck. "These women will not relent in their devotion to the teachings of devils who call themselves 'Good Christians.' Are they good Christians who would see someone burn for unbelief? No! They are children of Satan and they do not care who they harm. They would take you all with them if they could. But know, if you abandon the vanity of these false teachings, the sufferings you will bear in this age will be trifling and the glory that you will join will be immeasurable."

Again, he looked over his audience. The prisoners remained sullen. I didn't understand, since not all of these people could be charged with heresy, could they? Some of them must be thieves, cutpurses, surely. We knew there were bakers here who had given short weight. The sermon was wasted on them. I could tell that this monk was speaking in elegant French, although I could not follow every word, but he must know that it was not the language of his listeners. Fournier shouted a crude repetition in Occitan, but his voice was coarse and his words were coarser. The preacher went on.

"Confess, my brothers and sisters, come back to the Church. You will be welcomed back. When I am through here, my colleague Pere Vincent and I will remain. We will hear your confessions. We will forgive you in the name of the Church. We will be kind and gentle. But know, it is not enough to confess your own error." He was setting the hook. "If you truly seek forgiveness, you must tell us who you know who has sheltered these heretics. You must tell us the names of others you know who may be heretics, anyone who has said anything at all that the Church would find untrue. You must tell us their names and their families' names and you must tell us where they live. And," he paused again, briefly, "if you know where these traitors to salvation keep their treasury, you will not only be forgiven, but rewarded.

"Brothers and sisters in Christ, spare yourselves the pain that these two will suffer." He waved at the two women again, but they stood up more erect than before. "Because, truly, tomorrow morning, you will follow us to the graveyard and you will see these two pernicious women given over to the flames. You will see them burned alive for their crimes. And they will have no burial, not in holy ground, not in unholy ground—no, their bones shall be left to the wolves and the winds." A shudder ran through the crowd, I think they are more frightened of being left unburied than burned.

"After the *exemplum*," Fournier stumbled in his recitation and looked to the monk, who merely nodded. Fournier just repeated the word as he heard it and the sermon went on. "…of the flames, you will all be examined again. Let what you see teach you the error of this belief. Come forward, come home to the Church and you will be spared that awful fate. That is the end of today's lesson."

When Fournier had finished putting the French into Occitan, the monk took one look at him and one at the crowd then turned on his heel and left the stage. The two women were dragged roughly down as well and tugged towards the stairs to the dungeons. Everyone started to stand up and walk around, speaking to each other in low tones.

I was wounded to my core. This was Sunday. It had been a long time since I'd heard a Mass. I had hopes. I had hopes of the sacrament. I was no heretic. I was a devout monk on the road, and I desired the Eucharist and I was being denied it. I suffered.

The crowd, I noticed, seemed confused and lost as well. Perhaps it was the same emotion that I felt, I don't know. It certainly seemed they had gotten no spiritual comfort from that French monk. I saw one prisoner approach Fournier, perhaps meaning to offer a confession, but the invitation was ignored by most people in the yard. They milled around. Zaid surveyed them with a jaundiced eye.

"They are sheep," he said.

"That's what Christ called us. His sheep," I answered. "And he has said that if one lamb goes astray, he would seek that lamb. That is what these monks mean to do, to free people from heresy."

"So they say. I think they have more interest in treasure here on earth than in heaven." He spat on the ground and walked away.

A few of the people began to circle around me. One or two knelt, opening their hands in that odd gesture I'd seen before. They all shared the delusion of my captors, that I was some heretical high priest. Still, these were children of God and they were looking for comfort.

At first, I didn't know what I could do for them. I suppose I should have urged them to go to monks and confess any sins, to seek the forgiveness of the Church. I didn't see how that would be of any real comfort to them. I felt the secret pocket. For whatever reason, the small book had not been taken from me. I reached down, pulled it out into the sunlight, and opened it.

I read to the circle of prisoners from the Gospel of John in a language they could all understand unaided. I might as well have walked into the flames right then.

6
The Flames

The prison remained restless for the remainder of the day. People gathered in small groups and spoke nervously to each other. No one could be certain that one of these people might name them to the French Inquisitors and consign them to the flames in order to save themselves.

There seemed to be more contact between the men and women as the day went on. Arnaud seemed to have found his girl from our forced march and I heard snatches of their little *tenso:* "I come towards you with my skirt lifted…" answered by, "I approach you with my trousers lowered…" The two vanished from my sight and I gathered they had grown tired of just singing about these things.

The day passed slowly, taut with tension. At least Zaid was spared. It must have been out of respect for the Lord's Day that the torturers were given a day of rest. Instead, we sat around contemplating the fate of two women that we didn't know and wondering what was going to become of us.

"I see no way out here, Itzal," Zaid said for the third time after we had shared some bread at midday.

"Have some faith, Zaid, truly," I answered. "These are monks of my order. They must have sent a messenger towards Spain by now. It's not their fault that they didn't send their fastest messenger. My people will send word and we will be released."

"I think that, at best, they will let you go, my friend," he said. "They seem to enjoy having me for a plaything."

"You talk as if they were cruel for the sake of being cruel. They are trying to save souls."

"Then why do they put *me* to the pain? There is nothing wrong with my soul. I am a good Catholic. I don't deny the Eucharist. I don't deny the Church. They have tried to make me say things I don't believe and I refuse. That doesn't stop them."

It was hot and close in the stone courtyard. I walked over to the barrel of water and splashed some of it on my face, then rinsed my hands, rubbing them together.

"They must have their reasons," I replied, although I didn't really believe that.

"I think they want me to inform on others. Ha!" he spat out a laugh different from his usual menacing chuckle. As if I could. None of these people know me. None of them trust me. They will talk about the condemned women, but only because those two have nothing more to lose. I don't even know where any of these prisoners were born except for Arnaud. That one likes to talk."

"Oh? I'd noticed that, but he hasn't told me much. Where is he from?"

"One of the small villages in the mountains. Somewhere near the baths of Aix-les-Thermes. They say the hot springs there are very healthful. Or Arnaud says they are. He says people travel from all over to take their waters. I prefer to steam and sweat, myself."

"At home, in the priory, we are only allowed cold baths in river water once a month."

"I thought you were rather ripe when we met," Zaid laughed, more like himself. "Perhaps we will live long enough for you to feel that river again." He rose from his heels and walked into the cooler, shadowy reaches of the stone corridors.

***

I don't think anyone slept well that night. Zaid just sat, squatting on his heels, his back to the stone wall of our cell, rocking slightly. I stretched out on the fresh straw that had been thrown in the door that morning, but I was tense and nervous. I woke and slept and slept and woke, haunted by dreams. I dreamed of the village of my youth, of my brother, of the witch that I had seen on the pyre. As I watched, she opened her arms towards me and her face changed. First it was just a strange girl, then it became the face of my sister-in-law, her belly big. Finally it became the face of Alais, framed by a white wimple. I sat up in a sweat. Zaid was staring at me placidly, still rocking lightly back and forth. I lay back down, but sleep did not return.

We were called to wakefulness by the sounds of hammers against metal. I gave it no thought but knelt to my morning office, looking at the gray stone, trying to think of nothing. Guards came around and summoned us. We saw what the noise was—now every prisoner was wearing manacles, even those who had been unfettered before. Some of the people were obviously unused to the chains; you could see as they tried to rub sleep from their eyes and banged their faces with heavy, leaden links.

We were formed in lines, two by two. There was a wooden wagon in the courtyard and we lined up behind it. The taller Dominican climbed onto the wagon and recited a morning prayer in Latin that went ignored by most of the prisoners. The two women were dragged out from whatever hole that they had been stored in for the night. They still wore the paper vestments that looked dark in the early morning light, and dark parodies of miters had been placed on their heads. They also had chains around their hands and shackles on their ankles. They moved weakly, swaying slightly from the weight of the metal on their hands and feet, but they managed to show off an impression of dignity nonetheless. They were shoved roughly onto the cart, and at a word from the shorter monk, the large gates to the prison swung open and our grim procession began to move.

***

The tall Frenchman carried a gold cross on a staff as he led our way. The wagon rolled through the heavy gates of the prison into the narrow streets of Carcassone. The noise of the metal rims on the small cobblestones was enough to wake the heaviest sleeper. We filed out after the wagon, and townspeople, grimly, silently, came out into the street and followed behind us.

We turned onto a main avenue, broad enough for us to spread out a little bit. A man in a black hood followed behind the wagon closely, and a smaller man carried a smoking pot. It wasn't incense but the fire they would use at the stake.

"Those are some of my playmates," Zaid said as he walked beside me. I nodded. Obviously, they were representatives of the secular powers. Monks were not allowed to shed blood, that task had to be delegated.

We rolled through the gates of the city's first wall, crossed the odd lawn between the two walls, and out through the second ring of stone. The road dipped down between two hills, so we stayed in shadows until we rolled up to the summit of a hillock and the sun rose, throwing light on us and the two women in the cart.

I caught my breath. I couldn't believe the cruelty they intended. I had thought that the paper vestments were darkened, perhaps colored a penitential violet or a fiery red, but I could see this wasn't the case. The paper was greased! It would catch fire quickly and cling to the women's skin before the smoke could suffocate them. It was meant to cause the maximum possible pain. It was the most monstrous thing I had ever seen, I thought, until we rolled over the next hill and came to the graveyard and burning ground at its top.

If the greased vestments were bad, the stake was worse. I had expected a log to be set among the faggots of wood for burning, but it wasn't a log. The stake was set into a platform and dry wood had been piled around it and that stake was iron. It would hold the heat, unbearably, to the women's backs as their paper clothes burned away their skin. I knew then, too, that they intended to keep the chains on their hands and feet and not tie them to post with hemp. There was to be no semblance of mercy for these hardened heretics.

We were arrayed in a circle around the platform, the prisoners forming the inner ring, the townspeople surrounding us. All the people from the town were sullen and quiet. There was palpable anger in the air, but I couldn't tell if it was directed at the criminals or the monks.

"They don't like these monks," Zaid whispered to me, reading my thoughts. Any sound louder than a whisper would have felt like disrespect, although I wasn't sure who or what we were respecting.

"Is that it?" I asked. "I thought it was just fear."

"It's fear, true enough. And tension. This fire will release something, but I'm not sure what."

"It will release the souls of the women, at least."

"Not before their bodies suffer."

"Perhaps they'll repent on the pyre. They can say an act of contrition and save their immortal souls," I suggested.

"Look at them," he replied. "They know their souls are saved. Their bodies will suffer, suffer terribly, but they don't care. Dompna Heloise, look at how she holds her head, weak as she is. She hasn't eaten anything for seven days, I know. I heard them try to force her to take food and she wouldn't. She has no more use for this body."

I looked at them as they were dragged roughly off the wagon and chained to the stake, surrounded by piles of black oak. Dompna Heloise held herself stiffly, offering neither resistance nor cooperation. Dompna Sybille was trembling and her face seemed more uncertain, but she did not cry out as they chained her to the iron stake.

The two women were mounted against the huge beam, back to back. Their chains were fastened. They wouldn't be able to look at each other for comfort. I saw the fingers of their hands interlock. I could see Dompna Heloise turn her head and try to say something to her companion, but no one could tell what passed between them.

"*Orate Fratres!*" the tall monk called out, leaning against his crucifix like it was a walking stick. "Pray, brothers!"

The crowd shuffled their feet. There was a noise of manacles clanking. We all bowed our heads and let the Latin pour over us. He first recited the *Pater Noster*, and I could see the women at the stake stiffen a little bit. It was the prayer that both churches shared.

He went on. And on and on. It was still more cruelty, really. The women were chained in place. They could see the oak faggots at their feet. They could smell the smoke from the brazier. They could smell the grease rising from their paper vestments and they knew what that meant. They knew what was coming. We all knew what was coming. And this monk, this interloper from the Northern Counties, droned on and on in Latin, reciting prayers that no one but I could understand, prayers of a church the victims had rejected to the point of death.

The townsfolk were growing restless, the prisoners less so. For us, at least, it was a break from the monotony of The Wall. For those who were being treated roughly, like Zaid, it was a positive release. But it couldn't continue.

"These women have been judged relapsed heretics!" the monk shouted and I was surprised to see Pierre Fournier standing next to him, echoing the words in Occitan. "The Church has submitted them to trial. The Church is merciful. The Church offered them many chances to recant their wicked beliefs. These chances have been rejected, every one. These women are wanton in their disregard for their own lives. It is their choice that they are bound here, to be dealt with by these secular authorities. Heresy must be burnt out so that it does not grow again. The earth must be scorched. We do this not for our sake, but for the sake of your souls. Your souls would be in danger if we let this foulness flourish. You are our sheep, we are appointed by the Church to care for you—"

"And shear us." I heard somebody mutter.

"We are entrusted with the care of your souls. For your heavenly salvation, we must perform this terrible, earthly act. May God have mercy on all of us. Monsieur executioner, do your duty."

The monk descended from the platform, followed by Fournier. They turned their backs on us and looked at the victims. Dompna Sybille was shaking visibly. She may have been sobbing. I could see her hands joined with those of Dompna Heloise tightly, knuckles white. The other woman surveyed all of us with disdain, or it may have been detachment. I don't know. Her back was rigid, and she showed no sign of fear.

The hooded man climbed up along with his assistant. They opened the firepot; the smaller man bent down and blew on the coals, coaxing a flame. The hooded man picked up a long-handled torch and touched to the fire. It must have been heavily oiled because it caught right away and burned with black smoke in the morning light. They started at one side of the wood and worked their way around from left to right, setting the flame to the kindling.

Slowly, we could see the fire build. Yellow and blue tongues licked at the wood, rising into the morning. A breeze from the river encouraged it. Dompna Sybille was writhing slightly, trying to make herself smaller, trying to keep away from those flames as long as she could. She was trying to contain the fear, but her throat couldn't keep it in and she began to wail. She tried to turn her face towards her companion, who was maintaining her stoic dignity. You could see fear in only one woman's eyes as she tried to pull away from the unstoppable pain.

There was a noise in the air. A rushing, pounding sound. We all assumed it came from the fire as it was building, causing a draft, a wind. In fact, the flames had taken hold and they were rising higher and higher, moving in towards the women. But that was not the source of the sound; it came from behind us—and in front of us. The earth was shaking. I wondered if it were an earthquake, but I couldn't take my eyes off the two women in the circle of wood, smoke, and flame. The pounding grew louder, more visceral, just as I saw the greased paper on Dompna Heloise catch a flame and begin to burn. Finally, she broke and screamed, but her scream didn't last.

Coming up in front of and behind us was a group of people on horseback. Something flew from behind me, over my head. I didn't know what until I saw the old woman sag against the stake, the horn handle of a hunting knife jutting from her chest, the flames reflecting off the bit of blade that extended below her breast.

Then the armed horsemen rode over us.

Part Three

The Mountain Villages

1
Our Rescue

"Spare the white monks!" I heard a high, clear voice call out and I felt relief. I knew I wouldn't be harmed. Then I remembered that I wasn't dressed as a white monk but as a heretic. I didn't have much time to consider things. I was knocked over and I rolled myself into a ball, trying to make myself as small as possible just to stay out of the path of the horses and the swords.

I assumed they were swords. I heard the clang of metal against metal and I heard men and women cry out in pain. I heard hooves pounding on hard earth and I still heard the flames crackling where the now dead women were consumed. I held my arms over my head and face and I prayed to Our Lady with all my heart. I'd never been in any kind of battle and my impulse was to run away, but both my hands and feet were in chains.

"Stand up, man!" someone shouted at me in Occitan. Then he added more softly, "*Bonhomme*, rise so I may free you." A hand pulled one of my arms away from my face, then another took my left arm and I was dragged to my feet, my chains clanking.

Two men faced me, the crowd boiling behind them. These were citizens of Carcassone, one man dressed as a notary, the other as a blacksmith, his face smudged with soot.

"Find a rock," the blacksmith said to his companion. The man fell to the ground and rose from between various feet with a large, flat stone. "Stretch out your hands, *bonhomme*, so that I may break your bonds." He showed me his cold chisel and mallet.

I stretched out my arms and pulled my hands as far apart as I could, bent over the stone. The man brought the chisel down and, with one heave of his mallet, severed the chain on my hands.

"Now sit, stretch out your legs," he instructed. I did as I was told and in a moment my shackles were broken as well. "That will do for now," my liberator said. "There are others to be seen to." He walked away as the notary helped me to my feet.

Looking around I realized that what I thought were sword blows came from the many hammers and chisels being wielded in the area around the pyre. This wasn't a battle, but a rebellion against the Inquisition. The only people who were being assaulted were the French men at arms. The two Dominicans had been bound and left untouched, although they were uncomfortably close to the flames.

Everywhere I looked, prisoners were being loosed from their chains. Some were plucking at the threads that held yellow crosses on their garments. Others were working to conceal their broken fetters in their sleeves. Citizens surrounded the prisoners so they could leave the killing ground unobtrusively. I kept looking around.

"Zaid!" I yelled and someone touched me on the shoulder.

"Here, Itzal. Let us go." He gestured towards some people on horseback. "They say they'll take us away."

We were lifted onto the backs of horses. I saw Alais and Pons among them, but I was set behind a broad peasant who smelled of sheep. Zaid climbed up behind Pons. I saw a few men bleeding on the ground, their faces illumined by the still-rising flames. We started to ride away. We were led by a small person with shockingly white hair, who moved us quickly into a brisk trot and then a gallop. There was someone flung across the saddle in front of the lead rider and I realized it was our jailer, Pierre Fournier. The hooves rang out on the stones of the bridge as we crossed the river and our group broke into several smaller contingents. Some turned north, some turned south. We rode due west towards the mountains.

***

I wasn't used to horses. There were none in my village when I was a boy, although once a year, a man came around with a swayback mare and his new iron plow to get our small fields ready. I must have been placed on the back of that beast when I was small, although I don't remember it. I remember riding on the plow itself, to make the blade cut deeper into the earth. These large creatures, moving so quickly, were frightening to me.

I felt the muscles move as the hooves pounded the summer-dry earth. The noise was overwhelming. Fortunately, we didn't ride for long.

It was perhaps an hour after the battle at the cemetery when the white-haired leader called a halt. We had climbed into the mountains, over a ridge or two, and then followed a valley that was formed by spring rains, although it was bone dry now. It climbed a short distance and then we turned around a rock and found ourselves in a large hollow space that was almost completely hidden from view. The riders reined their horses to a stop and one by one swung off their backs. I didn't have a chance to survey the group because Alais came running into my arms, and all I could do was hold onto her.

"Are you hurt, Itzal? Did they harm you? Were you wounded in the battle?" She kissed my face repeatedly as she asked her questions and I had no idea what I should feel.

"I'm fine, Alais, just fine. My wrists and ankles chafe, but that will pass once the fetters are removed. I took no cuts or wounds, just fear," I answered.

Around us, riders were unsaddling their horses, and the saddles and tack were being shoved into a crevice in the rock wall. Pons dusted off his tunic with his hands as he walked over to us. One man was tying some horses into a string of pack animals and starting to lead them out through an opening in the hollow.

"We will meet at the Oaks tonight, Prades," the small leader said turning in my direction.

I looked the person over and only then realized that the general in this skirmish was a woman. A small woman, dressed in doublet and hose, but a woman. Her shape was unmistakable. She had hair that was whiter than the snow on the mountains and her eyes were pale almost to the point of being pink. There was a sword strapped to her hip and a dagger thrust through her belt. She nodded curtly towards me and then turned her attention to her men.

"Yes, Itzal," Pons whispered proudly into my left ear. "That is La Lobita. She saved you, for you surely would have followed those women into the flames."

"Never. I'm no heretic," I answered.

"The French wouldn't care," Zaid said from my right side. "They didn't care that I was a good Catholic. They enjoyed asking me questions I couldn't answer and then taking my ignorance for guilt. Pons is right. We all would have burned."

"And now, what? We are fugitives?" I asked the trio around me.

"Yes, fugitives. I suppose that's the case. But we are not alone," Zaid said.

"Who are these people?"

"Some are fellow prisoners who escaped with us," Zaid said.

"Most are *routiers*, bandits, highwaymen, willing to attack anyone for sport and profit," Pons explained. "Some are the men of La Lobita. The tall one there, next to her, he is her right hand. I believe he is mute. And Italian, but I don't know for sure. I have only heard of him. I have never seen him before." His eyes were alive with the wonder of it all.

"She rescued us from fat Pieter and skinny Lorenzo," Alais took over. "She had been planning the attack on the execution anyway. She had hoped to save the two good women, but we were too late, they were already burning when we got there. All they could accomplish was a quick end to their pain."

"They were cruel men," I said. "I say that even though they are of my order and I believe they are doing God's work. They made sure that those women would suffer here on earth. Perhaps they were afraid that God wouldn't see things the way they did."

"Yes, they were cruel," Zaid concurred, working his mouth in small circles and rubbing at his wrists.

A fire had been built with dry wood while we were speaking. One of the men was heating a chisel and a small anvil had been produced from somewhere.

"Prisoners, step up!" La Lobita bawled. "We won't get anywhere while we still have remnants of the charming jewelry you were awarded. It will burn, but we will get them off you. Then we will move higher into the mountains. There will be a conference tonight at the Oaks. Everything will be made clear. Form up!"

Something about her said that you didn't disobey her commands. A line formed, then eight or ten of us who were there shuffled to the anvil, led by young Arnaud, grinning his cock-eyed grin.

***

As I started to rub my wrists, sore from the hot iron used to set them free, Alais ran over and took them in her hands. It was nice; her skin was soft and cool. She stopped, ran somewhere out of my sight, and came back in an instant with a damp cloth. She kept rubbing and soothing them, not making any intelligible sounds but murmuring to me as if I were a baby.

"That's lovely, girl," I said after a few minutes. "I'm fine. See to Zaid, his pains have been greater." She obeyed without hesitation, running off to find more water while I sat down and rested my back against the yellow wall of the hollow. Arnaud dropped down heavily beside me.

"Exciting, isn't it monk?" he asked, pronouncing the word 'monk' as if it were some kind of code.

"Exciting? Yes, I am not a man of battles," I answered.

"Of course you're not, you are a man of God."

"But won't there be a garrison looking for us? I still don't understand how we got away from Carcassone without any troops riding us down."

"There aren't that many troops in the city these days, and those few there are were hampered in the streets. As I understand it, wagons full of hay appeared in all the streets of the town. No one knows how it happened, but it did. No troops could make their way through the narrow streets in time. Remember, our battle was over in fifteen minutes or so," Arnaud told me.

"It seemed longer."

"It always does."

"Still, by now they must have cleared the streets. They must be out searching for all of us."

"They will be in time. But they won't find us. You see," he pointed to another string of horses being led away from the hollow by two big peasants, "they will be looking for a large troop on horseback. Now, there goes a pair of horse traders on their way to Albi. We broke up into small groups right away. When we leave here, we will be five people with a mule—a monk and his man, a maid and a pair of companions."

"You sound like you have it all planned out."

"I don't," he answered. "She does." He pointed towards the small white-haired girl.

"You said a mule?" I asked.

"Yes, Fra Itzal, your mule is here, with its precious panniers and all of their contents. Your books included." He reached into his pocket. "Here, you should eat this, we'll be moving soon." He handed me something and I put it to my lips. It was a piece of salted fish and it was delicious. I hadn't known how hungry I was.

Zaid squatted down next to us. "That was very neat, wasn't it?

"Obviously well-planned," I agreed. I turned towards Arnaud. "Tell me, why did she specifically shout orders to spare the monks?"

"A lesson from Montsegur," he replied. "It was killing Inquisitors that led to the siege and the massacre. Pursuit would be less hot if they were spared."

"They deserved to die," Zaid spat.

"Perhaps," Arnaud agreed. "But more of ours would die that way. It's better like this. People will go back to their families. Many will cross over to Aragon or Catalonia, maybe even Castile. Some might go down to Lombardy, where there are many good Christians. They will blend in now, along the way, and be spared the burdens these foreigners would impose." He sounded like he was about to make a speech, but the one they called La Lobita came over to us.

"*Bonhomme,*" she addressed me. "You are unharmed?"

I nodded.

"Good. You are strong enough to travel, then?"

I looked at Zaid, Alais, and Pons. Arnaud answered for us.

"We are all strong, Dompna," he said.

"Never call me that!" she said angrily, raising a hand, then lowering it. "You know where we will be meeting? The Oaks?" she asked him.

"I was there once," he said.

"Good. Lead these four there. That is your penance."

"What? Have I sinned?"

"I know your family, boy, you are all of you sinners," she replied.

I looked at her face and realized that she was older than I had thought. There were lines around her mouth and a scar on her left cheek that was years old. There was a weariness in her pale eyes but a strength in her light form.

"All men are sinners, lad," I added.

"Listen to the holy man," La Lobita told him and then rose, walked over to the one remaining horse, mounted, gave the inert body of Fournier a poke, and then rode through the mouth of the hollow, singing a fierce song as she left us:

d'Hom, petit val tos senz ni t'artz
Si perz t'arma per tos enfanz

Per l'autrui charbonada t'artz
E l'autrui repaus t'es enfanz... ♪

"Those words seem familiar..." I started.

"These people remember many songs, Fra," Pons said. "You will complete your mission." He smiled at me through his broken teeth.

"Go get the mule," Zaid told him and in a very few minutes we were, all five of us, on the road again.

2
To The Oaks

♪Man, there's no value to your life or art
If you give up your soul for your children
If you get burned for someone else's meat
And their repose becomes your grief...♪

"Those weren't the words I remembered, but they were like that," I said as we turned around a dry creek bed and started our climb into the mountains.

"Many of the songs are alike, Fra," Pons offered. He was leading the mule with our panniers rocking on its back, all of our stores intact. Alais and Arnaud trailed behind him. "I do not know that one. The tune sounded like Bertran de Born, but the words have the sadness of Peire Cardenal. He lives, they say, perhaps someday you will be able to ask him about it."

"Perhaps," I answered, quickening my pace to come up beside Zaid. "Why are we leading? It's the boy who's supposed to know the way."

"He'll stop us if we go wrong. The two young ones want to chat and tease each other."

"Oh," I said, surprised. "But I thought she was in love with me. She gave me that impression this morning and at the prison."

"Maybe she is or thinks she is, which is the same thing. But I think she misses the May bonfires and all the sweet, physical play that goes along with them. Arnaud is lusty enough and closer to her age."

I grunted and shrugged my shoulders. I knew very little of women or girls. The creek bed grew steeper and rockier. There were scraggly trees offering little shadow. The leaves were more yellow than green. It was hot; even the gnats and flies only made the laziest of attempts to bite us. It was just past the hour of Nones and the sun was almost straight overhead. It was hard to believe all that had taken place since the first light of day.

That brought me up short. I had neglected all of my offices for that day. I reached into the pocket of my green robe for my psalter and pulled out the other book. I remembered it was the Gospel in its forbidden form. I slipped it back into its home and began to recite my Matins prayers from memory.

***

We worked our way up the creek bed for another hour or more. We stopped speaking to each other as the climb grew steeper and the afternoon grew hotter. Footing was getting difficult for our poor mule, and both Pons and Arnaud had to struggle to keep the beast moving. Finally, we decided to call a halt for a meal and a siesta.

Arnaud hobbled the mule, although it seemed hardly necessary. It wasn't going anywhere without us. Zaid and Pons searched through the panniers for food and drink. Zaid produced a water skin and doused his head before drinking deeply.

"Apologies, *bonhomme,*" Pons said. " There is nothing but this ham and bread."

"That will be fine," I answered.

"But flesh?" he looked at me in amazement.

"I'm a monk, I keep saying, not a *parfait.*"

"Of course you're not," Arnaud laughed, showing that he didn't believe me. Alais pushed the men out of the way of the baskets and relieved them of their burdens. She carved a couple of slices of ham, broke off some bread, and grabbed one of the flagons of gray wine.

"Come," she ordered me. She led me up the creek bed a few feet to where a large boulder had fallen. We rounded the rock and were hidden from the sight of the others.

"No doubt the *bonhomme* will be instructing her in the faith," I heard Arnaud say behind me.

"No doubt," Zaid agreed. I heard the sound of stale bread breaking.

***

"Drink this," Alais said, pouring wine down my throat quickly. It was tart and refreshing and it went right to my head.

"Now eat, Itzal, eat," She instructed.

She used a small knife to cut the ham and fed it to me piece by piece, taking a bite for herself every now and again. She continued to pour wine into my mouth until she decided we were finished.

Our little bit of shelter was at least shady. A black oak teetered on the lip of the cliff above us and the boulder itself afforded some comfort. Three or four flies circled lazily above us but left us alone. They would be after the mule soon enough.

"These rebels, outlaws," I started as I finished eating. "Do they think they can beat the French?"

"Of course not," she tapped my face gently. "They can save a few lives here and there. The French have won. The crusade is lost."

"But they could not save those two good women," I said.

"There was no saving them nor would they have wanted it. They had begun the *endura* in prison. They were going back to God. But La Lobita was able to see that they did not suffer too greatly."

"This La Lobita..." I began, but Alais put a finger to my lips.

"Do not talk about any other woman," she said.

"Not ever?"

"Not now," she replied, closing my mouth with a kiss and then opening it again with her tongue.

After a certain point, there is no turning back. Alais singing woke me up:

♪*D'aisso-m farai plaidejaire*
Qui-n amor ha son esper
No-s deuria tardar gaire
Tan com l'amors n'a lezer...♪

♪*To this truth I am pledged*
He who loves should live in hope
He should never hesitate
To take the prize love offers...♪

I rolled over. My head was in her lap and thick from food, heat, drink, and, yes, love. She brushed my hair back off my forehead and then pulled a louse off the top of my crown and crushed it between her fingernails.

"Don't stop, keep singing. I know those words. But that's not how the song begins."

"You were asleep when I started singing," she answered, smiling down on me like an angel on the Virgin.

She hummed quietly. She may have kept singing the words, but I became unaware of them. The tune was light and as bright as the air. I felt like I didn't ever want to leave this place, this moment, but she had not gotten onto the next verse before we heard noises from the other side of the rock.

"We must move on, Fra," Pon's voice came around the boulder. "The Oaks are an hour or more away, and we must be there by evening."

"But I like it here," I started to say. Alais laughed and shifted her legs to stand and I had no choice but to raise my head. I stood and dusted the dirt and brown leaves of grass off my green robe. I helped Alais to her feet, she picked up the flagon, and we joined the others.

"Your religious duties are accomplished?" Zaid asked archly.

"Let's just get moving. Arnaud, lead us from here." And we turned our feet westward once again.

***

"Alais knows one of my songs," I said to Zaid as we climbed the ever-steeper defile left by the winter snowmelt.

"I'm sure many people know songs here. We will write them all down if we live long enough."

"Why shouldn't we live?" I asked, kicking some of the mule's droppings out of our path.

"There are the usual things, of course," Zaid offered. "We could be set upon by bandits or routiers. You could slip right now and roll back down the way we came and fetch up on," he looked back down the path we had just climbed and pointed, "that rock there and break your neck. We could take a fever and with no one here to treat us, we could linger uncomfortably and die. Dying is easy. It's tricky to live."

"There's more on your mind than accident, Zaid."

"True, true. You see how things have fallen. We are no longer in the good graces of the civil authorities."

"Through no fault of mine!" I spluttered. "I was taken prisoner. I was rescued by forces beyond my control."

"I know that and you know that. The French lords and soldiers won't care, I should think. If they catch us, they'll stretch us. If we're lucky."

I sighed and pulled myself a little further up, using the root of a tree protruding from the wall of the cut.

"I suppose you're right. But I could always appeal to my prior."

"If they give us time. If they don't execute us summarily. I also think we may have fallen out of the good graces of all of your church. Assisting in disrupting the public punishment of heretics. The bishops and priests will not look kindly on that. And I have experience of how forceful they can be in their unkindness."

"Yes, you do. But my prior…"

"Stop talking about your prior! We are well out of his reach. He is probably not even that powerful in Girona. He cannot help us here. By the time a message got there and back, we are tortured and dead, both of us! They may pray for our souls, but they will be sent on their way first."

"We're almost to the top!" Arnaud called out ahead of us. Alais had once again been walking with him, sharing her life and energy, while Zaid and I dragged behind with Pons, the old men all together.

"I'm sure you're right, my friend," I said to Zaid.

"Then there are these people we have fallen among. They are good people, but they are all rather desperate right now."

"Desperate, not dangerous."

"Not dangerous? You saw the fight at the cemetery. Many of these folk are as deadly as they come. And they are certainly heretics, or at least sympathetic to the bonhommes. If we are taken with them, then we will go up in smoke."

"I can see that. You are drawing a very bleak picture of our future."

"A realistic picture. Now, for whatever reason, most of those we've met seem to think that you, yourself, are a perfected heretic."

"But that's ridiculous. I'm a good Catholic."

"As am I," Zaid responded, dodging a small shower of scree sent down by those ahead of us. "Now, our companions, for the most part, seem to think that you are one of them as well."

"Don't be silly. Alais knows I'm a monk."

"And she's seen how you respect your vows," Zaid laughed.

"She has a power over me. I can't explain it."

"I can, but I won't. Pons knows you're a monk because you freed him in Beziers, and only a monk could do that. But he treats you more like a bonhomme every day. Arnaud and all the prisoners who were freed think of you like that. I don't think they would take it kindly if you revealed yourself as a Dominican friar, one of the Inquisitorial order, at this point."

"No, I suppose not."

"And, as I said, they are desperate. They could not let you live. Of course, I could probably talk my way into their good graces." He smiled slyly.

"I'm sure you could, my friend," I responded with a shrug of my shoulders. "What should we do?"

"We are among these folks right now. Stop insisting that you're a monk. Let them believe that you are a parfait, a bonhomme. Don't lie if that bothers you, just stop offering your Catholicism as a shield. It is not protection here."

"But I can't administer any of their sacraments. I don't know them."

"Then don't offer sacraments. If they kneel before you, give them a 'Benedicte.' If they want more, a Pater Noster will do. Don't offer comfort to the dying. Keep saying your office, if you must, maintain your duties, but keep them to yourself. Tread carefully among these folk, they are our only safety."

I nodded but said nothing more. The creek bed began to flatten out. We were reaching the summit. A few minutes later, we had emerged on a long plateau. We were able to turn east and see the forbidding double walls of Carcassone below us. I could make out a column of armed horsemen just north of the city, beginning to veer east.

"See, see!" Arnaud was shouting, excited. "We've fooled them completely. They haven't any idea where we are and where we are heading. They think we rode towards the country around Albi. The fools! The fat French fools!" He was jubilant in his gloating.

We stopped and rested for a little while at the summit. Arnaud assured us that we only had a short distance to cover now. I made Zaid take out the big leather book and copy down the music to Alais' nightingale song. It made me feel that I was still somehow on my mission.

***

I looked across that flat hilltop we were walking along, wondering where these oaks might be hidden. I couldn't see any trees anywhere. We made a turn to the north and walked down into a small fold in the hill and there, to our left, was a stand of stunted but mature black oak trees.

Pons, Alais, and Arnaud all straightened their backs just a little bit. Pons dusted the back of his tunic and Alais adjusted her headdress.

"We're here, friend," Arnaud announced. I couldn't make much sense of it. It was still a bare hillside next to some oak trees. Then he plunged between two of the trees and disappeared.

3
The Trial of Pierre Fournier

Pons grasped the mule's bridle and followed Arnaud; Alais pushed against the two trees and squeezed herself out of our sight. I looked at Zaid and shrugged, and we forced our way between the trees. It was tight, but we emerged more quickly than we might have thought into a large, open space.

Once it must have been a quarry, perhaps in Roman times. It was a huge bowl of stone carved into the hill. There were signs that stone had been cut, the walls were checkered with square and rectangular outlines that had been softened by years of exposure to wind, rain, and snow. Perhaps some of these had become the walls of Carcassone. The rocks at the top curved over the bowl, forming eaves topped with turf. I imagine that you wouldn't see it if you were on the hill above until you almost fell into it.

There were about fifty people milling around. A fire of green wood was burning in the center, throwing off almost no smoke. Some of the people were roasting bits of lamb on sticks. There were bottles of wine being passed around. I recognized some of them as my fellow prisoners. Some of them must have been our liberators.

Towards one end of the hollow, there was a flat cut platform in the stone that formed a natural stage. A ring of stones had been set out on it and there was a stake in its center. Wood was heaped around the stake and I began to fear for my life again. Before this could sink in, Alais spoke.

"I'll fetch you something to eat, Itzal. Say your evening prayers." Her tone was brisk and she hurried off towards the fire. Pons had found a flat sheltered area near the wall and was unbridling our beast of burden and making something of a camp for us. Arnaud was already among the crowd greeting friends and, one presumes, relatives.

"Go," Zaid told me, gesturing towards where Pons was at work. "The girl's right. Say your evening prayers, you may not have a better chance."

I was no longer sure of the day of the week, let alone of the year, but it was at least past the middle of July. I sank to my knees and recited a psalm for the feast of the martyr Saint Symphrosa, who died with her seven sons. "They just cried, and the Lord heard them, and delivered them of their troubles," I recited in Latin, keeping my voice low.

It didn't seem to matter; I began to draw a small crowd. They fell to their knees around me, opening their hands, apparently offering me some sacred homage. I was unsure of what to do. I prayed my office hurriedly and then stood up. By now there was a circle of fifteen or twenty people. I could only follow Zaid's advice.

"*Benedicte!*" I proclaimed, opening my hands to them.

They looked up at me, expecting more, so I offered the only prayer that I knew both the heretics and the Church shared.

Pater Noster, qui est in caelis; Sanctificteur nomen tuum, Adveniat regnum tuum…"

I prayed the whole prayer, finishing up with, " *…Ed ned nos inducas in tentationem."* Lead us not into temptation. One by one, the people came up to me, bowed their heads into my open hands and walked back into the group. They seemed satisfied. As they dispersed, Alais returned.

"Here is some fish, fresh fish I roasted over the fire. It's not salted, it was caught this morning. And here is some of the local wine from these hillsides. It will give you strength," she said handing me a leaf bearing the fish. I ate, hungrier than I thought. A shadow fell across me. I looked up, and there was the woman they called La Lobita.

"Monk, we must talk," she commanded.

***

She led me towards the stone platform at the western end of the quarry. A chestnut horse was hobbled there and someone's kit was dispersed around it. No one else was anywhere near it and this, I supposed, was her makeshift headquarters. She sat on a campstool and motioned towards a rock that would keep me eye to eye with her.

"I know what these people think," she began without preamble. "They think you are one of them, that you are one of their holy men, and they are hungry for that. I know that you are not. I know you are an enemy of these folk, however good they may be. You are a white monk, and you would see us all burnt."

"I would see you saved," I started, but she cut me off.

"Your word, I don't care. These are my people, though. I must care for them the best way I can."

"Are you their lady? Their sovereign?" I asked, trying to sort out this small society.

"I was. That is, my fathers were, my mothers were. Then the crusaders came. They took the lands from anyone they called heretics. My family was among them. And they changed the laws, what was once to be mine I could never inherit; it's not the French way. My brother set out to atone for our family. The legate that the pope sent said he would be pardoned if he went on crusade." I looked at her, surprised. "Not here, in Outremer, Jerusalem, the Holy Land. Had he come back, he might have had our castles back. They would never give them to a woman. They would marry me off to some Frenchman, and he would take it all, and I would have nothing and be nothing. That fate is one I refused."

She looked at me, her pale eyes almost daring me to contradict her. How could I? What did I know of the law of this land or the laws of the French?

"Instead, I fight the crusaders. I fight the Inquisition. I fight the French and I protect the people who were once mine. We will not win, I know that."

"Then why keep fighting?" I asked.

"Because someone must. And to lessen some of the suffering that they have caused. I want these people to live as free as they can and believe however they might. I don't care."

"Don't you believe? Aren't you Cathar?"

"I'm nothing. I'm La Lobita, the outlaw. Were I Cathar, I could not kill, and I must kill. It's the only way. But these people, they're Cathar, or would like to be. Most of them, maybe all of them, are what you monks call *credentes*. They believe, they obey as best they can, but they haven't taken the final sacrament, the *consolamentum*. That would mean severity and austerity beyond their poverty. Most of them can't live like that, but they want to die with that blessing."

"You're not asking me?" I started, but she waved her hand dismissively, then pulled up a jar and drank deeply from it before passing it to me. It was hearty red wine. I drank.

"No. I know what you are. I have also heard that you are kind. I ask only that kindness. There is someone in these mountains, a newcomer, we don't know who. But he is a traitor. He is turning over peasants and farmers to the Inquisition. He's sly and he's clever. He only strikes at those with land of their own. The shepherds are safe enough. We think he might be a priest, a Catholic, who pretends friendship. We don't know."

"So find him," I suggested.

"No, you find him. That's what I'm asking. You can't go back to your people, at least not to the Church around here. You're an outlaw for now as much as I am. Work with us in this. You can pass among the priests and you can pass among the *credentes*. You have an open face. People will trust you. Find the traitor."

"But I have a mission, my prior has—"

"I know, I've heard all about it. You must collect songs. So do that. You'll find plenty in the mountains, in every house and *domus*. I'll give you a song right now; it will be my down payment to you. I'll sing you a song that was written by that foolish poet, Pierre Vidal, who loved my grandmother, the one called La Loba. Pierre loved her, but Roger of Foix won her," she said, and then she started singing:

> ♪*Tart mi veiram me amic en Tolzan*
> *E tart veirai lo Pueg e Monrial*
> *Que remazutz sui de tot a'N Barral,*
> *Mon bell Rainier, que truep fin e certan*
> *A Na Loba, dona, quar no.us remis*
> *Dels heulhs vos plor e del cor vos sospir,*
> *Quan mi membra vostre cors avinens*
> *El dous parlars e la cara rizens…*

> *It will be long before Toulouse sees me*
> *And long before I see Puy or Montreal*
> *I'm staying right here, in en Barral,*
> *My beautiful Rainier, it's safe and certain.*
> *But Na Loba, lady, I sigh, remembering you.*
> *The touch of your body on my body*

And both our bodies together
And the soft stroke of your voice... ♪

Her voice was light and strong, it rang like silver in the hollow of that abandoned quarry, echoing back from the curved stone. The various refugees from the prison stopped their conversations and listened while I used a stick to scratch notes into the dust at my feet. Between the verses, I raised my hand and signaled to Zaid to come. He understood me and was beside me with the book and the sheaf of poems while I listened. The girl kept singing the praises a dead man had written for her grandmother, and they were beautiful.

She stopped and stood up; this slip of a woman seemed to tower over me as I looked at the melody I had written in the earth.

"There you have it, monk. Will you help my people?"

"Yes," I sighed and she walked away, leaving Zaid to copy the notes onto our vellum pages while I looked over his shoulder to make sure it was recorded correctly and the tune wouldn't be lost forever.

***

The sky began to turn a darker blue while Zaid and I worked. We were intent on the page in front of us and the notes I had taken in the dust, we didn't notice. We didn't notice that it began to grow quieter. We didn't notice the people moving towards the western end of the quarry. We didn't notice the fires being lit at one end of the platform or on the ground below. We were just drying ink, blotting it with coarse sand, when a voice rang out.

"My people!"

We looked up. La Lobita stood beside a fire of green wood towards the front of the platform, away from where the stake had been set. We walked to the edge of the small gathering of souls.

"My people!" La Lobita proclaimed. "My people, we have lost!" There were protests from below. "No, we have lost this war. We have no castles. We have nothing we can defend. We have no great lords who will defend us anymore, with their horses and lances, with their swords and strong bodies. They are too rich, they have too much to lose if they try to protect your right to your souls."

At this, there were some shouts of derision from the crowd.

"No, be kind, my people. They fought and bled for you for over thirty years and many of the best of them died for you. We must accept things as they are. We have no strong places to defend except the strong places of our hearts."

She looked over the gathering. They had shouted affirmation back at her. The smokeless fire cast her pale face in orange.

"We must be true, each to the other, Catholic and Cathar must live together; live *our* way, without the French. We can hide from them, and we can save ourselves, and," she seemed to be looking towards me, "our songs. But we must be true, each to the other. We must never turn our brothers and sisters over to the white monks. We must send no one to the flames. We will not rule our Toulousain, but we will inhabit it!"

Again, a cheer went up although I'm not sure they understood her.

"I said send no one to the flames. I mean the flames that belong to the Inquisition. We have flames of our own, and we will make traitors pay like they make us pay for our prayers. Those who abuse us will not be safe, especially not those who come from among us. Bring him up!"

There was a commotion among the onlookers whose faces were now in darkness, and a bundle was pushed up onto the platform, a bundle that writhed and tried to scream. It was a man. La Lobita pulled him to his feet and unbound most of his body, leaving only his hands tied behind his back and his feet hobbled together. Only then could I make out who it was; the jailer of Carcassone, Pierre Fournier.

He was an animal at bay, he was terrified. He looked to his left and saw the stake and the ring of wood and almost fell. It looked as if he were trying to vomit, but the gag in his mouth held it in. He lurched away from the stake but could get nowhere.

"We are a just people!" La Lobita proclaimed. "We will let you answer for your crimes. You, Pierre Fournier, your family came from Paris, but you are accused of treason against the Langue d'Oc. You are accused of trading in human flesh. You stand accused of turning innocent people over to the flames because they would not or could not pay you. Bernard Marty, Raymond Lizier, Jean Mars, come forward!"

Three men emerged from behind the fire.

"Is this the man who demanded your farms to save your fathers from the flames?"

"*Oc!*" the three said together, loudly and firmly.

"One count! You also stand accused of sending good women to the flames, including those two women murdered this morning, because they would not open their legs for you. Dompna Guillemette Pons, Dompna Raymonde Belot, Dompna Esclarmonde Azema!" she barked out, placing firm emphasis on the honorific titles. Three women stepped out in front of the men. "Is this the man who raped your sisters for your salvation?"

"*Oc!*" the women called out and Fournier writhed in his bindings, appealing to the women with his eyes.

"Two counts! You have starved your prisoners. Philippe Benet, Prades Pellissier, Arnaud Rives, Jacques Baille. Step out!"

Four men joined the group in front of the fire.

"Is this the man who stole your food? The food the bishop so mercifully," her voice was dripping contempt, "provided for you?"

The four men faced their jailer and agreed, less loudly than the others, "*Oc!*"

"That's three counts and ten witnesses. Twelve, if you count Dompna Sybille and Dompna Beatrice, who died this morning. They are enough to condemn you. That you have been nothing but a lapdog to these French who would kill us all is widely known. We don't care how many families your family has married into, you are condemned." She finished with an iron flatness to her voice.

The crowd was murmuring ominously. They were being worked up to a fever by this woman. She would grant them release soon enough.

"What is done to others should be done to you, I think." She went on in a more conversational tone. "Let us see. Perhaps you should be scourged before we consign you to your fate." She picked up a branch of green wood about as thick as an oxtail out of the pile around the stake and swished it through the air. It whistled sharply in the sudden hush that had come over the crowd. She swung it in his direction and he flinched, but she didn't let the blow land. "I think you are a coward, Pierre Fournier. I think you fear the idea of pain more than pain itself." She swung the branch through the air again, and this time, it landed on his back, tearing his tunic and raising, almost immediately, a welt. He would have yelped but for the gag. His eyes showed only terror and very little comprehension. The crowd yelled. "Do you think that was pain, jailer? Do you think you have suffered the way you have made others suffer? I don't think so." She brought the branch down on his back once, twice, five times. Fournier fell to his knees. She pulled him up by his gray hair.

"I don't think we can make you suffer enough. You are vermin, you should just be exterminated." She cast him back down on the stone. She gestured to two men who had been in the darkness behind her. They came forward and lifted Fournier by his elbows, dragging him towards the stake. He kicked his bound feet and twisted his body as much as he could, but there was no freedom for the jailer.

One of the men held him straight; the other ran ropes around the center of his body. His hands were briefly unbound, then retied behind the stake. Fournier continued to struggle although it was obviously no use. This man was already dead and he should have known it.

"It will never be said that we are not just, that we do not let the accused have his say before we dispense our justice. Oh," she turned to the figure at the stake, pulling his head by his hair so she could look into his eyes, "we do not have fine Latin phrases and the blessing of the pope. We will not record your name in any book. You will be forgotten by all but us. Still, we will let you have your say before we do to you what you have done to so many others."

She ripped the binding cloth from around his lips and pulled the gag out of his mouth. He coughed once, twice, then spat at the ground in front of him. It looked like blood. Then he called out a single word.

"*Consolamentum!*"

All the eyes in that rockbound hollow turned towards me.

4
Deaths and Exits

I was grateful for the darkness. I wasn't easy to see in the shadows; still, I could feel the crowd turn in my direction. I gripped Zaid's shoulder.

"What should I do?" I hissed in his ear.

"As little as possible, Itzal," he replied, keeping his voice low. "This man can't be saved, not his life. Don't pretend he is anything other than a corpse."

"I know, I know. They will kill him no matter what I do, even if I were to preach some impassioned sermon, and I've never preached in my life. But the man deserves some kind of comfort."

"If you say so. I disagree. I think the woman's right, he's vermin."

"He has a soul, Zaid," I whined.

"Again, if you say so. I don't think it can be saved. Look at him. He thinks by calling for the heretic's sacrament he can save his miserable body. He's a worm."

"I can't perform the heretic's sacrament!" I was sweating. "I don't know what it consists of, how it's done. I'm not sure I would do it if I could. I'm not empowered to administer any sacrament."

"They don't know that, Itzal," Zaid assured me as the crowd pressed closer to us. "Just mouth some Latin words, don't make the sign of the cross, and be sure to place your hands on his head."

"What?"

"I know that much. They find the sign of the cross offensive and the *bonhommes* console people by the laying on of hands. You can do that. Perhaps that will give him comfort. I don't care. If it makes you feel better, make sure your prayers are orthodox."

"*Bonhomme!*" La Lobita called from her position on the platform. "Come up here." She got down to one knee and reached out to me. I had no choice but to take her hand. She pulled me up beside her.

"This *man's,*" she pronounced, covering the last word with venom, "life is forfeit. There is nothing you can do to stop that."

"It is against our religion to kill!" I shouted, desperate.

"You will not kill," she assured me, almost sweetly. "You may offer him some spiritual comfort. We know, all of us," she waved an arm over her head to include everyone in the quarry, "that after taking your sacrament, he would undergo the *endura* and die anyway. It will just happen faster, that's all. Go. Console the prisoner."

"You won't burn him?" I asked.

"We will spare him that. More than he spared ours," she assured me. I saw Fournier visibly relax.

I could feel the flames from the platform bonfire warm against my face. I thought I was more visible than I had ever been in my life. Fournier was kneeling on the sandy rock, still bound, panting but relieved there would be no flames for him. As I approached, I remembered the women from this morning—only this morning—with their oiled paper vestments and the cruelty he had conspired to deliver them to. I almost turned away.

I am a monk. I have a duty to Christian souls. I walked over to him. I looked into his eyes. They were fearful but he seemed grateful to me. Tears were carving canyons in his face and dampening his small beard.

"Courage, my son," I said to the older man as I searched my memory for words that might comfort him but not alarm the crowd of *credentes.*

"*Si ambulem in medio umbrae mortis no timebo mala; quonian tu mecum ex, Domine. Virga tua, et baculus tuus, ips me consilata sunt.*"

"Though I walk through the valley of the shadow of death," I recited the psalm from memory. I said it each morning. They seemed like the right words to say. The people watching, including Fournier's victims standing around us, accepted them.

"*In te Domine, speravi, non confundar in aeternam: in justitia tua libera me eripe me.*"

I continued from another psalm. He would be delivered to some sort of justice. I no longer knew if it would be the Lord's justice. I placed my hands on his head and continued my prayer until the end. Fournier breathed more easily.

"Are you finished?" La Lobita shouted.

"Praise be to God. He is as saved as he can be here," I replied.

"Bind him!" she ordered, and he was dragged, kicking at first, then digging his heels into the dust, towards the stake.

"You said you wouldn't burn him!" I objected.

"We are true to our word. Philippe, Prades," she ordered and two of her men kicked the fuel away from the stake.

"This will be better. We will all take part in the end of Pierre Fournier. Everyone, find stones. *Bonhomme*, you should turn your back to this. Arnaud…" she began, but Alais pulled herself onto the shelf of rock.

"I'll take him," she said, and she led me down to the quarry floor and took me to the shelter of its smooth-cut walls.

***

I faced the cut stone, my head bowed. Alais had her arm around my shoulders and was murmuring to me as if I were a child. I recited all the prayers for the dead that I could remember. The fire flickered behind us, throwing off heat and tossing huge shadows on the surfaces of the rock wall in front of me.

I prayed. That was all I could think to do. Pierre Fournier was an evil man, I knew that. He had caused much suffering to these folks and to their families. Still, he was a Christian soul; he had been part of the arm that enforced the laws of the Church on these lands. He had, in that at least, been a good Catholic. He had called for a heretical sacrament in the end, and for that, I sorrowed because he chose to condemn himself to hell. It was his choice. It was what was going on behind me that made the tears stream down my face.

I saw nothing but gray and sandy stone, my green tunic, the dark gown that Alais wore, the white of her wimple. But what I heard. What I heard. Names were called out, the names of the accusers. Bernard! Raymonde! Esclaramonde! After each name, there was a sound of throwing, of throwing hard, and then a dull thud. At each thud, Fournier made a sound. At first, he called out. He called out for mercy. Thud. He called on God. Thump. He called on family. Crack. When his female accuser's names were called, he tried little pet names. There was a staccato rain as if whatever woman he had appealed to had thrown a handful of stones. His ten accusers were through and I heard the movement of the people below. They came up one by one without being named, and I heard rocks being hurled at the man who was once Fournier. The real force came from the crowd, I heard bones breaking. I heard the sound of sharp rocks hitting soft flesh. Sometimes I heard a stone go wide and skitter off the gravel across the platform. Once, someone must have hit the stake, which rang almost like a bell. I felt the vibration in my belly. The stones kept coming. Fournier kept crying out for longer than you might think. There were weak sounds, stones that might been thrown by old men and women, or it may have been Fournier trying to stand then falling back down. He called on his king. A sound of cracking teeth. He called on the Blessed Virgin. A soft sound, almost like a splash. He tried to call out obscenities but seemed too weak for it. Thud. Thump. Thud. Crack. He had long since stopped appealing to his executioners, but he did not die easily, that one. I wondered if he envied the dead women tied to their own stakes, knives in their chests.

I glanced back just once. There was La Lobita, standing as tall as she could, small as she was, looking down at the form in front of the flames. The people kept coming and rocks were sailing through the air, some landing wide, most finding their target. The woman's face was blank, but her back was straight as a spear.

I don't know how long it went on. I thought I had recited the entire Requiem Mass, but that couldn't have been true. I kept losing my place in the Latin and I would turn my head into Alais' shoulder. She stroked the back of my head, ruffling my vanished tonsure, but it didn't help.

Fournier wasn't making any more sounds, but the rocks kept being thrown. I heard them fall on flesh, on stone, on dirt. Finally, after what seemed like an hour but couldn't have been more than a few minutes, an iron-cold voice called out, "Enough!" There was a mumble from the crowd, but you could hear them stepping back, the crunch of pebbles as they dropped down from the shelf of stone that had become their killing ground.

Alais stroked my head one last time, then raised my face in her small hand and turned me towards the scene.

La Lobita stood over an inert form, half-covered in stones of various sizes. The flames from behind dyed both of them orange. What had once been Pierre Fournier was a mass of blood. Bone showed, white and cracked, through the flesh in many places, legs and arms were indistinguishable. Whatever he had been wearing was torn to shred by sharp rocks, and his teeth were scattered across the platform.

"The criminal is dead. He is punished," La Lobita pronounced. "But it means nothing. There will be others. Many more will take the northern money, the northern power. There are many Inquisitors. They will keep coming. We cannot stay here, although I know you would like us all to remain together."

The crowd, which was shuffling on the ground below the platform, stirred and murmured, but they were quiet now, chastened by what they'd done.

"When you leave," she went on, "go in twos, threes, fours. The roads will be watched. You may go to your village, you may go back to your *castra*, but carefully. Follow the shepherd trails. Go to your families but in stealth. If they have your names in their registers, they will know where to look for you. Do not fear. Do not talk of your faith except to one another. There is a *bonhomme* walking these mountains now. We are together, even though we have to find our separate paths. Now—" she held up her hand.

"Now there is only one more thing before we go back into the night," she said. They looked at her, expecting—what? Instruction? Hope? She couldn't offer that, only her formidable presence in that slight frame. *"Bonhomme!"* she called out to me.

Confused, I stepped forward.

"These people must be forgiven," she stated flatly.

"What? How can I forgive this?" I asked, having the sense to keep my voice down so that only she heard me.

"Don't worry, they know what to say," she looked me in the eye, then took a firm hold of my shoulder and turned me to face the now silent crowd.

I looked down at them. They looked like anyone, shepherds, farmers, shoemakers, merchants, notaries, coopers. They all started together, in sing-song voices, to pray together in Occitan:

"We have come before God and before you and before the ordinances of the Holy Church that we may receive pardon and penance for all our sins in thought, word and deed. From our birth we ask of God mercy and of you that you pray for us to the Holy Father of Mercy that He forgive us. Let us worship God and declare all our sins and numerous offenses in the sight of the Father, the Son, and the honored Holy Spirit, of

the honored Holy Gospels and the honored Holy Apostles, by prayer and faith and by salvation of all the upright and glorious Christian and blessed ancestors asleep and here present, for their sake we ask you, Holy Lord, to pardon all our sins.

Zaid, who had appeared next to me out of nowhere, nudged my right side and whispered my part into my ear.

"*Benedicte, Parcite Nobis. Amen,*" I repeated. The people went on with their prayer, asking forgiveness in the most contrite terms, and I repeated the blessing. I looked down at Zaid. I noticed blood at the hem of his garments and some on his face. He, too, had cast his stones. No one here was without sin.

The crowd finished chanting. I started to move my hands in the sign of the cross, caught myself, and spread them wide over this makeshift congregation in a final blessing. They seemed comforted. I have no idea what God might have thought, but these people, at least, felt relieved of some of their burdens as they dispersed and gathered their belongings. Zaid and Alais led me back to our mule. Zaid picked up the book of music from where he had left it.

"We must go now," he said softly.

"Where? Where can we go now?" I asked.

"Into the mountains. Pons and Arnaud will guide us," he answered.

"We, all of us, have family in the villages," Alais said. "They will feed us, and you will give them comfort. It has been a long time since we've had a true *bonhomme* here."

"But I'm not..." I started, but my heart wasn't in it. It was no use. I was marked as a heretic holy man among these people forever. Even Alais, who had sinned so happily with me, seemed to have forgotten who I really was. Zaid shrugged. Pons took the hemp bridle and led our animal to the opening in the quarry.

"*Bonhomme!*" La Lobita called.

I turned towards her.

"I won't be far. If you find out the name we need, there will always be ways to get it to me; don't worry. And these people will help you find your songs."

I just nodded and then followed the others through the narrow opening between the oaks.

5
Towards the Castra

The darkness was almost tangible outside the quarry. No hint of the bonfires escaped and there was nothing besides the pale stars to light our way. Pons held onto the hemp bridle and led our mule down the rocky path. He turned us west and I could see a half-moon rising behind us.

Arnaud was still with us. That surprised me. I assumed he would have family among that group who would take him in and shelter him. He walked beside Alais, speaking in low but light tones. Still, there was something more serious about him now, and he didn't look quite as young as he had been on our journey to these oaks.

"We will not go far tonight, Fra," Pons said. "I know a little hollow near here, there's a bit of an overhang and a spring for water. We can sleep there. We will be far from the roads and out of sight.

"All right," I sighed. We trudged on behind him. Zaid walked beside me.

"So now you are a heretic," he said with his sly smile.

"For now, my friend, that is who I must be. I suppose," I replied. "You seemed to know more of their lore than I would have thought. How did that happen?"

"I have lived and roamed around this part of the world for most of my life," he said. "I have met the heretics, many of them along that Roman road as they made their way to Lombardy or Catalonia, where it is safer for them. I sit around their fires. I listen to their talk, if not their sermons. I have seen something of their rites. I pay attention."

"It proved a good thing. Do you think they would have turned on me if I hadn't been able to offer them comfort?"

"I don't think so, Itzal. They had expended their fury. And though you may not be one of their *bonhommes*, you are a good man and La Lobita knows that. You had her protection all the time."

"I wonder why." I shrugged. Pons was leading us down a long slope and I had to focus my attention on my footing. We spoke no more.

***

We had been climbing steadily for a little over half an hour. The path was narrow and overgrown with sage and wild thyme. The branches were fragrant but punishing as we pushed them aside. They would snap back into our faces with force being still young and green. Pons turned off the path leading the mule up a dry wash into the side of the hill. There was a trickle of water flowing on the downhill side. We turned around an outcropping of earth and we could no longer see the path.

"This will be safe enough," Pons announced. "Let us eat and rest. The day has been long." It was a masterful understatement. He tied the mule's bridle to a tree that was growing almost horizontally out of the rock and lifted our panniers off of its back. Arnaud was scratching around on the ground and I realized that he was gathering firewood. Alais took my hand and led me away from the rest.

"Let them make the camp, Itzal," she said softly to me. She pulled me by the hand around another turn in the wash and we were completely hidden from the others. She turned herself into me, pulling her headdress from her hair and letting it fall free. She reached up to my face and kissed me. The kissing didn't stop for a long time.

***

"We shouldn't do this," she said to me much too late for it to have any meaning. "You have taken vows."

"Vows that your religion says have no meaning. Vows that are sinful in their taking," I teased her, stroking her hair away from her small face.

"I don't know about religion anymore. My mother was perfected. It is not easy living with a perfect mother. She was good and holy and she looked after people and animals. She sent me off to that house in Narbonne. I should have been better, I should have tried harder, but I missed the songs and the games. All that kissing around the bonfires at midsummer. Perhaps I am just too young. My mother became holy after she had married my father, after she'd had all of us, my brothers and sisters, after she was all dried out." She pouted her lip at me, sighed, and buried her face in my chest.

"There are brothers like that at the priory that I came from. They have played at the ways of the world and think to save their souls in their old age. And to eat, now that they are too weak to work." I shifted her weight and she moved into a sitting position. I picked up some pebbles and tossed them at the rock wall across from us. "But you don't seem to think I'm a *bonhomme* now?"

"You are not one of them, I know," she said. "Still, you are more like them than you think. You will comfort people who need it, who have had no comfort for a long time since Montsegur."

"But if I am to be one of these holy men, surely we shouldn't do what we have just done." I tried to keep a smile in my voice, lifting her chin to look into her eyes and then kissing her softly.

"Vows don't matter, Itzal. Goodness does. You are neither of their church nor ours now. You are a shadow cast by both. You will do what God gives you to do. That is what matters. I am only one of the things that God has thrown your way."

"As a temptation or reward?" I asked.

"I think God will let you decide that," she laughed lightly. "With my help." She began to climb up my body again.

"Come out, you two!" Zaid shouted at us, appearing from behind the corner of stone. "Come join the rest of us and have something to eat."

We both rose. Alais brushed some leaves from the back of my green tunic and turned her back to me. I dusted off the back of her dress, straightened it, and brought the hem back to earth, and we went to join the others. I noticed that Zaid had found time to reshape his little beard. We were all seeing to our appearances.

***

Arnaud was already showing the effects of wine as we came into the circle of light offered by his small fire. Alais immediately set about finding something for me to eat. She searched through the panniers and found two of the fresher loaves of bread and several pieces of salted, freshwater fish. She carried these to me and then wrested the wine jug from Arnaud.

"I grow weary of all salted stuff," I complained, although I felt truly content with the world at that moment.

"Tomorrow, Itzal," Alais replied, "we will have time, and I will soak away the salt. You will see, it will taste as fresh as if it were caught this morning."

"Don't be silly, girl," Arnaud said. "Tomorrow we will be in the *castra* of Pexiora. My mother's cousin will feed us then. There will be plenty to eat. And you won't have to see to it, you'll be her guest."

"Your mother's cousin?" she arched an eyebrow. "Do you mean the de Castres? I thought they were still in the village of that name. They are my second cousins," she clarified, leaning towards me.

"No, not them, they are still in Castres. No, I mean Raimon Serni and his wife, Na Guillemette. It is Na Guillemette who is related to my mother. I think Raimon's brother married your aunt, though."

"He left her. He became a freebooter, a mercenary. I think he is fighting up north somewhere these days. He left her swelling with their third child. I think he grew weary of the life of a shepherd," Alais explained.

"What's wrong with a shepherd's life?" Pons asked, almost offended. "You're out of doors, away from prattle. You can pray if praying is what you like. And there's no one to tell you what to do or when. Unless you're out there alone so long that the sheep begin to speak." He stretched his hand out for the wine. I passed it to him and Zaid laughed.

"Perhaps that's why I choose to wander the roads," he said. "Itzal, play your guitarra for us."

"Play, Itzal," Alais seconded with tenderness in her voice. "Play something pretty. Perhaps we will sing something, too."

Zaid fetched the instrument from the mule and handed it to me. I tested the strings and tuned them as best I could, separating the notes from the sounds of crickets and night hunting birds.

I stroked the strings idly, picking out a low, slow melody. I wasn't thinking of anything at all, just the night, just her mouth, just the night. I was letting go of everything that had happened on that long day, from death in the morning to death in the evening. I stopped, a thought jumping into my brain.

"I only saw one horse at the Oaks," I said. "But I would swear in a court of law that there were more in the raid this morning."

"There were nine horses this morning," Pons answered. "La Lobita has a secret place where she breeds horses, over in Gers, I think. That's under the flag of the English king. They leave her alone there and she leaves them alone. She has stock left from her parent's castle and from her brother's warhorses. The ones he left behind when he went off crusading. She deploys them quickly and then sends them off to hide again. She doesn't want the French to find them."

"It seemed like more than nine," I commented.

"It would," Zaid observed. " They made such a racket. That was the idea, I think. They came out of nowhere and from all sides of the hill. It seemed like an army. There were only four men at arms guarding all of us, and they didn't have any horses, remember? She didn't need an army. She just needed everyone to think it was a larger attack than it was."

"I guess you're right," I agreed. I resumed strumming and picked up the tempo. I slid my fingers further up the neck of the guitarra, raising the pitch.

"Keep playing like that," Alais said with a smile. "Arnaud and I can sing you a song that will go with it." She nodded to the boy and he stood up between us and the fire, beside the girl. He looked like I did when I was about to recite a lesson in front of the village priest, waiting and a little frightened. Still, his face lit up when Alais began to sing, and he bobbed his head along with her melody:

♪*Gui d'Ussel be.m pesa de vos*
Car vos etz laissatz chatar,
E car vos I vulgar tornar
Per que sabatz d'aitail razos... ♪

Her voice was bright and lively. I kept up the rhythm, playing quickly and the tune was jaunty. She sang on, wondering why the troubadour refused to sing, and then Arnaud answered her:

♪*Dompna Na Maria, tenso*
E tot cant cuivba laissar
Mas aroras no puose estar
Q'ieu non chant als vostres somos... ♪

Arnaud's voice was much sweeter than the other morning when he exchanged sexual taunts. He was singing a reasoned debate, or rather, telling the lady that he had given up that kind of argument but would sing if she ordered him.

They went on, trading verses, debating whether the man or the lady was greater in love, before joining their voices together to sing that both were equal if both equally loved. They finished and stood side by side in front of the fire looking very serious for a long moment before they were overcome with gales of laughter. Zaid and Pons applauded and I kept strumming my guitarra. Wine was passed to the singers and then around the group.

Pons stood up and asked me to play more slowly but in a jaunty way, something like a hunting tune. He sang us a long song about Reynard the fox and how he tricked the hunters and eluded them. The verse was not very good but the story entertained us. It was clear that Pons thought that the hunters were the French and that Reynard represented either the people of the South or La Lobita herself. He finished and bowed stiffly from the waist. It was obviously something that he'd memorized long ago.

The fire was burning down to embers and Zaid turned to me and asked, "May I?"

He took my guitarra and started to play with the strings and their tuning.

After a few moments he had the feel of the instrument, and it was under his command. He started singing slowly and sadly. His voice was governed by his nose and the song had a plaintive wail to it, although none of us could understand any of the words he sang. All we knew was that it was very sad and very slow. I leaned my back against the wall of the wash and Alais curled into my shoulder. I don't know when we fell asleep, but all of us did.

* * *

One of those troubadour's larks woke us in the morning. The sun had just found its way to where we slept and we rose, shaking the stiffness from our limbs. I swung my arms in looping circles to bring them back to life after the weight of Alais resting on them all through the night.

Zaid was shaving with a neat little razor I hadn't seen before, watching his progress in a piece of polished steel. I bent over and looked at my face. The gash was healing nicely; there would be a thin white line on my cheek, for memory's sake, but I was not disfigured.

We each tore a piece of bread and ate it quickly. I knelt down and recited my Matins psalm while the other saw to their needs and gathered whatever we'd unloaded from the mule and placed things back into the panniers. We were off in good time.

Arnaud led us back to the main road for about half a mile and then turned up onto a narrower path, about as wide as a hay wagon. The day grew hotter as we walked. No one had much to say.

We had been traveling about two hours when Arnaud suddenly stopped. He held up a hand and the rest of us grew still as well. I saw nothing and heard less, just a light breeze tickling the long grass and the lonely call of a bird circling high above us.

"Quickly, quickly," he said, motioning us off the rutted track. "Kneel, all of us must kneel—not you, Fra, everyone else. And face him," he instructed, pointing to me.

"What is it?" I asked while everyone else obeyed the boy's orders.

"Up ahead—" he began.

"I see them," Zaid added. "Who are they?"

"They look like *routiers*, robbers," Arnaud answered. He shaded his eyes and peered across the meadow in front of us. I could just see motion up there and the glint of sunlight off something metal, perhaps. "Probably they are renegade mercenaries with no battles to fight. Fra Itzal, is there a book in your robe somewhere?"

I felt around and pulled out the little book that was not my breviary, the one that had come to me with the garment. "Yes," I answered dumbly.

"Open it. Read from it," he ordered.

"Read what?" I asked.

"Anything, anything at all. Hurry, they're coming." He knelt in front of me as well after quickly wrapping the rope around the mule's felt. He held his hands, palms upward, open towards me. The others did the same.

They came down the wagon track, skirting the meadow. There were three of them; one had a sword at his waist. The others had daggers stuck in the ropes that bound their garments and the biggest of them carried an ax. His face was cratered with smallpox scars. As they approached us, I saw the one with the sword put a hand to his weapon. I heard it slide in its scabbard with a cruel sound.

"Read something," Arnaud hissed, holding his hands up high.

"…and then shall the Son of God sit on the right hand of his Father and the Father shall command his angels, and they shall minister unto them and set them among the choirs of angels, to clothe them in incorruptible garments, and shall give them crowns that fade not…" I read as the party approached us. I wondered what this nonsense was, these Occitan words that sounded like a Gospel but were clearly something else altogether.

The party of armed men came up alongside of us. "*Bonjour*," the one with the sword said in French. I bowed my head and continued on, seeing Arnaud prompt me with a nod. "…and seats that cannot be moved. And God shall be in the midst of them, and they shall not hunger nor thirst anymore."

"Heretics," said the swordsman to his companions.

"Should we kill them?" The big fellow asked, as if we weren't there, stroking the edge of his ax.

"We might save the Inquisition some trouble." The answer was thoughtful. "No, no reason. What has the Church done for us lately? Besides, these people never have anything. They all take vows of poverty or some such nonsense."

"There's a girl. We could…" The man with the ax made a gesture with his fist while letting his voice trail off.

"Didn't you get enough last night? And again this morning? Don't be greedy. There's no point with these people. They don't even have meat. Let's just leave them be. They'll be cooked soon enough, I should think."

"*Benedicte, parcite nobis,*" I pronounced, hoping it sounded enough like a prayer.

"We could at least take their mule," the third suggested as they all ignored us while we knelt there, right in front of them, praying, harming no one.

"*In nomine Patre, et filii et…*" I began, but Arnaud shook his head quickly, trying to attract no one's attention but mine. I realized my mistake. Even these ruffians would recognize the beginning of a Catholic Mass. "*Bendicte, parcite nobis,*" I repeated.

"Amen." My little congregation answered.

The men stood there for a long moment, eyeing our mule, then the one with the sword, their leader, obviously, shook his head, and they moved on past us.

The big man slipped the ax back into his belt and looked back. He made a gesture with his hand that I couldn't make out at first. So he made it again. He held his palm closed, then opened his fingers slowly and blew across them. In case I missed the point, he waved his fingers upwards. The motion was like the movement of flames. I got his message.

6
Pexiora

"They are fools," Alais laughed after the men had vanished behind us. "We could have had the treasure of Montsegur for all they knew."

"Quiet, girl," Pons snarled. "Don't speak of things you don't understand."

"I understand treasure, old man," she teased back. "I know that none was found after the siege. I know there are rumors."

"Lies, spread by fools," Pons went on, glumly. "There was nothing left. Nothing at all. There was no treasure at Montsegur."

"But three got out," Arnaud said, scratching at the scar tissue under his eye. "Everyone knows that three were sent away."

"One went to Lombardy, boy. Two died. And none of the three had any treasure. The one who got to Italy had a book. That's all."

"You know a lot. Or pretend to." Alais was rude.

"I was there, girl. You were not. I saw the bodies."

"It doesn't matter," I inserted, trying to keep a bit of peace. "We are safe and that's what counts."

"Safe for now," Pons advised. "But we should move quickly. Where there are three there are probably more. These *routiers* travel in troops. The sooner we reach some *castra* the safer we are." He picked up a branch from the ground and used it to switch the mule's backside, although I didn't see the animal move any faster.

Still, we managed to pick up our pace. We ascended around a bend, past the edge of the meadow and we came across the handiwork of the men who left us in peace.

Smoke rose off the hay wagon, or what had once been a hay wagon. It was coal and embers now. There were three bodies nearby. An old man had been decapitated; the head had rolled beneath the bole of a nearby black oak. A boy lay next to the headless body. It looked like he had been killed with daggers since his body was covered with stab wounds, many of them shallow. It must have taken him a long time to die that way. Beyond him was a girl, or what was left of her. She was naked and young, probably no more than fifteen. Her arms were tied above her head and her legs were spread. Blood trailed down smearing both her thighs. There were remnants of a campfire next to her. She was probably kept alive all night for their entertainment. She was thoroughly dead now. One eye dangled from its socket and it looked like she had bitten off her own tongue. I turned away but managed not to be sick. Arnaud proved to be less plucky.

"We can't stay here," Pons urged. "There may still be some of these beasts around."

"We should bury them," I said. "Some decency, please."

"Not if we want to live," Zaid agreed with Pons. "We should just move along."

"Time for a prayer, please, something. And cover them with branches, at least," I pleaded.

"All right, all right," Zaid agreed. "But hurry."

***

We left them there, covered with branches and charred hay. I had muttered a quick *Requiecasat*, but nothing more was done for them beyond rearranging their clothes and placing the severed head close to its former body. We traveled on quickly, in grim silence. We crested the top of one ridge and were heading down into another valley.

"There it is," Arnaud said, pointing across the valley in front of us. About a mile away as the nightingale flies we could see the *castra*. It was a small, walled village with a short tower built onto a flat shelf about halfway up the side of the defile. The walls surrounded houses on three sides and a sheer cliff rose up behind it on the west. It looked tiny but easy to defend.

"The crusaders didn't get this far," Arnaud told us as he led us down a steep path. "The mountains were too much for them, they couldn't move their armies. The siege engines couldn't get far enough away to land stones inside the walls. They had enough trouble with that at Montsegur." He was almost boasting.

I looked up at the squat tower. Most of these *castra* were built on the remains of Roman encampments. You could see why that empire had chosen this position.

It commanded the whole valley. Of course, it didn't look like there was much in the valley. There were fields on its floor and a small stream, but I could see nothing that suggested commercial importance. Still, I was a monk. What did I know?

It took us most of the morning to get down to the valley floor. There didn't seem to be anyone tending the crops on the flat land on the bottom, but it was high summer and the fields didn't require much attention. Lavender and sage bushes stirred in the light breeze that sluiced down between the mountains. The air was fresh and lively and we could almost forget the vision of death we'd seen that morning.

The road wound back and forth, switching back along the western slope as we rose towards the *castra*. When we were about two-thirds of the way up, Arnaud stopped us.

"I should go ahead and greet my mother's cousin. Na Guillemette will be generous enough to us, I'm sure, but it would be rude to bring so many strangers into her *domus* without warning. I'll be back." He almost ran up the track towards the walled village.

We sat down by the side of the path with nothing to do but rest. I extracted the codex from the panniers and looked over the songs we had recorded so far. I saw that Zaid had copied down the duet that the two younger people had sung the night before without my asking him. I closed the book, resting it against my knees. I leaned back against a stunted oak tree and I dozed off for a bit.

***

"Take this," Arnaud ordered shaking me to wakefulness and handing me a broad, thin piece of wood with a leather strap attached to it. I stood up and draped the strap over my shoulder. "And this." He shoved a wool comb into my hand.

"What's going on?" I asked

"Nothing," Arnaud responded. "But we must make you seem less a heretic before we enter the *castra*." He looked me over. "Let's make that collar a bit more open, too." He took a small knife and split the cloth to my chest. "Sixtus, take some cloth from Alais and wrap it around your head. We want you to look like you come from below Catalonia."

Zaid complied, quickly forming a turban out of Alais' headscarf. Arnaud looked him over. "Alais, Pons, and I are all right as we are. Let's go."

We continued up the slope. A few hundred yards below the village there was a trough made of stone with a pipe leading into it. There were a pair of sticks and some stones, presumably for beating laundry. We kept on and reached the gates in the wall. Arnaud shoved it open. The *castra* was laid out on a square around a central fountain. The tower had been converted into a church and so served as a defense against enemies below and the fires of hell. The homes lined the wall on three sides with two larger ones built into the cliffside, along with a stable and small barn, but something was missing.

There was no one there. At least, there was no one in sight. After a moment, I made out several small heads peeking out from behind a corner across the square. They looked at us but held their place. Then one by one, they ran out, and it became clear that the only population here were young children. They all looked to be under twelve years old. About fifteen or twenty of them spilled out and they were shy of us, but one of them ran right up to Arnaud. Another relative, no doubt.

"Where is everyone?" I asked for the group.

"Inquisition!" came the answer from what I had taken to be a pile of rags next to the fountain. The pile moved and rose. It was a woman, or what had once been a woman. She looked old and walked bent over from the waist and her body was marred by leprosy. There was no way of knowing her actual age. "They were called. All of them. The priest took them all to Castelnaudry."

"The Inquisition summoned an entire village?" Zaid asked.

"The whole parish," the leper woman hissed. "Everyone from here and from the outlying farms. If there were shepherds in the hills or mountains, they were to go as well, although I don't know if they heard about it." She ran a rheumy eye over our little troop and then performed that ritual that was becoming familiar to me. She knelt down and opened her hands in my direction. "*Bonhomme,*" she said.

I held my hands over her head and pronounced a *Benedicte*. I stopped my hands before they formed the sign of the cross.

"You must hide," she told me, rising. "When the people come back, they will have sworn an oath. If anyone comes back."

"But oaths don't mean anything, old woman," Pons said.

"These will. These are oaths of death. They will have to turn over any *bonhomme* that they see. Turn them over to the white friars, or they will burn themselves. They will make them swear, the white monks." Her voice was laced with hatred.

"I am a cousin—" Arnaud began.

"I know who you are," the hag said. "Na Guillemette will shelter you, but you mustn't let him be seen too much by the children." She pointed her claw at me.

"When did they leave?" Pons asked sensibly enough.

"Yesterday morning," came the answer. "They may be back tomorrow. Not today. Even so, the children might tell their parents. They might talk about the strangers when their parents return."

"All the children are here, with only you to care for them?" Zaid asked.

"Me, and my husband," she replied. "Guihart!" she called. Another pile of rags came to life in the corner of the square. It approached us.

It walked across the square towards us, pausing to kneel next to the fountain and drink. It rose and we could see that it was a man, taller than the woman but just as scarred by disease. His nose was eaten away and he only had one ear left. His eyes were open, and a deep clear blue. There were scabs all over his face and arms, but his hands were white and unmarked by the illness. When he reached the woman, she struck him.

"Guirhart, you know better than that! We don't drink from the fountain. We use our dippers." She produced a ladle from somewhere within her voluminous skirts. He didn't say anything but somehow communicated with the woman. "I know there's no one to see but the children. Still, they could tell someone. Where will we go if we can't stay here? Have you thought of that, old man?"

"He doesn't talk," she said, turning to us. "The people here take care of us. They left us to mind the very young ones while they are gone. The Inquisition doesn't care about the likes of us. We are already damned and marked by God. They can do no more to us."

"You are not damned, sister," I said, trying to keep the revulsion from my voice.

"You are a good man," she replied, not using the formal term. "I know the true God doesn't damn us, but these preaching friars, that's what they think. Let us find a place to hide you so that no one gets hurt." She reached a hand towards me and I stepped back. She shrugged and turned, waddling across the square. We followed.

"If one of the children speaks to you, you are a wool-carder," Arnaud instructed. "Sixtus—"

"Zaid," I corrected. "Call him Zaid unless we're in front of an Inquisitor."

"Zaid, then, is a merchant from the South, Catalonia or Aragon. He is looking for good wool."

"It seems elaborate. Why not just say I'm a monk?"

"Because you are wanted now, monk or not. Besides, everyone knows you are a *bonhomme*."

"But I'm not," I insisted, knowing it was useless. We were led to a door at the far end of the square, near the cliff face. The leper woman opened it for us and we followed her inside. There was a stable to our left and behind us, and a house to our right. We were in a small, enclosed yard, walled and sheltered by the cliff.

"This is where Dompna Guillemette lives," the woman told us. "You go into the stable, I'll have the children bring some water over, and then you can wash off the dust of the road. Come out when they have gone." She left us there.

Pons led the mule into the stable and I followed. The space was empty except for hay. The light was yellow as butter and dust and hay floated through the air as we entered. It was cool and smelled of animals and old root vegetables. It was very comforting.

We heard the door outside open and a little bit of laughter, then it closed again.

"You can come out now," Alais called. We emerged into the sunlight, Pons carrying our panniers over one shoulder, holding onto them as firmly as he could with his thumbless hands.

"Here, sit by me and I will wash and shave you." I must have looked alarmed because the girl quickly reassured me. "I'm not a barber, but I have brothers, or did have when I was in the wider world. I know how to shave a man. Trust me."

"Can you renew my tonsure?" I asked, sitting on a stool close to the wall.

The yard was sunny but cool from being so close to the stone of the cliff. It was a luxury just to sit after all our traveling and to know that I didn't have to go any further until the next day at the earliest. I tilted my head back and felt cool water flow over my hair and face. The torn green tunic got damp but I didn't mind.

Alais must have borrowed Zaid's razor because I felt a blade on my chin, scraping away the pitiful excuse for a beard that had sprouted on my face over the last few days.

"Before I can shave a tonsure for you, I should get these lice," Alais said. Her fingers searched my scalp and I could feel her pick creatures from my hair and heard her crack her nails on them. I closed my eyes and recalled being a small boy and how my mother would perform this simple, everyday task for me. The sun flowed down on my upturned face and I felt very safe.

Alais eventually shaved away a little bit of hair off the top of my head and it was my turn to take care of her. I sat behind her and as she tilted back, poured water over her yellow hair, then searched her scalp. Arnaud emerged from within the house with a loaf of bread and a small wheel of white cheese. We feasted, then leaned back to nap in the sun.

Later, the sun started to head toward the cliff behind us, and I extracted my guitarra from the panniers. I strummed it idly at first, tuning the strings, and then I picked up the pace. The tune grew wild and it caught me, although I had no idea what I was playing. It was just the joy of the afternoon and the rest and the warmth and the food. I finally stopped and looked around the yard.

Everyone was smiling. Alais clapped her hands. I saw the male leper crouched in a corner, watching me closely. I hadn't noticed him entering. After a moment he reached out those curiously white hands towards me.

"He wants the guitarra," Arnaud suggested.

I shuddered with revulsion at the thought of that diseased body coming into contact with my instrument but took pity and handed it over to him. He pulled his sleeves tight around his wrists so that none of his sores would come into contact with the neck or frets. He started to play, and he played wonderfully.

The first song was slow, almost dirge-like. His eyes were shining, but that was all that was left of what had once been human. He finished his first song and started another one, livelier, lighter. Then, from somewhere outside the wall, we heard a rich contralto voice singing:

♪*L'autrier jost'una sebissa*
Tobei pastora mestissa
De joi e den sen massissa

Si cum filla a villana
Cap e'gonel e pelissa
Vest e camiza trelissa,
Sotlars e caussas de lana… ♪

7
Beatriz Sings

The song flowed on through the warm afternoon. We sat still and listened as the story of the courting knight and the shepherd girl was sung. The girl was no better than she should have been, but the knight didn't seem to notice. It was a lively tune and a funny *canso* full of clever rhymes. All of us in the courtyard smiled.

Pretty soon we heard the voices of the children from the other side of the little wall.

"Dompna Beatriz is singing!! Na Beatriz is singing!" You could almost hear them jumping up and down. The song ended, and we heard the voice of what could only be the old leper woman say, "Scat, shoo. There'll be more singing later. Not now. After we've had our supper and the moon is high. You know I like to sing when the moon is up. Go, see if there are any beans so we can make a good supper."

The children must have scattered because the woman came through the gate by herself.

"I am sorry, *bonhomme*," she said to me, kneeling. "The children like it when I sing, and I don't sing very often. Life is hard and sad."

"I know that life can be hard, but songs lift everyone's heart, sister," I replied. "Who made that *canso*?"

"It is a very old song, *bonhomme*," she said. "It was made by Macrabu almost one hundred years ago. I know many songs and so does my husband."

I looked at the leper holding my guitarra. It was hard to believe that he knew anything at all, but I had heard him play and there was joy in his fingers when they stroked the strings.

"He knows how to make music," I commented.

"He was a *troubar*, sir," she explained. "He made many songs of his own. He fell in love with me and, because I was poor, I became his wife and his *joglar*. Even when we were young, he had a sorry singing voice, although he made many good verses and songs."

"What happened to you?" Zaid asked. I hadn't noticed him coming over.

"Times, the war," the woman shrugged, shedding a light dust of old skin. "We both got sick, got this disease. Guirhart stopped talking. That was five or six years ago. I know what he thinks and what he needs. They are kind to us here. Sometimes I sing but it has been a long time since I heard him play."

"You say that you know many songs, sister?" I asked.

"Many songs. Songs my husband made for me," beneath the diseased face I saw what might have been a blush, "and songs that other people made."

"Sister, I have been sent to find the music for many of these old songs. Would you sing for me? Can you read? I can show you the songs I would like to hear."

"No, *bonhomme*, I never learned the trick of reading. My husband can, but it will do you no good since he doesn't speak. I remember songs. I keep them here." She tapped her temple.

"Will you sing what you know?" I repeated.

"You are as bad as the children. I will sing after the evening meal. You can listen from the roof since you should not be seen. You have brought a guitarra my husband can play. That will make him happy. Rest now, I will bring food when the sun goes down."

She walked over to her husband, lifted my guitarra from his hands, and brought it to me with a bow. I could read sadness in his eyes as he gave up the instrument. She took his hand and led him out of the little yard into the square, to look after the children.

***

"Was that one of our songs?" I asked Zaid.

He had the codex out and the sheets with lyrics and was sorting through.

"I don't think so," he replied after a little time. "It's very like one or two here, but it isn't one of them. Still, we can record the melody and let others fit the verses."

"Pons has said that some of these *troubars* would set different words to the same tune. It doesn't matter who made the tune, I don't think. I don't think my prior will care. As long as we have words and music together, we have done our duty."

"Your duty, Itzal," Zaid reminded me. "I am a free traveler, and I owe nothing to any order or any man."

I thought this seemed a bit harsh, but I didn't say anything. I decided that the leper woman was right; it was a good time to rest. The sun was high and hot, but there were cool corners in the courtyard. I folded myself into one of them, and Alais folded herself into my arms, and we both dozed through the afternoon.

***

I woke up to the smell of a stew. Rabbit, if I wasn't mistaken. With fresh herbs—wild thyme perhaps, and sage. The sky was growing darker, more purple. Stars were starting to pop out like pinholes in dark vestments. I could hear the sounds of the children clattering bowls and spoons. Supper was about to be served.

Alais and Arnaud had vanished somewhere. Zaid was sitting on a stool, mending his sandal. Pons came out from the stable, chewing on a piece of straw.

"Don't worry, Fra," he said to me. "You will have food soon. I know you can't eat the rabbit, but Alais has found some nice perch for you."

I was sick of fish, salted or fresh. I wanted that rabbit. With everyone convinced I was a perfected heretic, I wasn't going to get any. I sighed and offered up my suffering for the sins of the many. As suffering went, it wasn't too bad.

A few minutes later Alais emerged from the house into the yard with a flat piece of bread holding the perch and a small pile of lentils.

"I'm sorry, Itzal," she started, "the lentils were cooked with the rabbit, so there will be broth. I know your soul forbids—"

"My soul does not forbid that, except on fasting days, and I don't think today is one," I interrupted, putting up my hand. "I admit, I'm not sure what day it is exactly, but we'll say that it's not one for fasting. I don't mind a little broth with my lentils."

She set the bread on my knees and I picked up a piece of fish with my knife and ferried it to my mouth. Weary as I was of these creatures, it was a beautiful meal, dusted with dried herbs from inside the house. The lentils were rich and soft. I washed it down with a cup of cool gray wine from a wooden cup.

"I knew some *bonhommes*," Pons said, "who would not drink from a cup if it had touched the lips of one who had just eaten meat."

"Even if I were what you think," I said, "that is carrying things too far." I finished the food and then ate the bread that held it. I drank off the last of the wine and leaned back against the wall of the little yard. I was content enough.

"I have inks and pens," Zaid said. "We should hide on the roof if there is going to be singing. Arnaud found us a dark lantern we can see by."

I roused myself and went over to the ladder beside the barn. Zaid and I climbed it and lay down flat on the roof below a low parapet that sheltered us from view of anyone except the night birds circling between us and the stars.

***

"Raimon," I heard Beatriz's voice say, "run and fetch your flute. The one Guirhart made for you. You can play with us. Guillietta, you know where the wood blocks are? The one I use to clap the laundry, they're down by the trough. Go get them, they will help. Oh, oh, and Prades, go to the church, Pere Michel keeps a little bell in a box behind the altar. That will sound pretty, too. Go, all of you, and hurry back. We will start singing soon."

There must have been a fire built in the courtyard because we could see flickering orange light below us. We heard the sounds that groups of children make as they start to settle down. Then I heard the strings of my guitarra sound, a full chord. There was a moment's pause and I could hear two strings pulled into tune.

"Are we all ready?" Beatriz asked. Apparently they were because the music started. "We will play a little before I sing for you. Guillietta, start slapping those blocks."

First came a steady beat from two pieces of wood. Then the strings of my guitarra sounded below us in a quick, lively rhythm. I could only imagine the notes he was finding. Finally, a wooden flute entered the group.

They played a lively country dance that could have been from anywhere—from my boyhood in Basque country, from the plains before the sea, anywhere from here to the Rhone. It was the kind of tune that peasants played when they danced at midsummer or to greet the spring or when someone got married and there was plenty of food and wine. The rest of the children were clapping along with the wooden blocks, and somebody must have started to dance because there was laughter and shouts of encouragement.

It was going to be a festive evening.

The players didn't stop all at once, but the guitarra came to a rich, full chord and then the strumming ended. The flute went on a little bit longer and so did the clapping. Then it all stopped and we could hear the breathless laughter of the children.

"Now sing, Beatriz," said one young voice. I couldn't tell if it belonged to a boy or a girl.

"What shall I sing?" she asked and you could almost hear the smile in her voice. From where we were, it was easy to forget the devastation that disease wrought on her body.

"Sing something sad," said a little girl's voice. "Sing something very sad."

"All right, Guillietta, I will sing a *planh*. This *planh* was made by Bertran de Born a long time ago. It is a lament for the death of the young English king, even though it was Bertran himself who started the war where the king got killed. Or so they say. Still, it is a sad song, and we like English kings, don't we?"

The children cheered and I flipped furiously through the loose pages in front of me. I knew I had seen the name mentioned. The dark lantern cast a narrow beam of light across the paper and I felt triumph rise in my chest when I saw the name of Bertran in large, formal letters at the beginnings of a number of songs towards the middle of my collection. I signaled to Zaid that he should pay close attention. Beatriz started to sing in a low, slow tone:

♪*Si tuit l-el marrimen*
E las dolos e-il chativer
Qu'om anc agues en est segle dolen
Forssen ensems, sembleeran tuit leugier
Contra la mort del joven rei engles
Don reman pretz e jovens doloros
E-il mons escurs e tenhs e tenebrous
Sens de to joi, plens de tristor e d'ira...

If all the grief and bitterness
If all the sorrow and evil chance
That ever walked this grieving world
Were pulled together, it would be light

Against the death of the young English king
Worth is fallen and youth is sad
The world is overshadowed and overcast
Absent joy, full of sorrow and wrath... ♪

The song ran on, sadder and heavier as it went; telling us how there was nothing sadder than the death of a young rich man. The music was wonderful and the rhymes were ingenious, but I kept thinking of the dead family we had seen that morning. Perhaps, I thought, their deaths deserved a song and that the world had lost something else special when they had been raped, tortured, and killed. Still, Beatriz has a singular voice and I couldn't help but be moved as she sang the dirge. The children, restive at first, grew more still with each verse until they were completely silent when she sang for the last time, "Absent joy, full of sorrow and wrath."

Everyone was quiet for a moment, and then Beatriz clapped her hands again and said, "Enough sadness. I will sing about what makes me happy. This *canso* was made by the Monk of Montaudon. You remember that one, Guirhart my love?"

Apparently he did because the strings came to life right away.

It was another lively and jaunty tune, and the little bell tingled gaily in the dark night. Beatriz gave something like a laugh and then began to sing again:

♪*Mont me platz deportz e gaieza*
Condugz e donars e proeza
E dona franca e corteza
E de responder ben apreza
E platz m'a ric home francqueza
E vas son enemic maleza...

I like sports and I like gaiety
Feasts and gifts and games
And a lady who's full of courtesy
Not afraid to say what she means.
I like a lord who's honest to me
And evil to his enemies... ♪

The song went round and round with a catalog of what the monk loved most in life. It was mostly about food and drink, but the copy I found included more than a few verses about carnal pleasures as well, although Beatriz seemed to slur through those. Zaid scribbled furiously, copying down the bouncy but oddly circular melody. Even out of sight of the singers, I couldn't help but smile at the song.

Guirhart kept playing a long time after Beatriz stopped singing. The flute, clapping blocks, and tinny bell built up to a mad sort of climax, with everyone playing at once, loud and out of time before it collapsed like an overloaded bridge into peals of laughter.

"It's time I sang a love song, I think," we heard Beatriz say, "because love is what is most important, after all. I shall sing a *canso* made by Dompna Castelloza not that long ago and not that far from here."

> ♪*Ja da chantar non degr' aver talan*
> *Quar on mais chan*
> *E pietz me vai d'amor*
> *Que plaing e plor…*
>
> *I should have had my fill of song*
> *The more I sing*
> *The more I fail at love*
> *Tears and care*
> *Make me their home…*♪

She sang in a sweet, plaintive voice, the lament of a lady who loved someone who was treacherous. She would stay true no matter what, no matter how much it hurt, and she would never betray him. She would live on kindness and courage if she had to. The melody was inventive, with repeated themes, and Guirhart's playing on my guitarra was constantly surprising.

They sang on into the night. Once Arnaud took a turn along with Beatriz to exchange the verses of a *tenso,* a dialogue between a knight and a lady on the nature of life and love. Zaid copied the melodies as quickly as he could and I kept trying to find the words in our collection. By the time the singing stopped, we had collected seven more songs that matched our pages, as well as several other stray melodies we would try to match up in daylight.

"It is far too late and all good children should be in bed," Beatriz announced. "Come, come follow me. You, young lady," she must have been speaking to Alais, "help me to get these hellions to sleep. We'll stay in Na Lombardas's *domus* tonight, in the great room. Won't that be fun?"

There were sleepy murmurs of agreement in the high-pitched voices of children and I heard the gate open and the shuffling of feet. It sounded as if Alais had picked up at least one child and was carrying him off to bed.

I was stiff and weary myself after our long day, I stretched my arms over my head and then stood up, feeling it must be safe. Below us, in the courtyard, Guirhart was still strumming on the guitarra idly. I swung my arms back and forth as I rose, and just then, Arnaud must have kicked the fire because flames shot up, showing my form, a shadow against starry skies.

From down below, the guitarra played on, and then a voice that didn't belong to Beatriz, a voice of no quality at all except sincerity, gave out a song:

♪Be'm degra che chantar
Quar a chan coven alegriers
E mi destrenh tant cassiriers
Que'm fa de totas partz doler... ♪

8
Flight

It was as if sorrow itself were floating on the warm evening air. The voice was cracked, almost as broken as the lands we had crossed. His song, about how he should not be singing, went on. Songs should come from gladness, not sorrow. This was a song that should never have been made.

> ♪*Mo sen, mon gauch, mon desplazer*
> *E mon dan e mon pro ver*
> *Qu'a penas dic ren ben estis*
> *Mas trop suy vengutz als derriers…*
>
> *My sense, my joy, my folly*
> *Have all fled, I cannot make a verse*
> *For all this sorrow —*
> *I was born after my time had gone…*♪

I stood riveted. I glanced down at Zaid and was pleased to see that he was sketching out the melody as fast as he could write while I tried to remember all the words about the so-called Christians who had ruined this world, about the double death that loomed over everyone here, the loss of their lives and the loss of their world. The final, prayer-like coda, asking the Virgin and God for justice, love, and mercy almost tore the air. And then it stopped.

I only had ears for the song; I hadn't heard the shouts of the children.

"A miracle! A miracle!" they shouted, running away from Alais and the old leper woman to the source of the music. "It's a miracle. Guirhart can sing! His silence is over. Look! That must be a holy man! He must have cured him. A miracle!"

The children burst into the little courtyard and surrounded Guirhart but he was silent now and might remain that way forever. I looked down from the roof and saw that he had set down my guitarra and buried his face in his snow-white hands.

"Holy man!" a little girl shouted. "Holy man, come down and make him sing some more!"

There was no more hiding, that much was certain. I walked to the corner of the building and climbed down the ladder. The children surrounded me and I felt like I'd entered a sea of little limbs and voices.

"You cured him, you cured him!" some of them were saying. That was not true and they could see it. His skin was still diseased. He was weeping soundlessly and you felt that his silence would never end.

"Thank you, *bonhomme*," Beatriz said, coming to my side. "I have not heard my husband's voice for over five years. I told you he wasn't much of a singer." She went on, disparaging him, but her eyes were alight and her face was moist.

"It was no miracle!" I insisted. "I'm not a *bonhomme*."

"So you say, and I will believe you if you like," Beatriz answered. "But it isn't safe for you here anymore. You must leave before morning. The children must not see more of you, and their parents will be back tomorrow evening or the next morning, if not sooner. You must be higher in the mountains before they return."

"I'll pack the mule," Zaid said as he stepped off the ladder.

"What day is it, sister?" I asked Beatriz.

"I believe it is a Sunday," she answered. "Although I don't keep close track, and it's difficult with the priest gone. It is no saint's day that I can think of. I think it is a Sunday in ordinary time. It's August, I remember that much. When the grown-ups return they'll begin making hay."

Sunday. I hadn't been to Mass since before I was locked up in Carcassone. I had neglected my office for the last few days.

"May I go into your church and pray? I heard you say it was unlocked."

"It is open, *bonhomme*. You may use it, although there is a crucifix. I know that's against your teaching."

I just shrugged my shoulders. I'd lost this argument. I turned to Zaid who was loading our animal.

"Please finish our packing. I need to be in a church for a little while. We will leave when I'm finished. Tell the others, or any of them who want to keep going with us." Zaid nodded his response.

***

I walked across the square past the fountain. Beatriz was wrangling the children into one of the houses to the left of the church, trying to calm them down after the miracle. I pushed open the heavy door and inhaled the odor of hundreds of years of incense and humanity. It was familiar and comforting. I made my way up the dark nave and knelt down at the altar rail. It was too dark to see the pages of my psalter, so I recited a series of prayers from memory, along with a heartfelt act of contrition.

By the time I lifted my eyes up to the Lord, I was wracked with sobs. I couldn't make sense of what had happened to me. I was a monk. Not a very good monk, not very learned or pious, but a monk. I was a member of a chapter of the order of preaching friars, the Dominicans, the locally hated white monks. How had this order come to fail at its mission so miserably? How had I traveled so far from myself? At least I was still gathering up the songs. I was following instructions. But I could also feel my Catholic faith falling away from me, like the flakes of skin off the two good and sad lepers. They were somehow the heart and soul of this town that was composed entirely of children for the moment. And even those children posed a threat to me. But these were good people, even if they were heretics. I mourned my loss of certainty and I wasn't able to accept the freedom being offered to me, and not just because that freedom meant danger. I was mourning that loss through that hour in the dark, in a deserted church. I don't know when I stopped reciting my psalms. I found myself surrendering to that one prayer both faiths shared and said out loud, in a cracking voice: *Pater Noster, qui es in caelis; Sanctificetur nomen tuum...* I ran on to the end of that and then found myself reciting my childhood prayers in my almost forgotten Basque tongue. Finally, I gave up words altogether and just laid my head against the altar rail.

Alais found me there, I don't know how much later. She placed her hand on the back of my head and I started upwards. She reached down and lifted my hand off the rail. I turned towards her and stood up slowly. She wrapped her arms around me and kissed me hard, almost fiercely. Her hands were sliding down my body. I stopped her.

"Not here, woman. Can't you see this is a holy place?"

"It is not holy to us, to you and I. Besides, no one will see us." Her hands were making their way to the rope that bound my tunic.

"No! It is holy to me. Besides, even if it weren't, it's holy to someone. We must go. They say we should be gone before the first light."

She sighed but gave up her efforts. "Yes, we must. We mustn't let the adults see the direction we take. The children are certain to tell the story of the *bonhomme* who miraculously cured Guirhart's voice. The priest will make them tell the Inquisitors and you will be burnt."

We stepped out into the square. The night was black with washings of stars decorating the heavens but offering almost no light. I wondered about something, so I asked the girl as we made our way to the gate where our small party was waiting.

"You are all so convinced that I am one of you, a heretic, a *bonhomme*. You feed me nothing but fish because such men will not eat meat. Yet you play these games with me. Aren't they forbidden, too?"

"They would be, but because of my condition, I suppose that it's all right with God and everyone."

"What condition? Are you sick, girl? I never knew."

"I thought Na Carenza told you when you paid for me. It's nothing too sad. It's just that I cannot have children. I am barren. That is why my parents sent me away. But I didn't like it in Narbonne. I like it better with you."

"I like to have you here, too. But still, the things we do…"

"Well, since we can't bring another soul into the evil world, it is just amusement, isn't it? It can't be terribly sinful to enjoy the flesh if it makes no harm, brings no one else into suffering, don't you think?" She tilted her chin towards me and I could only smile in that darkness. I no longer knew what ruled in this world in which I was wandering.

***

Zaid, Pons and Arnaud were all surrounding our mule near the gate of the *castra*. Guirhart and Beatriz stood next to them. Pons was clapping his thumbless hands together against the chill of the night, and Zaid was blowing on his fingers, but the others seemed used to the climate.

"My husband will guide you through the night. He will take you the quick way so that you will be high up and out of sight early. Just send him back to me in the morning," Beatriz said to me with heartbreaking tenderness in her voice.

"We will do that, sister," I answered softly.

"I could lead us," Arnaud protested. "I could guide us if it weren't so dark. I used to play in this place when I was a little boy. I know the ways of cliffs and mountains."

"I am sure you do, boy," I said. "Did you leave anything for your relative, for Dompna Guillemette? We ate her bread, after all."

"No. I have nothing, *bonhomme,*" he replied, embarrassed.

"Take this, then," I said, giving him a small coin from the purse. "Leave it on her table."

"Perhaps more," he wheedled. "I have filled your panniers with some of her wine and some things from her smokehouse."

"Fine, here," I said, handing him a second coin. He ran off across the square and returned in less time than it takes to shoot an arrow. "All of us who are going are here?" I asked, surveying our little group. "Let's go."

Since Guirhart didn't speak I wasn't sure how he was going to guide us, especially considering the depths of the darkness, but his solution was simple enough. Arnaud grasped the rope that held the rags on the leper's body; Alais held onto Arnaud's girdle, I took hold of her skirts. Zaid held onto the rope around my waist with one hand and the hemp bridle on our mule with the other, and Pons followed, his hand entwined in the mule's tail. All of us would make it through the darkness, or none of us. I felt as if we were trapped in a parable out of the Gospel of Saint Matthew. We filed through the gate and turned left clinging to the *castra's* wall. We turned and circled the settlement, keeping one hand against the wall. Where the walls met the cliff we turned next to a bush of fragrant lavender. The cliff face was on our right and a narrow path, not visible from within the *castra,* was cut into the sheer wall. We climbed, with stray bushes between us and a long fall, through the hours of the early morning. As the sun began to paint the sky pink behind us, we reached the top.

We halted at a signal from the now visible Guirhart. His hand raised, we all caught our breath. The sun rose a little higher in the sky, turning our ghostly forms into substance. I looked back down the way we had come and was grateful to the darkness. The path we had followed was less than a foot wide in places. I'm surprised the mule made it at all, and I was glad that Pons was there to keep its rear legs true. Guirhart didn't let us linger, just giving us enough time to catch our breath and take a drink of water, then he led us into the hayfields that grew on the summit of the cliff.

The yellow grasses were higher than Alais' head and we moved through them like swimmers, making good time and enjoying the fragrance of green growing things. For the moment, I felt that we were safe, although I knew we weren't.

The bowl of grass we traversed began to rise and we emerged into full morning, climbing the side of a green hill. I looked up and saw that it quickly became a mountain. We started to follow a path worn by generations of shepherds and their flocks. You could almost smell the sheep, although we knew there were none nearby. We pressed on and climbed higher. We could see the edge of the cliff behind us but not the village below it. We had stopped clinging to each other's belts and were spaced out now. Zaid looked back, shading his eyes against the morning light.

"There!" he called out.

I looked where he was pointing but couldn't see anything at first. "What? Is there something there?"

"Look," he answered. "The village is returning."

I stopped and followed his gaze. It was hard to fight the bright August sun but I began to see them. In the distance, coming over the lip of the opposite hill, the high side of the valley across from the *castra*, I saw sharply etched forms, like they were cut out of dark paper against the bright light, incredibly small, almost like ants against the green valley edge. They were being led by someone or something taller. I realized it must be someone on a horse.

"See!" Arnaud said, spitting on the earth. "The French priest rides."

I looked again and saw that the rider was clothed in black, not the brown homespun of the flock he led. There was a wagon at the rear of the little column. It seemed that there might be some people in that, but I couldn't be sure at that distance. There wasn't much movement in that wagon.

"The priest rides," Pons said, "and so do the wounded. Some must have already been punished. If they were forced to walk, they would bleed to death. I wonder how many thumbs the Inquisitors collected. I wonder if God is happy with their lost limbs." His voice was more bitter than the boy's had been.

"Let's keep going," Alais was almost pleading. "We don't need to travel much further today." She was looking to the leper and he seemed to nod.

We kept climbing up the hillside that seemed to grow steeper with every step, then we turned, rounded the hill and lost sight of the returning villagers. We kept up a good pace for almost an hour, Guirhart setting our speed but never uttering a word. Finally he led us up a narrow defile that was formed by the spring runoff. It twisted a bit and turned and we found ourselves behind a wall of rocks. The old man held up his hand and stopped. We stopped with him.

He waved his hand in the air. It seemed to mean that he was leaving us here. He knew, as we did, that if he were not in the village when the priest returned there would be more questions than could be comfortably answered.

Pons tied our mule to a little beech tree and then threw himself onto the ground to rest. The others followed him. Guirhart turned towards me and I thought I could read a request in his eyes. I walked over to the animal and extracted my guitarra. He took it in those odd, white hands and sat down on a stone.

He tuned the instrument deftly and started to strum it lightly. Then his long, nimble fingers plucked out a melody, a note at a time, a trick I'd never learned. I listened closely. It was the same, unbearably sad song he had sung for us the night before. I was prepared to hear him sing it again, but he didn't. He just played through the notes once, twice, and then varied them before returning to the beginning of the tune. Then he strummed the strings softly again. He bowed and handed me back my instrument. I bowed as I accepted it.

He stood up and decorously dusted off the seat of his tunic. He looked at me, his ravaged face very close to mine. I knew that it held a soul, a great soul, and that I was lucky to have met this man, both for his nimble guidance in our escape and for the music he had given us. He knelt down before me in the familiar attitude, his head bowed, his hands held wide. I placed both of my hands on the stringy hair of his head.

"*Benedicte, parcite nobis,*" I pronounced.

He stood up, smiled through his broken teeth, and then vanished around a bend in the defile as if he had never been there at all.

9
Transhumance

We were all weary. None of us had slept. Still, Alais had to make sure we all had something to eat. She pulled bread, cheese, the by now dreaded smoked fish, and a small miracle, a new ham, out of our panniers. She broke off chunks of two-day-old bread, doused them in gray wine, and passed them around. She handed me some cheese and a bit of fish, then cut slices of ham for the rest of our party. Zaid, seeing my face, slipped his ham over to me as I passed him my fish, and I had meat for the first time in days. The bottle of wine got passed around two times and the girl began to put everything away. All of this was accomplished in silence except for the songs of the morning birds and the rustle of hot wind in the trees at the lip of our little shelter.

"Someone should keep watch to see if anyone heads this way from the village," Zaid said.

"I'll go first," Arnaud volunteered. "My night was quiet, at least."

The rest of us just grunted in agreement. I went behind a rock and started to stretch out. Alais stopped me, took off her dress and rolled it for a pillow, then lay down beside me in her shift. She leaned her head into my shoulder and went chastely to sleep in moments. So did I.

***

The sun was high when I stirred. Alais had rolled off my shoulder and was snoring lightly on the grass, the innocence of sleep having betrayed her. I rose and dusted myself off. I walked to the mouth of the wash where Zaid was sitting on a rock, keeping watch and shaving. The small steel mirror glinted in the sun and his razor scraped softly as he shaped his mustache.

"Is there any movement?" I asked him.

"Nothing that I could see. No one coming this way. I saw the villagers enter the *castra*. They dispersed to their houses. I didn't see anyone leave the walls. They are probably resting today. They will begin making hay tomorrow, and that is hard work, I'm told."

"You've never done it?" I asked. It seemed odd how little I knew of this companion.

"My family were merchants. We did not farm. We bought our food in the market. We kept chickens in the yard and my mother grew herbs and taught me how to use them. All I know of farming is what I've seen as I pass through other lands."

"When I was a boy, we all farmed. It was a small village way over to the west. I made hay. I tended the town ox sometimes—there was only one and we all shared it as our beast of burden. I looked after sheep and goats. I milked and made cheese."

"I'm sure that is what built your exemplary character," he replied with a half-smile. "Still, it is not a necessary experience."

"No, I suppose it is not. It's just that I thought it was universal."

"You've seen enough of cities now to know better," he said and he turned his attention back to his chin.

I decided to go off by myself to recite my office. I knelt behind a rock a few paces beyond where Alais lay sleeping. I opened my psalter and recited the words written on the page in front of me, but whatever faith I once had was gone. It had vanished like smoke on a breezy day and I could think of no way to bring it back. I tried to consider the wounds of Christ, the tears of his mother. I was not touched. I contemplated the pains of Hell and even they did not move me. I thought of our founder, of Dominic, in ecstatic prayer, contemplating the Virgin, the vision of the beatific. It was a lovely thought, but it did not move my soul. I wondered if anything ever would again.

***

We passed the whole day and night there, gathering our strength. There was a quick squall of rain in the afternoon, the kind you sometimes get in the mountains. We sheltered under the stunted trees but dried quickly as soon as the sun came out and the hot winds blew over us. Alais made a meal over a small fire that did not give much away. We drank wine and made idle conversation without even discussing what the next morning might bring. After sitting in the cool darkness a little while, Alais took my hand and led me to a sheltered spot. She lifted her shift and then my tunic, and we did what men and women have always done. Her skin felt lovely against mine, but I felt that I wasn't really there.

Everyone was stiff and slow to rise the next morning, the dampness left by the storm having reached everyone's bones. Still, we managed to rise, pack our supplies, load the mule, and only then considered our direction.

"We can keep going up this wash," Arnaud told us. "It will take us to the top of the mountain. We can look around from there. I think we should head west and maybe a little south. My village lies across the Ariege, north of Pamiers. I'd like to go home."

It seemed as good a plan as any. We trudged up the narrow defile and came out, as predicted, on top of a rounded mountain. There was one lone black oak tree. Alais darted behind it as soon as we reached the top, full of too much water and wine from our breakfast. The rest of us looked back the way we'd come. We could still make out the walled *castra* we had left and the road that ran from it. There seemed to be almost no traffic. You could see what might have been villagers moving in the hayfields. It was as quiet and peaceful a scene as you could wish for.

Alais emerged and we set out down the other side of the mountain. It was an easy, grassy slope. We turned one little switchback on the trail and we saw someone.

"Wait," Pons cautioned, holding up his four-fingered hand.

"It is nothing, no one," Zaid offered. "Not every person we meet is in the pay of the Inquisition. Look, it's only a shepherd."

I saw a compact, dark man dressed in brown homespun moving about three sheep along with his staff.

"Hail! Greetings! You there!" I shouted out.

The fellow stopped and leaned against his staff until we reached him.

"Hello," I said. "We are traveling here and we could use a path. Can you help us?"

"I am going a little beyond Pamiers," he answered in Basque. I was surprised.

"That's our general direction," I replied in the tongue of my childhood. "But we prefer to avoid the main roads and cities."

"I know many lonely routes. I have just come down from the high mountains where my master's sheep are grazing for the summer. I will go back there before too long. We will be moving them to the lowlands for the winter. I will return for that, the transhumance as it is called."

"Will you guide us?" I asked.

"I will go along and keep you right. Who are you?" he asked. "I am a shepherd, as you see. My name is Peru, Piere in the local tongue."

"I am Itzal, these others go with me. We are harmless."

"I don't think that anyone is harmless these days. But I will lead you towards Pamiers and around it if you like. And I will lead you in such a way that you won't be seen."

"Thank you," was all I could think to say, and we fell in alongside him.

***

He was true to his word. He led us through that day by narrow tracks that were obviously formed by the movements of sheep. We did not see another living soul all that day. We made camp in a little hollow near the top of a mountain. I moved apart to go through the motions of my office while Pons and Alais prepared a meal. Zaid was leafing through our codex, trying to make the notation as neat as he could and Peru just sat down and began carving a stick with his knife. The sheep formed their own group.

"Peru," I heard Arnaud ask as I slipped behind a tree and sank to my knees, "whose sheep are those?"

"They belong to my master, Prades Clerges. Or they did. I am taking them to my sister. She lives in Comus. Her husband died in prison last year. She can use them. Prades won't miss them. He does not know how many lambs we birthed last spring."

I ignored the talk and recited my empty psalms one more time. I was not sure how much longer I could keep up the masquerade. After my prayers, I gathered with the others around a little fire. They ate ham and bread; I had cheese and salted fish again. The bottles of wine made the rounds. I thought about bringing the guitarra out but decided I was too sad and weary to make music. Alais avoided my eyes as we ate. She retired early, off by herself. We were all footsore, but we felt safe in our little mountain dell, so it was an early night for all. Arnaud banked the fire and we all took to our blankets.

It was late when I felt someone next to me. Alais was prodding me awake.

"Come with me. I need to feel you again," she said, and she took me by the hand and led me back to where I'd said my prayers.

"Why so secret? Everyone here knows you share my bed," I said, whispering as her motions indicated quiet.

"The shepherd does not. I am sure he thinks that you are pure and holy. Let's not give him any cause to gossip. I know how shepherds talk. It will be all over the Aude and the Ariege and even in the court of Foix if he suspects anything. I don't care for me, but for you and for the church."

I sighed and pulled her towards me and we played our gentle play with each other's bodies through the late hours, saying our Compline prayers with our flesh.

***

A low mist rose from the grass the next morning. Gray ghosts made by dew rising to the warming sun teased our vision as we started out. Peru led the way and I stepped up next to him.

"I was hoping you would choose to stay in front," he said to me in Basque.

"I wanted a chance to go back to the language of my childhood. It's pleasant, sometimes, to remember back to the days when we were too small to sin," I said, smiling, recalling with pleasure my sin of the night before.

"Yes, I suppose it is. But I wanted to speak to you of important things. Of matters of the soul," he began.

Behind us, Arnaud, shooing the sheep ahead of him with his hands sighed and said, "God save us from a shepherd who wants to talk." He slackened his pace, and the others fell back a bit, too, giving us room to converse on our own.

"I know you are a *bonhomme*," he began again. "The mountains are glad with the news that a true perfected soul is among us after so long."

"No one is perfect, my son," I said, deciding not to fight the delusion that the local population suffered under.

"Perhaps not, but you've been through the baptism of the Holy Spirit. You are a creature of fire, not of flesh. And you must be wise as well as holy. And clever, or you would be more a creature of ashes than of flame."

"I am lucky, that's all. I have good companions who are smarter than I am and who know the ways of these hills and mountains. Companions like you," I said, nodding towards the small man.

"So you say. I say you walk with God." He remained silent for a while as we walked. The sun rose higher, the mists grew a little thinner, although the rising vapor reminded me of ghost stories my brother used to tell me during the dark of the moon.

"I wanted to ask you," he went on after a while, "about the transmigration of souls."

"What?" I asked. I'd never heard of any such thing.

"Metempsychosis," he said, speaking a language that made no sense to me.

"What is that word?"

"It's Greek, so they say. It means the same thing. How souls pass from one being to the next. From sheep to horse to bird to woman to pig to man. One soul taking many forms until it can escape from the round of life in which the Evil one has entrapped our essence."

"You seem very learned for a shepherd," I offered, thinking it a compliment.

"The mountains are lonely. We have time to talk and to think. We listen to holy men. We listen to monks. We listen to anyone who is passing, who has something interesting to say. We even listen to Moors, like the one who travels with you. They know many things."

"I do not know of Moors in general, but Zaid is wise and clever. And a good Catholic."

"So he would have you believe. They are all heathens at heart. If you trust him, that's enough for me. But it is this passage of souls I wonder about. Why, for example, do fish have no souls?"

"I don't know what you mean."

"They must not have souls. You, the *bonhommes*, will eat fish, so therefore they could not have souls. You will not eat that which has a soul. That is your rule."

"If you say so," I answered, waiting for him to go on.

"The question of fish is idle. We talk about it on the long summer nights. Some think it is because they cannot live in air, and the soul is a function of air. Myself, I don't know and I don't care about fish particularly. But I do want this to be my last life trapped in this sort of flesh."

"Then obey the commandments, pray, and make a good confession every so often. God will look after you."

"Oh no, there's more to it than that. There must be."

"Not really. But you must not sin. For example, I heard that these few sheep that are traveling with us do not belong to you. They belong to your master."

"They come from his flock," he replied, kicking a stone that bounced off ahead of us and caromed off a stunted tree. "He will not miss them."

"Still, they are not yours. You should not take them."

"I know you're right. Still, my sister can sell the wool and eat the meat. She is in greater need than Prades Clerges."

"That is not for you to say," I reprimanded him, trying to look like my old prior did when he lectured the novices.

"It is a small enough sin. I can live with that. I can live with a great deal. It is dying that bothers me."

"We must all die, my son. That is the price of breath."

"See! There it is again, the breath! I knew we were onto something. But I want to make a good death and I can only do that if you offer me the *consolamentum*. There is no one else who can do that. But I cannot take the sacrament and still enjoy the flesh. I am puzzled."

"I have heard that many wait until they know they are about to die to submit to the sacrament. Or they choose to die after receiving it."

"I have seen that. An old woman in Comus. I saw her take the blessing of the Spirit and then she starved. But she was very old and did not have much left to live for anyway."

"Tell me what her ceremony was like," I asked. I was thinking of the poor, benighted jailer whom I'd failed so dismally.

"But you must know. You have performed it. You have had it performed over you."

"I know, my son, but I have seen various forms. I want to know what you saw. How the hands were laid, what words were said, what happened. Each *bonhomme* has learned things a little differently. I would conform with my brethren. I want to be sure that I can end the, the—transmigration of souls."

We walked on through the morning, the Basque shepherd telling me the details of a sacrament that I had been taught would send his soul to hell. He thought it the only road to salvation. The sun rose and the mists burned away. The day grew hot as we climbed over the next crest.

10
Conversion

I listened to him most of the morning. I listened as he recited little bits of the Gospels of Saint Matthew and John, quoted lines from the Epistles of Paul, and told me about the laying on of hands. He recited in a singsong voice, obviously searching his memory, trying not to leave anything out, to recall everything that he had heard or seen. His words were in the language familiar to me from childhood, not disguised in Latin, not made falsely high-minded. He spoke with a simple faith and I could feel my soul change.

"Wasn't your ordination like that?" he asked, finally.

"It was brother, but simpler. We were in a small house," I lied, "and we were hurried. There were white monks of the Inquisition coming for us. The man who brought me into the grace of God burned only days after his hands had touched my head. I was very sad."

He shook his head and made small clicking sounds through pursed lips. "We live in troubled times, *bonhomme*. It is terrible to burn for the faith but worse to lose it."

I nodded and bowed my head. My hand went to the book in its secret pocket, not my psalter, but the madman's bequest. I could see him throwing himself into the river. I knew what his gift was for now, and I was grateful.

"You say the whole region knows that I am walking these hills—how is that?" I asked.

"You were not the only one to see the jailer die. People scattered. People talk." He shrugged.

"If everyone knows, why am I still free?"

"The people want a *bonhomme* in these mountains. Most of the parish priests don't mind. At least not the ones who were born in these parts. They are not very good priests, I'm afraid, but they are good sons and good brothers."

We stopped in the heat of the day under an oak tree taking a bite and a sip at the wine bottle. We drowsed until the sun headed west and the breeze came off the sea, far to the south. The sky was still bright but we walked away, still avoiding the main roads, following the shorn grass that sheep left behind them. I dropped back and walked beside Alais, taking her hand every now and then. I knew that I was a different man and that I could understand her faith. She didn't know, but she enjoyed my attention.

***

"We'll stop here," Peru announced holding up his hand. We had reached a hollow dip near the top of a smallish mountain or a large hill. There was the sound of rushing water nearby. "We will need to cross the road between Fanjeux and Pamiers on the lower slope. Then there will be the river to ford. Don't worry; I know a place well upstream from one city and downstream from the other. We should sleep early and rise early. If we cross before the gates of the cities open we should be able to go across that road unseen."

Pons tied the reins of the mule to a beech tree and threw himself on the ground next to the beast. Zaid pulled off the panniers and Alais rummaged through them for food. Zaid set them on the ground and sat, using the baskets to rest his back.

"That ewe needs milking. The two lambs are weaned," Peru said. "But her udders are heavy." He set about to milk the animal before looking for anything to hold the liquid. Alais located a bowl in the panniers, I never knew where that came from, Dompna Guillemette, no doubt.

"I'll fetch water to cool the milk," Arnaud offered. He headed off towards the sound of the river.

***

When he came back he was holding his outer tunic in front of him, bulging and dripping with water. His once white undershirt was stained and torn but he didn't seem to mind. He was smiling broadly.

"Look, not just water, but supper, too," he laughed, showing his burden to Pons. The old man reached into the improvised vessel and slapped out two fat trout that writhed on the grass, their speckled sides reflecting silver in the late afternoon light.

Alais clapped her hand. "Fresh fish, so much nicer than the salted!" Our entire little group seemed delighted. She took Zaid's knife and set about cleaning the catch while Arnaud and Pons built a small fire.

I extracted my guitarra from the panniers and tuned it quietly as the sky grew slowly darker. It went a green-tinged purple and then fell to black as the sun sank suddenly beyond the mountain that sheltered us. By that time, I was strumming chords and plucking notes. Alais was simmering lentils in milk and building little baskets of twigs for roasting our trout. Zaid sat apart, looking sullen, cleaning fish leavings from his blade.

"Do you sing, *bonhomme?*" Peru asked me.

"Not well," I replied. "But I am in these mountains to listen to songs. I'm collecting music. I let others do the singing. The girl has a pretty voice, and the boy's is strong. Most of the songs he knows are rather crude, though."

"I know a tune or two," Peru started.

"I'm not interested in Basque songs," I interrupted. "I know many of them from my childhood, and that isn't my mission. I am looking for the songs of this country, the songs that seem to be slipping away."

"They are, *bonhomme,*" the shepherd answered, "but I know one or two of them as well."

"That's fine. We'll have supper, sing a little bit, and then say our prayers and sleep. We can be off before first light if you can guide us in the darkness."

"No worries about that. I am more sure-footed than my sheep, and my eyes are sharper," he answered, laughing.

***

The meal was fine and festive—trout roasted over beech wood, lentils with a little wild garlic steeped in sheep's milk, all washed down with gray wine. Everyone seemed to be in a lovely mood except Zaid who brooded away from the fire. We pushed aside the knives we'd used and tossed the leaves that had served as plates into the coals. I rubbed my fingers clean on the grass, picked up the guitarra, and strummed a little bit.

"Where are you leading us, Peru?" Pons asked over the music.

"I'll take you into those mountains on the other side of the valley. There are many there like you. We'll go to a village called Saisons. They have a new priest and he is, let me say, sympathetic. He seems to take care of heretic and Catholic alike. Especially the women," he leered in the darkness. "He doesn't question the faith of any woman who takes off her smock. Of course, the men in the village seem to disappear, and they are not all of them shepherds. The priest is growing fat." He was almost cackling.

I looked over to Arnaud and nodded. He paid close attention.

"Saisons is not that far on the other side of the river, but it is hard to reach. The road winds below it," Peru went on, "but only footpaths will take you up into the square. We will be able to approach it without much danger of being seen. Now, you said something about singing?" He looked over at me.

I was still idly strumming the guitarra. "You said you knew a song or two," I suggested. "How should I play for you?"

"This is a very serious song," he said, "but the pace is very lively." I strummed a bit faster. "Yes, like that but—" he began to clap his hands in an odd rhythm. I took his cue and tried to play to it. He warbled a few notes. It was a complicated melody, but I was able to follow it after a few wordless minutes. I looked to Zaid and saw that he had a pen in his hand.

♪D'un sirventes far en est son que m'agenssa
No-m vuolh plus tarzar ni far longa bistennssa
E sai ses doptar qu'ieu n'aurais malvolenssa
Si far sirventes
Dels fals, d'enjans ples,
De Roma, que es caps de la dechasenssa
On dechai totz bes
No-um meravilh ges, Roma, si la gens erra,
Que-l segle avetz mes en trebalh et en guerra...♪

The melody was tricky, but there were a lot of bitter verses to this song, and both Zaid and I had plenty of time to learn the tune. The vitriol this simple shepherd was pouring on the Church of Rome was astonishing, blaming it for all the ills of the world, denouncing it for war, for greed, for lust, for the poverty of the South. Peru sang his song in a biting tone, the bitterness was palpable, but the music was astonishing. It was intricate but inspiring, lively and serious at the same time, and his voice seemed to stoke the flames of the fire in front of us.

It was a long song, and I kept playing along with him, although even in my newly converted state, I had twinges of conscience at his denunciation of what had been my own true Church until very recently. Still, the artifice carried me along. Alais and Arnaud clapped their hands in time and Pons offered cheers of encouragement at some of the fiercer charges. The song didn't so much end as simply run out of energy. Peru sat down and leaned back, reaching for one of the bottles, out of breath, and I let my fingers slowly come to a stop over the strings.

"I think that may be the only song we need for this night," I observed. "It has worn me out, and it looks like it's done in our guide. Let's sleep for a few hours before setting out."

Pons moved to bank the fire so there would at least be warmth in the morning and the rest of us took to our blankets.

**

Someone was shaking me to wakefulness before I even slept, or so it seemed.

"Rise, *bonhomme*," Peru was saying softly. I sat up and rubbed my eyes. It was still quite dark out, the sky was alive with the late stars. There was a hint of graying to the east.

One by one the shepherd was rousing our party. Without many words but grunts, yawns, and stretches, we rose and rolled up our blankets quickly. We stood around the fire, passing bits of bread, washing them down with cool sheep's milk left over from the night before.

"Come, come, we must start," Peru urged us.

There was some grumbling, but we all began to move. Pons took the halter of the mule. I felt the codex in the bag slung over my shoulder. Alais reached out and touched my hand quickly, lightly, so as not to arouse the shepherd.

The path was narrow and we could barely see it by starlight, but Peru seemed as sure-footed as he'd claimed, and we wound around the top of the knoll and down the other side. We walked single file, each with a hand on the shoulder of the person in front of us, with Zaid bringing up the rear.

The gray light grew behind the hill as we made our way down. We could make out shapes when we reached the flatter ground. We remained quiet as we crossed the flat earth of the valley floor; I was trying to remember my Matins prayers and recited them in my head for the sake of form and habit. We heard motion ahead of us just as the sky began to show pink.

We had reached the road from Fanjeaux to Pamiers. At least, that was our fair assumption. It was a road. There was traffic moving along it. We stopped and waited while two shepherds shooed a small flock towards the south. There was a wagon pointing north that waited by the side of the road, heavy with dew-damp hay. We muttered greetings, but no one had any interest in others traveling at this early hour.

The sheep passed us and the wagon creaked as the ox strained to get it moving again. We crossed between the two parties. We headed west and the land was falling away behind us.

"Aren't we missing one?" Peru asked, a little way from the road.

I glanced around our party and saw that Zaid had fallen behind us. It looked like, though it was hard to see in that dim light, that he had stopped to talk to the shepherds on their way to Pamiers. We stood and waited and after a few minutes, he made his way down to us.

"I wanted the news," Zaid explained as he reached me. "I wanted to know what kind of alarm had been raised in the country and to find out if anyone was watching for us."

"Well," Pons asked, his voice brittle and weary, "what did they say?"

"The Inquisition is on guard and most of the roads are being watched. That's all they had to say. No one specific is a target, although there is a rumor," he bowed his head towards me, "of a *bonhomme* in the area, and he is much sought. But no one knows where he is or what he looks like."

"That's all to the good," I said.

"Yes, yes, it must be, but let's keep moving." Peru urged us on. He turned us north and we were walking parallel to the road. "We have about a mile to go before we reach a place where we can cross the river. We'll be safer in the mountains on the other side. The Inquisitors don't like it there. Rumors of witchcraft abound, and ghosts with secret powers are said to have hiding places there. And that's how the people like it in those mountains."

"All right, all right, you don't have to push us," Arnaud answered, and we walked wearily towards the north, the sky glowing red to our right.

***

We trudged on. The river rushed to our left but the current seemed to become more placid as we walked upstream. The river spread out and the bottom could be seen slick, green, and rocky. The sun came over the horizon and shot its beams through the water.

"Here," Peru said finally. "We can walk across right here. The stones are flat and the water is shallow. Still, it can be tricky. We'll all hang onto a rope. The mule can anchor us at one end. I'll take the other."

The water glinted, almost silver in the early morning. Arnaud pulled a piece of rope out of our panniers—he had supplied us well out of his cousin's *domus*. Peru handed one of the lambs to Arnaud and the other to Zaid. "The ewe can make it on her own. She's strong," he observed. I picked up Alais and had her ride on my back. There was no point in all of us getting wet and my sandals would dry faster than her flimsy leather shoes.

Peru shooed the ewe in front of us and we walked gingerly through the water, each with a hand loose on the rope. The current was cold, rushing around our ankles. Towards the center of the channel, it reached up to our knees, but no more. I felt my legs wobble a bit but was able to keep my balance with Alais on my back and one hand more firmly on the hemp line.

"A little bread, I think," Peru said once everyone was safely across the Ariege. "Just to restore us before we climb into the mountains." Pons was coiling the rope as Alais slid off my back. I looked at her fondly but said nothing.

We pressed on. We climbed the slope of one foothill. The track was narrow and steep. We kept walking for hours. Down one hill, up another steeper one. We always stayed midway up the slope for some reason, but the trails left by sheep were always there.

"There," Peru shouted. "There is Saisons!" He was pointing at a rocky mountain a bit ahead of us and to our right. I could make out the shape of some buildings towards the summit. "See, the road winds over that way." He gestured, sweeping the valley with his arm and I looked away to the left. "But it doesn't quite lead us there. We'll be fine."

He laughed. The way was still steep, over a rocky, narrow defile. Trees were growing out of the side of the mountain almost horizontally. Peru pushed the branches up over his head and started to stride forward. He didn't see the root crossing the track. His foot caught, he teetered for a moment, waving his arms, grasping air instead of the branch of the tree. He caught one, but it tore away and he fell down to the rocks beneath us.

11
Consolation

I started after him but Arnaud grabbed my tunic.

"You'll never get him back up here," he said. "The man's dead."

"We don't know. We have to see." I answered.

Peru had fallen head first, hitting the steep slope about two-thirds of the way down. He turned over and slid down into the gully. His form lay motionless below us, a splash of red near his left hand.

"Even if he's dead, we should bury him. Recite some prayers."

"If it suits, *bonhomme,*" Arnaud replied. "We'll use the rope."

He brought the length of line out of the panniers and tied one end to the baskets. Alais and Zaid held the animal still. Arnaud led the way down; I was in the center with Pons following above me. We lowered ourselves backward into the little valley, but the rope didn't reach all the way down. It was too deep and steep for that.

When we had to let go, Arnaud showed the way. He turned over onto his back and slid down the last half-furlong, digging in his heels to slow his descent. I followed and Pons came after, yelling as he slid, whether out of fear or some kind of pleasure in the speed I couldn't tell.

The bottom of the narrow valley was strewn with rocks, some of them smoothed by winter run-off. Both of Peru's arms were at strange angles as we approached him and there was blood seeping from his head. He lay on his back with his eyes wide open to the morning sky. He wasn't yet dead, but he would be soon. Anyone could see that.

I bent over him. "There's no help for you, man," I told him softly.

His eyes stared up at me. There was a prayer in them.

I reached out with my hands and placed them both on his forehead. I reached into my soul for all the devotion I could find there.

"Will you keep the commandments of God? Will you continue to your end? We have hope that you will receive life eternal."

"I have this will," Peru whispered, hoarse but joyful. "Pray to God for me."

"*Parcite nobis,*" I pronounced. "Good Christians, we pray you, by the love of God, you grant this blessing and the blessing of the Holy Spirit. We pray your death be a good death."

"*Parcite nobis,*" he responded, his voice growing thin.

I gestured with my shoulders to Arnaud and Pons. They took my point and knelt beside us. Together, we prayed. "By God and by us and by the Church, may your sins be forgiven, and we pray to God to forgive you them."

"Amen," he breathed.

"*Adoremus, Patrem, et Filium, et Spiritu Sanctum,*" the three of us intoned together.

"Thank you, *bonhomme,*" the dying man exhaled. "Burn my flesh, I beg you."

I looked at the others, bewildered by his request.

"It is the only way, Itzal," Pons told me. "We can't bury him, we have no tools. Besides, if his body were found by the white monks they would disinter him and desecrate the grave. It is what they do with heretics."

I looked down into the man's eyes and nodded, but he could no longer see any of the troubles of this world.

Arnaud was already gathering dry branches; Pons began to build a palate of smooth rocks. I closed Peru's eyes and murmured a *Pater Noster* over him.

***

We left him there on the rocks, the greasy black smoke rising from his body. Arnaud had covered him with wood. His clothes were dry and dirty and they went up right away. We labored back up to the rope and pulled ourselves, weary and silent, along the slope back to the path. There had been no choice, I knew. He could not be saved and we couldn't have carried his body with us. If what Pons said were true, there would have been little point to it. I still felt heaviness in my soul for a man I'd known only a day. I hoped his soul went where he wished it to go; although I was no longer certain of what might be true.

Arnaud coiled the rope and stowed it in the baskets. No one said anything. Pons made a small sound with his mouth to get the mule moving. We followed slowly, a small and forlorn procession. Alais took my hand.

The sun rose higher and the day grew hot. We wouldn't reach the village before midday, we could tell. We paused at the foot of one mountain and made a silent meal in the shade that lingered there.

I lay down after a bit of bread and wine and tried to sleep through the heat of the afternoon, but sleep remained a stranger. It was as if I could still smell the smoke from Peru's body. Alais stroked my forehead from time to time and looked down on me with sad eyes. Her kindness touched me but it didn't help. All of us were restless. No one could lie still and we soon started to shake off the crumbs and make our preparations for traveling on. Nothing was said, we just seemed to agree to move.

We climbed up the mountain in front of us and over a shallow saddle. Our sheep path stayed true. We were above the main road, which we could survey just below us. It was deserted at first, but then we noticed movement coming from the village ahead of us. It was a white horse moving at a great speed. It seemed an odd enough sight that we all just stopped and watched it as it approached. After a short while, we could make out the rider, it was a boy in a white smock with a broad-brimmed white straw hat that somehow managed to stay on his head.

"Are you the *bonhomme?*" he called up to us as his horse reached the spot below us. He'd reached it more quickly than we'd expected.

"Yes!" Alais shouted down. "He is!"

"You must ride with me. It is my grandmother. She is dying. She wants consolation. Come. Hurry!"

"Don't you have a priest?" I yelled.

"There's a priest, but he's no good. And he's Catholic, he is not a good Christian."

"You go, Itzal," Alais told me. "It is only kind."

"I will. Arnaud, do you know where to take those sheep to keep them safe from the she-wolf?" I asked.

"I know someone that needs a new shepherd," he replied.

"I'll ride ahead. You'll be in the village before nightfall," I said, and I leaned over to kiss Alais chastely on her cheek.

"Hurry, *bonhomme*," the boy urged me. "My grandmother will not last long. She doesn't want to go to hell."

"I'm coming," I said, pulling the leather satchel over my shoulder. I half slid, half walked down the slope, and attempted to mount the horse behind the boy. I was clumsy and the horse wouldn't stand still. Finally, the boy pulled me up himself, turned his animal around, and started pounding along the dusty road to his village.

***

I struggled for balance on the back of the horse. I tried to hold onto the boy, but he was small and didn't offer much of a counterweight to my body. I almost slipped off once or twice. I wasn't used to horses, and I don't think I'd ever been on one that was galloping like this one. It was a large animal, powerful and well-muscled from what I could tell. The hooves pounded on the road like a drum.

We rode down the slope of the mountain and up the gentler slope towards the village. We started to pass through some well-tended fields, mostly millet, and a vineyard. I could see the half-harvested hayfield beyond the buildings that made up the town.

"What's your name, boy?" I shouted over the racket from the beast.

"Bernard!" he shouted back over his shoulder. His heels pounded against the flanks of the unsaddled horse, his small hands holding the rope reins loosely but maintaining perfect control.

"You say your priest is no good, Bernard?" I felt like I should make some conversation with the stranger.

"He has only been in our village a few weeks and already he is collecting rents from three households. He says he is doing God's work, but my grandmother doesn't believe him."

"What about your mother?" I asked.

"She died. She got sick and she died. My father was killed when the French came when I was very little. I live with my grandmother. She is very holy."

We were slowing down. The horse came to a trot, panting. Both sides of the branch road we were on were lined with vines bearing fat, almost black grapes. We turned up a trail that led from the feeder road into the town. The horse was walking now, I breathed easier. I could hear the lazy buzz of bees and smell the ripeness of the grapes.

The village was surrounded by a low wall, resting on the crest of a green hill. It was arranged around a square like most of the villages I have known, with a church anchoring one corner and a large house anchoring the other. The boy leapt off his horse as soon as we entered the walls, practically knocking me to the ground on his way. I slid down the side of the animal and tried to stand. The boy slapped the animal's rump and it trotted across the square, apparently certain of where it was meant to go.

"Come, *bonhomme*, we must hurry." He was tugging at my sleeve, leading me diagonally towards a smallish, whitewashed house on the western edge of the town. Oddly, this seemed to be another uninhabited village. The square was deserted. I hadn't seen anyone in the fields. Still, the boy tugged at me and I surrendered to his urgency.

We reached a house—he almost kicked open the door—and there was much of the population. At least, the house was full of women, most of them older. They were almost silent as I entered, but I thought I detected a collective sigh.

"She lives, Bernard," a woman with iron-gray hair said softly to the boy. He just nodded and led me through the parting sea of women.

There was only a bed in the inner room of the house. A window looked over the low wall of the village down the western slope of the hill. I could smell lavender.

At first I thought the bed was empty, then I realized it held the form of a very tiny, very ancient woman. Her cheeks had fallen in on themselves, her few wisps of snow white hair trembled in the little breeze the window allowed. Looking into her face I realized that she was blind.

"Grandmother," Bernard said with terrible tenderness, "I have found you a *bonhomme*."

"I thought they were all dead," she breathed faintly.

"No. I really found one. They were right, there was one on the mountain," the boy answered.

"Sister," I said, "I am here."

"I can no longer kneel to you, *bonhomme*," she said with an apology in her feeble voice.

"There is no need, sister. *Benedicte*," I offered.

"I am dying. Lay your hands on me and say the words. I beg you." There were tears coming from her blind eyes. I don't know if they were tears of sorrow and fear at the prospect of death or joy in my arrival.

"Bernard, bring in Gauzia. There should be a witness. Be quick." Her voice was sharp with authority and the boy darted out of the room, returning in seconds, leading the iron-haired woman by her hand.

"Fabrisse," the woman whispered, kneeling beside the bed.

"There's no time. Just pray with us."

"Wherever two or three are gathered in my name," I recited quickly and clearly, "there I am in the midst of them. As the Apostle Paul said, you are the Temple of the living God. As God has said through Isaiah, His prophet, I dwell in them and walk in them." I almost sketched a sign of the cross over the woman, my hand showing its old habits, but I stopped myself and just held out my hand, palm down, over her forehead.

"Be it understood that your presentation made before this daughter of Jesus Christ confirms your faith."

"Amen," the sick woman muttered.

"Amen," her friend and grandson echoed.

"*Pater Noster...*" I began reciting the prayer from memory, grateful for its familiarity. I was calmer now and the room was cool.

"I deliver you this holy prayer. Receive it of us and of God and of the Church. May you always have the power to say it."

"I receive it from you and the Church," she answered.

"My sister, do you desire to give yourself to our faith?" I asked.

"Yes," she responded. "Yes, yes."

I knew the question should be asked three times, but she had already answered in the triple form.

"God bless you and keep you," I pronounced.

"Pray to God for me, a sinner, that He will lead me to a good end."

"God bless you and keep you and make you a good Christian and bring you to a good end." I placed my hands on the papery skin of the woman's face. Both Gauzia and Bernard exhaled sighs, apparently convinced that the woman's soul had just been saved.

"Good Christians, *parcite nobis,* we pray you, by the love of God, grant this blessing to our sister—" I looked to the boy.

"Fabrisse," he prompted.

"Fabrisse. By the love of God and the church, may her sins be forgiven and we pray to God to forgive them of you. *Parcite nobis.*" I said, turning may hands over, palms upwards.

"*Adoremus, patrem et filium et spiritu sanctam,*" all four of us recited together three times. Then it was obvious that the old woman on the bed had no more breath left in her. I reached down and closed her blind eyes.

12
Confrontation

The three of us stood there for a moment, each praying in their own way, I'm sure. I was vaguely aware of a murmur coming from the room behind us, but I was too caught by my own thoughts to think of it. I had just administered a sacrament that belonged to a Church that I had never joined, that I had no authority to offer to anyone. The act might be enough to send my own soul to hell. Perhaps I had just ushered the old woman into her own eternal damnation. That was what the Pope thought. I wasn't sure then and I'm no more sure now. I do know that it would have been cruel to withhold the words, to keep my hands from her sunken brow. I knew I had done what needed doing.

I heard a small cough behind me. It was a cough I knew, familiar. It was a sound that took me back to the hollow echo of a flagged cloister, the cool dark cells that I had left so long ago.

"What has happened here?" The voice came from behind me. I stood up, stiffened my back, and turned to face him.

His face was the same, marked by pox, slightly vulpine, but the boy had filled out in the last few weeks since last I'd seen him.

"A woman died, Fra Pedro," I said firmly. "You have ignored her spiritual needs."

"I have no interest in spiritual need, Fra Itzal, I never did," Pedro replied. "I didn't really have any sort of vocation. And I have almost no interest in old women unless they're rich."

"Yet this is your parish."

"You call it that. It is my little kingdom. You know that I'm not a priest," he answered, leering at me.

"And now this village will know. Your reign will end," I said.

"I don't think so, Itzal—I'm sorry, *Fra* Itzal. One heretic is dead already. Two more corpses will make little difference."

"You'd kill all three of us?"

"I don't think so, I don't think I'll need to," he answered, moving forward, his limp somehow adding power to his stride. "The woman." He swung his hand out with a speed that I had never seen and knocked Gauzia to the ground. Her neck made a snapping sound. The woman didn't make any sound of her own, "will die easily, I think. Oh, look, she is already gone." He kicked her in the belly with his strong leg. She slid across the floor, but there was no noise from her. "The boy is known to be hysterical. He is given to delusions. He claims he had a vision of Saint Luke last Michelmas. He only needs to die if it is his choice."

"And what about me?" I asked, not really afraid.

"Well, you *are* a heretic now, aren't you? A heretical holy man of all things. And you, such a good Dominican." He shook his head, smiling almost kindly towards me. "I can just turn you over to the Inquisition at Pamiers or Fanjeaux. You will burn prettily and I will be rewarded."

"I didn't come here alone," I countered.

"Yes, you did. Or you might as well have. Oh, I know there are others who traveled with you, but you came into these walls with only the boy. If your companions keep coming, well, they're heretics, too, aren't they?"

I could only stare at him, bewildered by his audacity. I was also baffled to see him on his feet. Finally, I had to ask the question. "Aren't you dead?"

"Only to you, Itzal, and I had hoped, to our prior. I never really liked the cloistered life. There was no room for power, at least not for the likes of me. You could move up if you liked sleeping with boys, I guess." He looked me up and down and licked his lips. "I didn't mind that part so much. The older brethren didn't care about my pockmarked face when I had my back turned to them and my habit above my waist. No, that was pleasant enough, but it never would have gotten me what I wanted."

"And what you wanted was…?"

"Power, wealth, women. What does any man want? With a parish like this, a village of my own, I had all of that. The women came to me to confess. The penance I offer can be quite pleasant. The men confess also. If they're willing to pay, their penance is light as well. If not—well, the Inquisition isn't far and it doesn't take all that much to convict a man of believing in God the wrong way. Then the man gets burned and I get his property. I have three houses already. And a vineyard!" He laughed. "I did leave you. I meant you to think I was dead if you followed. I gather you followed." He looked the question at me.

"I followed," I replied.

"It was only a pigeon that died, so don't fret over that. I knew that you'd want to see some blood. I killed the bird and used it to weight my habit. I knew that you'd never climb to check on my body."

"I might have. Someone stopped me."

"I may have passed him on the road. I kept below the track, but I heard someone lead the mule away. I only had time to take one of the coin purses. I wanted to keep everything. The codex would have fetched a pretty price in Toulouse. I wasn't greedy enough to do anyone harm."

"Not then. But now?"

"No, I'm not greedy, but I enjoy my place here. I might have let a real heretic go on his way. What do I care how people pray? But you, Itzal, I'm afraid you have to die. I'm sorry."

"I can expose you to the Inquisitors."

"They will not believe you. I am known to them as an enemy of the heresy that haunts these hills, and all that goes with it. You are not. Weren't you among those who broke out of Carcassone? I heard there was someone there who kept insisting he was a monk."

"That was me."

"Of course it was. Only you would think that was a defense. Still, you see, you will be condemned. It's rather sad. I don't dislike you, Itzal, but you are not convenient for me. Bind him!" He barked the last two words and a pair of burly peasants emerged from the doorway behind him. They tied my hands behind my back with a coarse rope.

"Oh, and I'll take that," Pedro reached over and lifted the satchel off my shoulder. "It is a pretty codex, and it will still fetch good money in Toulouse. They can always scrape the pages blank, no matter how much you've written in it." He gestured and the two men pushed me through the front room of the house into the bright light of the square.

Alais and Pons had arrived. I could see the mule near the gate in that low wall. Zaid was sitting on the parapet, playing at shaving again, tilting his knife and his little polished piece of steel. Light flashed to the valley below.

The peasants shoved me across the square. I looked at Alais and she looked back at me, but there didn't seem to be any way she could help me right then. Pons nodded at me and I felt reassured.

"Take him to the Church, he'll be safe enough there," Pedro instructed. "Then bring out those old women. We'll burn their bodies here in the square. They will make an example to anyone who thinks they can leave the true Church behind." He was almost spitting the last word. "The house will be confiscated."

I was hurried roughly across the square which was filling up with the population of the town, and then shoved through the open door of the church and left there on the cool stones, alone in the darkness.

**

It must have been somewhere between Nones and Vespers. I didn't remember how long it took to gallop to the village and administer the sacrament, but my conversation with Pedro was quick and clipped. I righted myself and prayed in that deserted chancel.

I'm not really sure what I prayed for, or to which God I prayed. I didn't know if I was praying for the salvation of my soul or the preservation of my flesh. I prayed that Pedro would be punished for his sins, but in any church, that was an unworthy prayer. So I prayed to be forgiven for that prayer.

The darkness grew more palpable around me. Time passed and I had no idea what was going on in the village outside. I heard vague sounds. It might have been some sort of construction. It might have been people gathering wood and tossing it onto a pyre. I didn't hear any human voices for an hour or more. Then I heard the disaster.

It started as a rumbling sound that made no sense to my ears and forced me to abandon any pretense of prayer. Then there were voices shouting and I heard screams and wails from the women in the square outside. The rumbling continued and then became a heavy clopping on the stones of the square and I realized it must be the sound made by horses.

"In the name of the Inquisition, by order of his holiness the Pope!" a voice shouted in French, "this entire village is condemned for heresy!"

"No!" A distraught voice shouted. It was Fra Pedro. "No, it is my village. Mine! I was finding the heretics. I have a prisoner here, a heretic priest. Take him. Just leave me the village."

"You've done well," the other voice proclaimed. "You have served the Church. You will have a place in Pamiers."

"No!" Pedro wailed his despair. He didn't want to be part of a community; he wanted a small place to rule.

"Is this pyre ready?" There was no response. "Bring out the bodies of the dead heretical women. And bring forth the prisoner."

The doors of the church opened and two men at arms walked through the door. Though it was close to sunset, the light was blinding to me. I could make out pikes in their hands and some form of armor, probably leather, but no faces. I was lifted roughly by my elbows and brought out into the remaining daylight.

My eyes adjusted and I could see the form of a huge pile of wood in the center of the square. There was no stake and that seemed to bode well. The population of the village was at the east end being held in check by three or four men at arms. Two tall Dominicans in white habits and black traveling hoods were bawling out the orders in French. There were two armed knights in graymail that caught the last rays of the sun from second to second, making them glow like something out of another world.

Pedro stood beside the Dominicans, clamoring to keep his fief. Next to him and away from the crowd of villagers, Zaid stood. That made no sense.

I was thrown to my knees near the stack of dry wood that towered over me. It looked like a huge, brown haystack, and it seemed as dry as any tinder.

Three men at arms emerged from the house of the dead woman. Two of them carried her desiccated body on her bed. The other had Gauzia's limp form slung over his shoulders like a sack of turnips. I saw the Dominican, who had yet to speak, reach out towards the wood with a torch, and flames started licking the bottom of the pile.

"Throw them on!" the other monk shouted.

I watched in horror as the bodies of the two women were tossed onto the bonfire. The townspeople gasped and little Bernard cried out wordlessly.

"Throw him on as well," the monk ordered. "We'll have a trial later. Pere Pierre here can supply all the testimony we'll need. Best to get the execution over with."

Insanely, I wondered who Pere Pierre might be. The two men at arms picked me up by my bound arms and feet, swung me back and forth three times, and tossed me onto the woodpile as if I were a rag. "Oh, Fra Pedro!" I said out loud as I arced through the air.

I felt the wood give and heard a little bit of it spill as I landed. A sharp stick jabbed me in the back. I wasn't comfortable. The bigger logs were rough and chafed at my face. I knew it wouldn't be a problem for long. I could hear the flames begin to crackle below me. The smell of the smoke was almost sweet. I was facing the sky, which was darkening quickly as the sun sank behind the mountains to the west. I wondered how much it would hurt.

Then I remembered the witch I'd seen burn when I was younger. And I remembered her screams. It thought about the women at Carcassone and the mercy that had been shown to them by the Inquisition. At least I wasn't wearing oiled clothes. Of course, my green tunic was filthy—it was greasy, stained with my sweat and oils, and the oils from Alais' skin, where her form had pressed against mine. Perhaps I should think of her.

I couldn't see any flames yet, although smoke was rising over me into my sight. If I lifted my head and craned my neck just a bit, I could make out the end of the bed that held the dead form of Fabrisse. None of this would matter to her. She had already died comforted. There was no comfort for me.

And I didn't mind that and I wasn't sure why.

My psalter slipped out of my pocket and fell open. I laughed at the sight of it and thought, *Well, let that one burn, there are plenty of those. I wish I could save the other, though, the book hidden next to my flesh.* That would burn, too, and be lost forever. So would the songs, all the songs I'd written down. The pages would be scraped clean and the book used again. All of Zaid's hard work, all his copying of notes would be gone forever. Why was Zaid standing with the Dominicans?

I thought it was taking an awfully long time for the fire to come and consume me. I felt like Isaac, being sacrificed by my own church or what had been my church. I laughed again. If anyone could see me, they would have been certain I'd lost my mind, and maybe I had. There was certainly no reason to hold onto it.

I looked to my right and saw little tongues of flame begin to lick their way through the wood. I saw them kiss the branches with blue and then yellow and then orange and this light fascinated me and entertained me. It was getting warm, but I was used to heat.

Time had become a different kind of thing for me right then. It was stretching as I watched the delicate dance of flames. I saw the edges of the psalter start to turn brown and then black. The sound was still only a light crackle. I was surprised by that, I thought it would roar, but I'm glad it didn't.

Because it was just about then, as my book of monkish prayers started to glow orange, that I heard the sound I'd been waiting for, so much like what I'd heard from within the little church.

Much like it, but louder and heavier, more intense. Perhaps the wood amplified it. This was not a group of three or four horses, pounding their way up the sides of the hill. This must be what an army sounds like, I thought. The ground was rumbling, I could feel it through the wood and flame; the whole bonfire shook from it.

I thought I heard voices singing fiercely over the pounding of the hooves, but I may have dreamt that in my odd state. I lifted my head and turned towards the gate and the low wall, across the empty side of the square. The wall seemed to vibrate with the sound; it shook as if it were alive.

Then it stopped. It was almost as if the whole world was holding its breath through that long moment. I know that I was, but that was because the smoke was finally starting to make my eyes water.

Still, I kept my gaze focused on the wall and then it happened.

Riders, ten of them, twenty, I don't know how many, thundered up and goaded their horses to jump the wall. They seemed to fly through the air before landing with a sharp ringing on the stone square.

Arnaud had gotten through.

La Lobita was here.

13

Dispensation

♪Massas e brans, elms de color.
Escutz traucar e desguarnir
Veirum a l'intrar l'estor
E maintz vassals ensems ferir....♪

I would swear I heard singing, loud, raucous voices singing of joy in arms and battle. I realized that I couldn't possibly have heard it. Not over the pounding of the hooves, the scrape of steel, the screams from the people in the square. Voices shouted in French, in Occitan, in Gascon. in Basque.

I lay my head back down. I could no longer see through the smoke. I looked up at the greening sky being blackened by the oily fumes of the fire that was beginning to roast me. Still, I was laughing, almost buoyant. Perhaps the madman's garment had loaned me the release of madness, I don't know. I heard the fire roar up and saw yellow flames to either side of me. I could feel beads of sweat pop out on my forehead, along my arms and legs. I saw the flames lick at the hem of my green garment.

"Save the *bonhomme!*" I'm sure I heard that being shouted, although I have no idea who gave the order because that was the last thing I heard before I slipped out of consciousness, certain that I was about to die.

At least it's pretty, I thought, the orange light, the yellow light. At least I am peaceful for all of this noise. And then I thought no more.

***

I was being rolled against cool stone and then I felt water being thrown into my face. I coughed and sputtered. I woke up in pain. My right hand and most of that arm were burnt not quite black, the skin blistered. I tried to sit up but it hurt too much. I must have passed out again.

The next time I came to myself I was looking at stars against the blue-black sky. There was a sickening odor around me and I realized that it must be coming from my burns. I remembered what happened, the capture, the attack, the fire, the next attack. I don't remember how I was drawn out of the flames.

Alais looked into my eyes. She ran a damp cloth all over my face. "Does it hurt so very much, Itzal?"

"It hurts, girl. Will I live?"

"You'll live they say. It is only your hand and your arm. They may heal. No one will say. But you are alive now, this is over. You've been saved."

I wondered how she meant that last word, but I let it go.

"I'll fetch La Lobita, it was she who saved you, of course. I would have died with you, but I couldn't have saved you, and—" she started to cry," I wasn't brave enough. I couldn't leap into the fire. I'm sorry, Itzal."

"Don't be, Alais," I said as tenderly as I could, then with the pain and the effort. "It is not as easy to die for love as the songs would have you believe."

"I'll go get her." She vanished and I closed my eyes.

When I opened them, I was looking into the pale eyes of the woman warrior.

"Peace, *bonhomme*—"

"I am not—" I started.

"You were not before, but you are now. It doesn't even matter if you want to be," she said. "You have already paid the price."

I nodded weakly.

"Na Sybille!" she called. "Come, bring the balm. There is no one whose need is greater."

An impossibly old face looked into mine, a woman's. She shook her head and looked towards my right arm. She shook her head again, making some small sound through her lips, and then busied herself.

"The old woman knows things, Itzal," La Lobita said gently. "She will ease your pain."

I lay there and felt something rich and cool being spread over my burnt arm. The cloth was wrapped tightly around it. There were smells I couldn't identify but they mingled with the smoke from the fire and the sweat from my body.

"Can you stand, *bonhomme?*" The small outlaw asked.

"I'll try," I said and rocked my body forward. Alais took my left arm and helped and I found myself standing.

I looked around. The scene was amazing. The huge fire still smoldered and it looked like people were gathering more wood for it. There was a row of people lying on the pavement of the square, the wounded, I supposed. Two Dominicans were bound with their hands behind their backs, kneeling near the fire. Zaid was next to them, his hands bound as well.

"You are needed here first, *bonhomme*," she instructed and led me over to the people stretched on their backs. "These will not live. Lay your hands on them. It will give them comfort."

She was right, I knew. There were five or six of them, mostly old women. I knelt by their heads, one by one. I placed my hands on their brows one by one. "*Benedicte, parcite nobis,*" I breathed. I went down the line. The last one was Pons.

"Itzal, *bonhomme*," he said, wincing.

"Pons, what became of you?" I asked.

"A horse broke my leg," he answered. "Then one of those damned Frenchmen put a spear through my lung. I am dying."

"I am sorry, Pons, you have been my friend."

"Then lay your hands on me and give me your blessing because I know you for what you are, and you are a *parfait* no matter what you say." He tried to smile through his pain.

I placed both my hands, the burnt and the whole, on his wrinkled forehead. I closed my eyes and offered, "*Benedicte, parcite nobis.*"

He smiled up at me and answered oddly, "*Nunc dimittus.*" Then closed his eyes.

I stood up, held out both my hands over the wounded and the dying and began:

"*Pater Noster, qui es in caelis, sanctificetur nomen tuum...*" Everyone joined in as best they could until we all finished up, "*Sed libera no a malo.*" Deliver us from evil, indeed.

***

"Enough, *bonhomme*," La Lobita said. "You have a judgment to make and someone to see."

She led me across the square to where the Dominicans were bound. I saw the bodies of the armored knights lying nearby. The men at arms who had thrown me on the fire were sitting sullenly against the outer wall of the church.

Stretched next to the prisoners was the form of Fra Pedro. His eyes were open but there was blood and spittle dripping from the corners of his mouth. He would not live long.

"This one," she said, prodding Pedro with a toe of her boot. "This is the one we spoke of before. You did well to send the boy. His reign is over, but he says he knows you."

"He does, dompn—La Lobita," I answered and knelt down next to him.

"It was a short lordship, eh Pedro?" I said to him. His mouth moved but no words escaped his lips. "Perhaps God is just after all." I stood up and turned away. I stopped myself and knelt down next to him again. "I believe this belongs to me." I removed the satchel from over his shoulder, lifting his head to do it and dropping it back to the flags. I started to rise again but I saw something in his eyes. I wouldn't leave him like that. "*Requiescat in pace*," I said, tracing a sign of the cross on his forehead.

"What happened to him?" I asked. "I see no wounds."

"In the melee, as we came over the walls, that old mule over there," she pointed at my animal, "ran amok. It was kicking everywhere, and one of his hooves caught this evil man's chest, caving it in. He will be dead within the hour unless you'd like to make him suffer more."

"No," I replied, almost laughing. "No, being punished by the mule that came with us from Aragon is enough, I think."

The light from the fire was eerie as it glowed with coals at its heart. The flames had stopped rising, but with fresh wood being tossed onto the stack, that would change soon. The air was heavy with smoke, weighed down with the odor of the burnt bodies of those two old women. La Lobita took me gently by the hand and led me to the Dominicans and Zaid. I looked into the faces of the monks and realized they were the same ones who had presided over the Inquisition at Carcassone.

Zaid had a cut over his left eye. The blood had stopped but there would be a scar, you could tell. I wondered why his hands were tied, what he was doing among the prisoners. He didn't look at me as I gazed down on him.

"Do you know this man?" La Lobita asked me.

"He has been my traveling companion for some time now. He is my friend." I saw Zaid's head start back as if he'd been struck.

"He may have traveled with you, but I don't think he is any friend of yours," the woman said.

"I don't understand."

"This one has been leading these white monks after you ever since we left the Oaks. As least he did not betray that place."

"I still don't understand. He was traveling with me. He was helping me to collect songs. He has lovely handwriting," I ended, realizing how silly I sounded.

"His handwriting may be lovely, but he has left a trail of evil behind him. I think if you went back to Pexiora you would find two dead lepers."

I was shocked. Zaid had betrayed those two old people who'd been so kind to us?

"He kept the Inquisitors informed of your passage. He sent word to Pamiers when you crossed the river. He signaled to them as you climbed the mountains. He used his shaving mirror and knife to let them know where you were. Capturing a whole village of heretics would be a great triumph for the likes of these." She kicked the taller Dominican and he fell over onto his side.

I looked down at Zaid. He hung his head, ashamed.

"Is this true? Did you lead these men here to kill us?"

"Itzal," he looked up at me in that inhuman light, tears shining in his eyes, "Itzal, you don't know what they did to me. The pain they put me to while you rested in that prison. They are not human, those two. The men who do the evil for them are less so. They kept at me every day, finding new ways to inflict pain. A man can endure so much and so much only. I would have done anything to make it stop. You would have too."

I looked at his face and shook my head. "But once we were free—why did you keep it up? You were safe with us."

"Was I? You can't escape them. They are everywhere, they are legion. They will find you. They'll find you when you are sleeping and then the pain will begin again. You don't know, you just don't know, you can't. They will never go away and never let up. They broke me, Itzal; they broke me like a toy. I was once proud and brave and now…" His voice trailed off.

"He was your friend, *bonhomme,*" La Lobita said, "your companion. His fate is in your hands. If it were up to me I would kill him. Quickly, with no pain, but I wouldn't let him live. It is your judgment to make."

I didn't know what to say, either to the small, fierce woman next to me or to my companion kneeling at my feet. At least, I thought, he is not kneeling in supplication. That would have been too much. He is not begging for his life, or asking anything of me except that I understand what was done to him. I was never in that torture dungeon in the Wall. He was right, I couldn't know.

"Let him go," I said. "Let him go, give him a horse, one of your horses, so the French don't think he stole it. Leave him free to wander. It's what he does."

La Lobita nodded her head and one of her men cut the ropes that bound Zaid. He shook his hands once or twice to restore feeling and then he offered them to me. I reached down and pulled him to his feet.

"Go. Go and don't look back at any of us," I said, embracing him. "I am sorry for your suffering, but you must leave this land. Go to Lombardy, to Italy. Go back to Al Andalus. Wander, live, become whole again."

He embraced me firmly and briefly but said nothing. He stepped back and nodded at me, looking into my eyes at last. He mounted the horse that was brought over, kicked its sides, and rode out of that circle of light.

***

"Now these two," La Lobita pronounced, kicking both the monks. "These two are lost. There is no saving them. Most important, however," she said, reaching down for the book the rounder monks clutched, "there is no saving this. The names in this book, in these transcripts of false and unjust trials will be lost forever." She threw the book into the red coals of the fire. Sparks danced off the wood and flew into the air like moths. Then the flames licked the pages for a moment, and they burst into yellow and orange.

"You spared them once before. At Carcassone, you made a point to spare the white monks," I said.

"That was there," she explained. "The vengeance of the French would have fallen on the city, which has seen enough trouble. We have seen that vengeance before. But here, well, this village doesn't exist."

"Of course it does—" I started.

"No, Saisons was here for a season." She laughed. "It is a real village and these people have lived here for a long time. But we will make it as if it had never been. You see how they bring everything to fire?"

I nodded.

"They are burning what they can't carry. Then they will follow me into Gascony, where they will be safe enough. We will find them new homes. But there will be no stone left of this place."

"What is to become of me?" I asked.

"*Bonhomme,* you are welcome to join us, but I don't think you want that. No, there is a place here in these mountains that is safe. It is a place where holy women live. They know all the songs you want to learn, and they will teach you."

"Then I will complete my task," I sighed.

"You will complete it, but I would be surprised if you took what you learned back to your monks. God alone knows what will happen to you after this."

"Pray for me."

"My prayers won't help you much, whichever version of God you worship. You should go now. We are going to make these evil men suffer a great deal before we allow them to give up their souls to their God. They have much to atone for and we can't count on the fires of hell. We'll roast them slowly. You should not see that. It would scar you."

"I thank you for that mercy, La Lobita." I bowed my head to her.

"Enough, Itzal. The boy, Bernard, will take you where you have to go. Perhaps the girl will go with you, although I don't think she will like it there."

"I'll go. I am in your debt."

She looked at me and laughed. Then she walked away to see to her men and the preparations for the gruesome deaths of the Inquisitors. Bernard came to me and took my hand.

"We must go, *bonhomme*," he said softly. "We have far to ride. The mountains are deep and high."

He led me to where my panniers still sat. He tossed them over the back of my mule and then lifted me onto his horse, and Alais behind me. Bernard followed on the mule and we rode away from the village that was being erased from the earth.

14
The Last Songs

The night sky was painted with stars as we left the circle of smoke hovering over the village. Bernard was sure of foot and his eyes pierced the darkness. He led us westward down one side of a mountain then up another, steeper slope. We went on like that for a long time.

We traveled by night so that we wouldn't be seen by any living eyes. Bernard knew all his secret paths well. He was wise in the ways of the trails for all his youth. Each morning, we'd make camp in some sheltered spot and Alais would sleep next to me, working my body with her sweetness, almost sadly. Bernard looked after the animals and seemed to ignore us. He thought of me as a holy man who could do no wrong. Myself, I wasn't so sure.

On the third night after leaving the village, Bernard told us we would be reaching our destination the next morning.

"Then you are safe, Itzal," Alais sighed.

"As safe as I can be in this world. I am an outlaw to all that I've known, but I have no regrets."

"Itzal, I know where he is leading you, and you will be safe. There will be people there who can look after you. I can't stay there. I have lived among holy women before, and I have had enough of it."

I looked at her and I knew she was right. She was so young, there was so much life left to her. She would be safe enough among her people. Perhaps she would find a husband, although it wasn't likely if she was known to be barren.

"Where will you go, child?" I asked, brushing her hair back under her headdress.

"Bernard can take me into Gascony. La Lobita's people are there. I may be able to help them. It is English land. I will be safe from the French, at least."

"And what will you do?"

"I will remember you," she smiled. "Perhaps I will open a cook shop. I have a cousin in Gers. She will help me. If you wander that way one day, look for me. You seemed to like my cooking."

I laughed, thinking of all the fish. "Yes, you're a good cook."

"Then let's go on. I'll leave you in the morning."

I mounted the back of the horse one more time with some help from Bernard. My arm seemed to feel better. I had the use of my right hand. Alais and the boy had been slathering the burns with a pot of something they'd been handed before we left Saisons. Whatever it was, it eased the pain.

The morning found us deep in the mountains. I didn't see the opening at first. It was more hidden than the way into the Oaks. It was narrow, little more than a fissure. Bernard vanished through it with the mule and the panniers and then returned without the animal.

"It is through there, *bonhomme*. That is where the holy women live. I am not permitted, but they know you are coming."

"Thank you, boy, for all you've done," I said.

"Thank you for saving my grandmother's soul. Perhaps you can save mine someday." He mounted his horse.

"Goodbye, girl. I am grateful."

"Enough, Itzal. I am going. Pray for me." Alais mounted behind the boy. He kicked his heels into the animal's flanks and they trotted away. I turned to the fissure in the rock and plunged through.

***

It was a box canyon. This was the only way in or out. There were some sorry looking trees on its flat bottom, but the walls were limestone and sheer. I could see that they were pocked with caves and I realized I was in some kind of monastery. It made me think of the hermit fathers in the desert.

"Hello!" I called out. My voice rang off the walls and echoed back to me. No one came.

I stood there thinking I'd been abandoned, that there was no one here, and everyone who had led me here knew it. Perhaps it was a just fate for a false *bonhomme*. Then, from somewhere above me I heard a firm soprano voice sing out:

*♪Reis glorios, verais lum e clratz
Deus poderos, Senher, si a vos platz
Al meu companh statz fizels ajuda
Qu'eu la vi pos la nochs fo venguda
E ades sera alba...*

*Glorious lord, true light and clarity
God and ruler, lord of our place
Protect my companions, safe out of sight
While I guard through this fading twilight
Brighter than the dawn...♪*

Then came another voice, a bit behind the first. I thought it was an echo until I realized it was much lower, an alto, singing in a round. The whole verse was repeated, followed by feminine laughter. I looked up and saw two older women standing in front of two caves on opposite sides of the canyon. They leapt and climbed down faster and more nimbly than I could believe and stood in front of me on the shadowy floor of the place.

"You are the *bonhomme* that we've been told about," the smaller one said. She seemed to be in her fifties or perhaps older. She was short and very round. Her face bore all the marks of age, as well as scars that may have dated back to her youth.

"I am a monk, " I began, "or I was."

"We know," the other woman said. She was tall and sinewy, older than her companion. "Welcome. I am called Sister Grazide and this is Sister Bernadette. We are the last sisters of this sanctuary, open to God but hidden from men."

"It is much safer than a castle. Armies don't surround it. It doesn't attract any attention at all," Sister Bernadette said.

"I will take you to Dompna Esclarmonde," Sister Grazide offered. "She rules here, below God."

I looked at her, surprised by the name. "Surely not—"

"No, no," she laughed musically. "Not the famous Esclarmonde of Foix, she is long dead, as the world knows. This is just another holy woman with the same name."

The one called Bernadette took the halter of my mule and led it away. The other woman led me down the length of the canyon to a large opening in the limestone wall.

"He is here!" she called into the cave. Without waiting for any answer she led me inside.

There was a large chair with a small praying bench next to it. The walls of this cave were whitewashed and it was illuminated by a single candle. Seated in the chair was one of the oldest people I had ever seen. There was something about her, though, that immediately inspired reverence. I knelt before her and held my hands open wide, as so many others had done to me. She placed both her hands on my forehead and then said, "Rise, Fra Itzal."

I stood and looked at her face. It was as if sorrow had worn her face into a relief map of suffering. It was deeply lined, the skin sagging but still strong. There were cataracts clouding her eyes and I knew that she could not see well, if at all.

"You are welcome here. We have been expecting you for some time." She placed her hands on my head and I felt them rub the short hair of my old tonsure that was growing back in. "You will stay here with us for now. You will learn. You will learn of our church, which you have helped to save, even if you did not mean to, and you will learn the songs that you have sought."

"Thank you, Dompna," I replied.

"You will stay through the winter. When spring comes it will be over for the three of us. You will bury us here and leave this place. You will have all the knowledge you want by then and all the knowledge we want you to have. For now, let Sister Grazide take you to a cave. It will be your home. You will fast for three days there and recite the *Pater Noster*. Then we will talk again."

There was no question of refusal. I had no desire to struggle with anything more than my own soul. Grazide led me to a cave a level above the one we'd been on. It was clean and held a praying bench and a palate. There was a pitcher of water and nothing more. The woman left me there and I began to pray.

***

That was how I spent my fall and winter. The women had been there for decades I learned, but they were the last of their kind. I looked after them—I dug latrines, I fed them. They taught me all the songs I wanted to know, every one that my prior had given me to transcribe, and many more. I wrote them all down in the codex. Dompna Esclarmonde would instruct me in the Cathar religion each morning. Then I would read to her from that Gospel of John I'd managed to hold onto. Her eyesight was too weak for her to read for herself.

It grew cold in the mountains during the winter. Snow fell although very little found its way to the canyon floor. I kept fires going. I nursed Sister Grazide through a very bad chill, using lessons Zaid and Alais had taught me. We never wanted for food; there seemed to be something left at the mouth of that hidden canyon every week. The women did not need much to sustain them.

Christmas came and went, unmarked by us. The days began to grow longer again. I enjoyed the life there—the physical work, the spiritual comfort, and all the music. I played on my guitarra almost every evening and the two younger sisters laughed and clapped. Soon enough the light began to look like spring. One afternoon I was called to attend to Dompna Esclarmonde.

"Fra Itzal, is that you?" Her eyesight had all but vanished, but I was certain she could tell it was me from my odor.

"Yes, Dompna," I answered.

"Come here, sit next to me. There are some last things that I must tell you."

I pulled her prayer bench over next to that great chair and settled myself on its low boards.

"First, you must know that we knew of your mission almost from the first. Sir Raimon sent us word after your meeting. You were watched. You were guided and protected. La Lobita dogged your footsteps. Pons, the boy Arnaud, they were our friends too, and kept you safe. Our plans were carried out, and you were tested by the journey."

I didn't know what to say to that.

"Have you carefully written down all the songs that you've heard here?"

"I have copied them as I heard them."

"And you have learned to play all the notes?"

"Yes, Dompna."

"And you have written them so that someone else could sing the melodies and play these songs again, even if you weren't there to explain it to them?"

"I think so, Dompna. I have used the system that the Church—the Catholic Church—uses to record such things. Why?"

"Do you know of the ancients, Itzal?" she asked irrelevantly.

"No, not much. I have heard names. Perhaps some of the scholars at my priory but I—"

"No matter. I want to tell you about one. There was a man called Pythagoras long before our Savior was born. He excelled at numbers and he knew the mystical nature of the world, as much as one who does not know Christ." She coughed, loudly and long, and I saw myself in another room, what seemed a lifetime ago. I shook my head and she went on. "He alone knew the music of the spheres, the music the stars make as they move."

I looked at her, pondering the idea, but said nothing.

"You see, you have been carefully transcribing these songs thinking them all silly love poems, songs of war, conquest, and lust."

"I have found them lovely but, yes, frivolous," I replied.

"That is because you think the words are what matter, but they are not. We only make up the words so that we can remember the tunes. All the lore of our church is held in those melodies. Like Pythagoras, we have heard the music and we have used it as a code for our teachings. There are numbers in the notes, and the numbers can become letters, the way the Hebrews in Al Andalus use them. That is the secret we've been hiding. That is the secret your benefactor wanted preserved. We are all of us vanishing. It was the only way. Keep that book safe, Itzal. If you have children, pass it to them and teach them how to turn your markings into song. Someday, someone will know what it means, and we will be more than shadows cast by the flames of the Inquisition. Do not stay here but go back to your Basque country. You will be safe and you can pass the knowledge down."

I bowed my head to her, but she couldn't see me. "I will, Dompna."

"There is one more song for you to hear. Listen very carefully; be sure you can write it down. This one has no words."

Then for the first time, I heard her sing. Her voice was cracked and sounded as old as time itself. She sang a long, slow melody that sounded like it could make the sun rise at night or coax the moon down from the sky. I listened closely. I wrote the notes quickly, as quickly as I could. I copied that song of light on scraps of paper, on the dust, and in my heart. I copied it again into my book. When she stopped singing, it was as if all sound itself had ended, and everything had become silence.

"Tomorrow, Itzal, my sisters and I will begin our *endura*. Because we have learned that in music we can enter the silence. You will bring us no more food. You may pray with us every day. When it is time, put your hands on us. And then bury us. Dig the graves today. We would like to be near them."

I left the cave, heavy in my heart. I knew there was nothing I could say to these women to change their minds. Their souls had waited for this moment for years.

I took a shovel and dug three graves in front of Esclarmonde's cave. They looked stark and ugly as scars in the earth.

The women came out of their shelters and knelt next to them the next morning. They prayed silently for three days, eating nothing and drinking the water I brought them. I knelt beside them because I didn't know what else to do.

It was Bernadette who went first. That was a shock since she was the youngest, but on the third day, she just fell over onto her side. I placed my hands on her forehead and then one hand on her chest and felt the breath leave her.

I wrapped her in her habit and lowered her into her grave. The other two women were too weak to speak by then. That night, Grazide died. I touched her head and buried her, too. I tried not to sleep, but I couldn't help myself and I dozed off towards morning. When I woke up, Esclarmonde was dead too. I hadn't laid my hands on her, but she didn't need me to save her soul.

I shoveled dirt over her body. I sealed the graves with stones. I knelt and offered a prayer for their souls to any God who would listen. I was not sure of a church that asked these three saintly women to starve themselves to death, and I was no longer able to believe in the Catholic Church. I was alone now. Esclarmonde had told me I was now qualified, fully, to serve as a *bonhomme*, but all I hoped to be from this day forward was a good man.

I packed my book and my guitarra onto the back of the old mule who had miraculously survived the winter. I led him out of the dim light of the canyon onto the mountain trail. I looked up to the sun to get my bearings and did the only thing I could do.

I turned my feet towards home.

THE END

HISTRIA BOOKS

HISTRIA FICTION

Other fine books available from Histria Fiction:

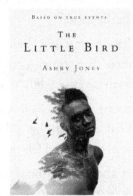
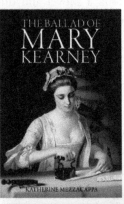

For these and many other great books visit

HistriaBooks.com